Lisa Clark's The Messengers seri[es] [...]
novel that pits the faithful and unluc[...]
Gospel against those that would silence it forever. Plucky Simon, our hero, is still recovering from the Arena, where in the first book he stood up for his faith at the cost of his safety. The second book finds him navigating both a world of betrayal—where friends aren't always what they seem—and his first love interest, a very welcome addition to the series. While the first book delivered high on the action front, *Concealed* falls more into the cloak-and-dagger genre, with Simon dodging a shadowy government that has infiltrated every facet of his life. Clark's strengths shine in how she lays out complex pillars of faith in a way that makes it easy for teens to understand the Bible. Simon and his close band of friends are noble characters for readers to root for, but are still flawed enough to be believable, and their dialogue reflects their always transforming faith. Overall, fans of this series will not be disappointed; *Concealed* delivers its theology with grace and its story with teeth. In this current day, where the future seems particularly nightmarish, *Concealed* is brimming with a much-needed hope, a hope in things unseen.

—*Colleen Oakes, Author of the best-selling Queen of Hearts Saga*

It was with great anticipation that I read Lisa M. Clark's second book in The Messengers series. In *Discovered*, I had been introduced to Simon Clay and the Messengers, and their stories drew me into a world where the value of the Word is far greater than what I give it in my everyday life. It was a compelling and convicting book. In *Concealed*, Simon's journey continues as he learns more about the truth he so boldly shared, and begins to realize the consequences of his boldness. Those consequences bring the greatest challenge he has yet to face: forgiveness.

—*Eden Keefe, Lutheran Women's Missionary League*
Vice President of Christian Life 2013–17

Lisa Clark's continued tale of faith under persecution is at once timely and timeless, driving Simon Clay and the rest of us to a fuller understanding of the apostle Paul's confession about life on this earth: "To live is Christ; to die is gain."

—*Katie Schuermann,*
Author of the Anthems of Zion series and Pew Sisters

If you loved *The Messengers: Discovered,* you won't be disappointed! Lisa Clark uses plot twists that give you new theories, confirm some you might have had, and change your ideas about the characters. I couldn't stop reading it because of the cliff-hangers and finished it in less than a day. It has even more action and excitement than the first book, and I can't wait for the third!

—*Simeon Roberts, Seventh grader, Our Savior Lutheran School,*
Grand Rapids, Michigan

Anticipation abounds as we join Simon and the Messengers on their next missions. As the ever-present government dangers lurk closer, how far will they go and how much will they risk to spread the Message? Clark's second installment in The Messengers series continues drawing deep, eloquent connections between the historic Christian Church and the modern life of believers. Encouraged and resolved in their own faith, readers ponder: What is there to lose? What is there to gain? YA and adult readers alike will delight in the risks and suspense as Simon twists and turns through both alleys and the maze of his own teenage years. An excellent continuation of a series that should be on everyone's shelf!

—*Elisabeth Tessone, Librarian, University of Central Missouri*

Simon Clay's faith in Christ is dangerous. Ironically, the government has been saying that all along, and they'll kill you to show you how seriously they mean it. Fresh off Simon's very public confession of his faith following on the heels of his own recklessness, Lisa Clark's *Concealed* adjoins the reader to Simon's struggle with the faith that puts those whom he loves in great danger. *Concealed* is a worthy continuation of The Messengers series and a welcome release for all those who have joined the Darkness.

—*Timothy Koch, Pastor at Concordia and Immanuel Lutheran churches, reviewer at TheBeggarsBlog.com*

Lisa Clark's latest edition to The Messengers series leaves us with the reality of the darker side of life and the questions that come out of facing this hard truth. It is a challenging but hope-filled reminder of what we are left with when all else in life is stripped away. Clark deals expertly with the questions of who God is and where He can be found in the light and the dark. Simon's story challenges us with questions of what is really worth it in life. What is worth our pain, what is worth our time, what is worth our energy, what is worth our tears, and what is worth our love? Clark's rich use of adjectives captures the light and dark of every day, of friendship, and of the unquenchable hope offered in a Savior who loves us through not only the triumphs, but the struggles as well.

—*Heidi Goehmann, Writer*

In *Concealed*, Clark gives us the safety of a well-told story in which to explore our own vows to suffer all rather than fall away from the faith. As we dodge, crawl, question, ache, sing, and pray alongside the fictional Messengers, their words and actions point us to the source of comfort and safety that transcends the borders of New Morgan—a Savior who has joined Himself to our real, broken world, Jesus Christ.

—*Christina Roberts, Kantor, Our Savior Lutheran Church, Grand Rapids, Michigan*

Prologue

The night sky afforded little light, and the cool air sent a thrill through the body of one who stood in the shadow of a building's alleyway alcove. One block away, an apartment building with a carpenter's workshop waited silently for two of its residents. The figure waited too.

If only I had come in time for them to leave, the stranger thought. *I could have followed them to their headquarters.* Instead, the wait would only confirm an inconsequential hunch.

No matter, the waiting figure concluded. *There would be plenty more nights of this to come.*

Step, step, step. Step, step, step.

There you are, the stranger smiled. From the security of darkness, the visitor watched two silhouettes approach. The shadow in the front was smaller, but not by much. As they approached, a patch of moonlight confirmed the identities of father and son.

Patiently, the stranger took in the movements of these two Messengers, watching their pattern of surveillance and stealth. The long wait was rewarded, and it took every ounce of willpower for the visitor to stay silent in the shadows.

Sure enough, the two turned to the side of the building. The figure moved quickly but with painstaking care to reach the corner in time.

Perfect. As the stranger peered around the edge of the neighboring building, one figure helped the other through a portal four feet above the pavement.

The wait was worth it. For the one in the shadows, this was the start of something new.

■ ※ ▓

The Messengers

CONCEALED

Lisa M. Clark

CONCORDIA PUBLISHING HOUSE • SAINT LOUIS

This book is written in thankfulness to God for the Jacks,
Charitys, and Simons throughout the ages.

Concordia
Publishing House

Copyright © 2017 Concordia Publishing House
3558 S. Jefferson Avenue, St. Louis, MO 63118-3968
1-800-325-3040 • www.cph.org

Written by Lisa M. Clark

1 2 3 4 5 6 7 8 9 10   26 25 24 23 22 21 20 19 18 17

Chapter One

The world is going to hell. It's bad enough that we're surrounded by a hostile government, that we must bow to dogs, but now our own kind raves around like madmen. Rejecting all they know, all I've taught, they blindly wander after a corpse. Who do they think they are? Who do they think He is?! Well. If the tomb is where they want to go, I'll be happy to oblige.

■ ■ ■

—*Right about now, not far away*—

Simon's life was normal. Mind-numbingly normal. He went to school, he hurried home, he did his homework, he went to bed. Day. After. Day. Now, sitting in his bedroom, he drummed his fingers on his history book, which lay open on his desk. Empty words stared up from the page, and Simon's stare was equally blank as the monotony slowly dulled his senses.

Except, of course, life *wasn't* normal. Less than two weeks ago, his life had been on the line as he stood in the middle of the large public Arena, on trial for what he had done. No, that wasn't true. His actions had been a catalyst, but the trial had little to do with any temporary pranks or subversive crime. Simon had been on trial for *who* he was, for what he believed. Ignoring the unreliable, carefully censored propaganda in the textbook at his fingertips, Simon let his thoughts wander through the recent history of his own life.

Simon pictured the crowds that had filled the seats of the Arena, swelling the space with anticipation, watching as he endured one of the most difficult battles of his life. He remembered his leg stinging from poison and punishment, providing him with barely enough energy to stand, much less defend himself against the taunts of society that invaded the battleground around him. Simon clenched his jaw as he recalled Mr. Gerald Burroughs, cochairman of the Department of Security and puppet of New Morgan's authority, looming above him from an imposing podium. Burroughs, as the appointed judge of the public trial, had been bent on fulfilling his duty to make an example of him—before eliminating him.

Simon scratched his head and let out a snort. By some turn of events that still baffled him, his testimony in front of Burroughs, the other government officials of New Morgan, and the assembled crowd had inspired a turn in momentum. The people watching from the stands of the Arena had an abrupt change of heart. The ringleader of the spectacle, at a loss for control and ideas, diverted attention to a different act. Within minutes, all evidence of the trial was whisked away, Simon was ignored, and the duel of massive Bots commenced. The crowd, now supportive of the brown-haired, olive-skinned teenager who had disrupted their government-controlled lives, still hungered for action and cheered as the Bots took the field.

Now, safe in his bedroom, Simon rubbed his knee, still sore from tumbling down a concrete stairway on the way to his trial. That day's Bot duel, he realized, was no more than a cowardly attempt to distract the crowd from the government's defeat. New Morgan's leaders would ignore this episode as if nothing had happened and restore the illusion of normalcy as quickly as possible.

With a shudder, Simon acknowledged that the government's need for normalcy was his current lifeline. If something were to happen to him, if he were suddenly to go missing, the absence of the now-infamous face of the Darkness would raise eyebrows from those who supported him during the duel. And so, he obliged in creating a facade of status quo in an effort to keep Security at bay for as long as possible.

Was it worth the trouble? The age-old question Simon's dad often asked echoed in his thoughts as he realized that his rogue acts of courage and rebellion were the reason he was separated from his newfound family, the Messengers. Swallowing back a lump in his throat, he closed his history book and walked into the open living space that comprised the living room, dining room, and kitchen he shared with his dad and the long-faded memory of his mom.

"How's it going?" The salt-and-pepper hair of Simon's dad lifted above the table, where he had been checking the stability of the four legs. A carpenter to the unassuming eye, Jonathan Clay had his own collection of secrets to conceal.

"I feel trapped," Simon said as he walked over to the couch facing the east wall of the apartment building and stretched himself across the length of it. He stared up at the tiled ceiling and exhaled. He knew his dad's question had more to do with homework than anything, but Simon was tired of holding back.

"I can't stand this, Dad." Simon struggled to summarize the past several months. There were other places he would rather be tonight; the couch served as a poor alternative. "I've always thought there was something out there, something more than New Morgan wants people to know. Then, as soon as I know the truth, I try to tell others—because that's what we're supposed to do, right? Then *bam!*"—he slammed a fist into his hand—"I'm locked out."

Simon kept his focus on the ceiling as he heard his dad's footsteps approach, but a quick glance confirmed that Jonathan had taken a seat on the smaller couch against the wall separating the living room from Simon's bedroom.

"It's a good thing we went to the City when we did," Simon admitted, thinking about his visits to the underground community that had provided a new world for him over the course of several months. His thoughts took him to the last worship service he was able to attend, just hours after he won his duel with Westbend. His chest tightened as he realized there was no way he could go back anytime soon. Grateful he and his dad had been able to make it to the City that night, Simon knew it was now too dangerous for them to leave the building after dark.

"Simon, do you remember Mark chapter eight?"

Simon had learned a lot about the Word over the past few months, and this room had become a classroom as his dad unpacked passages from a book the government did everything to suppress.

"Yeah, Peter had some crazy ups and downs at that point."

Weeks ago, Simon read Mark 8 under a tent in the middle of an underground marketplace, his friends Micah and Charity nearby. On that night, Micah had pointed out that Peter's testament of faith was met with Jesus' approval as well as His warning.

"Dad, that one part didn't make sense," Simon added, pulling himself to a sitting position on the couch. "Peter knows Jesus is the Son of God. But then Jesus tells His disciples not to say anything. Why would He do that?! I mean, how will people know of Jesus unless they have heard?" Placing this narrative from Mark in comparison to a passage in Romans 10, Simon was confused. It was Romans 10 that motivated Simon to take action and spread the light of God's Word in the darkness, beginning an exhilarating adventure just a month ago.

Simon watched as Jonathan leaned forward from his spot on the sofa and folded his hands. His dad's green-gray eyes were steady, reassuring, earnest.

"This wasn't the only time Jesus told people to stay quiet. You've been learning about His miracles. Often Jesus would heal someone and then tell them not to tell anyone."

"Why, Dad? I don't get it."

His dad smiled and sat back, folding his arms. "Okay, Simon. Tell me your story. Going out on any missions tonight? any big adventures?"

Simon knew his dad was going somewhere with this, but he smarted from the sting of reality. His only answer was a frown.

Jonathan didn't let up. "No plans, then? Why not?"

Now Simon could see where his dad was headed. "But Dad, I can't just do *nothing* while so many people are clueless to the truth."

The smile on his dad's face was small and knowing. "Nothing. You mean like what you're doing right now?"

Ouch. Point made. Simon's eagerness to spread the truth may have actually hindered his mission to do so, and maybe even hurt the mission of the Messengers. His stomach churned at the thought, and he rested his forearms on his knees as he bore the weight of his actions. *What have I done?*

"Simon, Jesus taught. He healed. He rested. He was never *not* working on our behalf. Even now, everything He does is out of love for us. But He knew that His most important mission held precedence over anything else that might distract, even other good things."

Simon began to ache with the truth that was setting in. "I really messed up, didn't I?" He looked directly at his dad.

Jonathan looked across the apartment, out the windows along the north wall. He shook his head slowly.

"Oh, I don't know about that. There is a time and season for everything. Your time of adventure sure sparked a lot of events, and I imagine we're still waiting to see how it all plays out. But we know that God works all things for the good of those who love Him. Maybe your actions ultimately left you in this time of waiting, but that's not necessarily a bad thing. Seasons come and go."

Simon had plenty to digest. His dad stood and walked over to pat him on the shoulder before leaving him to his thoughts.

Hours later, Simon still wasn't resolved on where he stood. After such an intense time of success and then failure, he now wavered during this eerily quiet aftermath. He lay in bed, struggling to fall asleep. Finally he kicked off his sheets in a fit of frustration and stood to take his post at the window. Moving the shade just enough to peek outside, he inspected the side alley below.

Simon ached at the empty scene that greeted him. No nighttime visitors. No mysterious shadows. No calls to action. But just as he stepped back to return to bed, something caught his eye.

In the glow of the streetlight, Simon noticed a long shadow stretch from his street into the alley's north opening. His heart leaped to his throat, but Simon knew no Messenger would be so bold as to stroll down Merchant Street right now. His heart plummeted when a figure came into view, the light catching the brim of a hat and glinting off of a badge. Security.

Simon retreated from the window, saying a prayer for the safety of his fellow Messengers who might be out on the streets. It would be another hour before he was finally able to sleep. But as he began to drift off, he thought he heard faint sounds of hammering from somewhere far away.

The morning came, bringing with it the last day of the school week. Fatigued after a restless night, Simon started wishing the hours away even before reaching the steps of the West Sector Preparatory School. Students flocked up the wide stairway, greeting one another with waves and chatter. In a few minutes, the tone would pulse and the day of muted learning would begin.

Simon had never been particularly social, preferring to be on the fringe, safely observing the world. But the past two weeks at school had consisted of an especially confusing mix of targeted attacks and concentrated neglect. During lunch break, Simon used to be able to sit wherever without notice. But on two occasions since his trial, students had moved out of his way as soon as he approached, as if creating a bubble to protect themselves from whatever was wrong with him. That was tolerable enough. Other times, students took great pains to show "interest" in him. While washing his hands in the restroom the first day back at school after the trial, he was suddenly caught in pitch-black darkness. A voice called from the hallway outside the bathroom door: "Hey, Simon! Like the *Darkness*?!" After fifteen minutes of pushing against the door, Simon was able to squeeze through and see that an old teacher's desk and a heap of chairs had been piled up as a barricade. He walked into the classroom, the lecture already begun, to the sound of muffled sneers.

Ms. Stetter made as much effort as possible to ignore Simon's existence, going so far as to "forget" to hand him a test sheet as she passed them out to the students. After ten minutes, he had summoned enough courage to walk up to the front and take the test that sat precariously on the corner of her desk. She refused to look up as he approached, but he saw that her ears were red as she hovered over her grading. Simon's own ears burned when he turned the test over to see that the space for the name was already filled out: *Nobody*.

Ben, a recently rediscovered friend, seemed to agree with Ms. Stetter. On three different afternoons, Simon called after Ben as they walked home from school to the same block. Ben only quickened his pace, putting space between them. In class, Simon would occasionally try to look back at Ben's desk when Ms. Stetter said something particularly ridiculous. Ben only looked down, freckles disappearing on his reddened cheeks.

One student, however, seemed more interested in him than before: Ella Maxon, who sat two desks to Simon's left. She offered a shy but encouraging smile every time he tried to capture Ben's attention. Her long hair was so blond it was almost white, and her blue eyes were cool and mild. Her friendliness caught Simon off guard at first, but after a while, he began to aim his glances at Ella instead of Ben.

During lunch break on Friday, Simon decided to preempt the inevitable neglect by sitting alone at a smaller table in a corner of the cafeteria. He poked at the processed meat of his sandwich and stared at the lunch tray.

"May I join you?"

Simon nearly fell off of the bench on his side of the table, but he braced himself against the wall behind him just in time. Ella tried her best to hide a small laugh, but she was not successful.

"Uh, yeah. I mean, if you want."

Simon attempted to drown his panic with a bite of bologna.

Ella sat opposite him and observed him carefully before taking a bite of her own sandwich. After a sip of water, she cleared her throat.

"I thought you were brave the other day." Ella took another bite. She didn't need to explain.

"Thanks." That was it? That's the best he could come up with? Simon's mind filled with words, but none of them came out of his mouth.

"So what does it mean?"

Simon swallowed. "I'm sorry?"

"The words. You know, on the streets. And that thing you said in the Arena. Other people knew it too. What does it mean?"

Simon stared at her, eyes and mouth wide open.

"There you are! I've been looking for you, Simon."

It was all Simon could do to keep from falling off the bench for sure this time. Ben stood two feet from the table, a huge grin plastered across his face.

"Is this a table for two, or may I join in the fun?"

Ella blushed and moved down the bench; Ben sat down directly where she had been and focused on Simon.

"Hey, I've been thinking. I'm getting behind on my studies again. What do you say to another afternoon at the library sometime soon?"

Simon's pause clearly annoyed Ben, who frowned while Simon tried to string words together that would create an intelligible answer.

"Well, yeah, Ben. Sure. That'd be fine. Monday, maybe?"

Ben shrugged and looked off to his left, talking to the wall behind Simon.

"Well, I'll have to take a look and see when works best. So, I've been reading this book on archaeology, and you won't believe what it said . . ."

Simon turned his focus back to his bologna as Ben filled the rest of the lunch break with his newfound knowledge on fossils and ancient pottery. Occasionally, Simon would glance at Ella, but she seemed completely tuned out as she chewed mechanically, eyes fixed on the corner of the room.

The afternoon sped along as Simon contemplated his two strange encounters. When the tone pulsed to announce the end of the school day, Simon had to rouse himself from his thoughts and grab his belongings.

The springtime air warmed Simon's skin as he walked out the school doors. He scanned the stairs for Ben's light brown head of hair among the mass of students on their way home. Ben passed to his left, racing down the steps.

"Ben! Hey, Ben!" Simon's voice felt strange in his throat as the message failed to reach its destination. Ben didn't pause for a moment as he headed in the direction of his apartment building. Simon made his own descent down the stairs and began his trip alone.

"Simon. Simon! Did you hear that?"

Simon sat up with a start and scrambled to make sense of his surroundings. After a moment, the familiar walls of his sparse bedroom came into focus, and Simon's eyes adjusted to the dark. His dad's silhouette was framed in the doorway. Just then, he heard a muffled *tap, tap* coming from the air vent. Simon looked to his dad in alarm.

"Get dressed," Jonathan said. "We need to take a look."

Simon hopped up and found his stash of dark clothing from the back of his closet. He grabbed a navy pullover and black sweatpants, pulling them on as he made his way to the door of apartment 2A. Jonathan was already there. He carefully turned the doorknob and eased the door open with as little noise as possible.

Simon walked out first and led the way down the stairs, heading for the workshop door, his heart pounding. This was it! They had a visitor again. *It's about time.*

"*Simon!*" Jonathan cast his hushed voice after his son in warning. Just before unlocking the door to his dad's carpentry and repair shop, Simon spun around to look at his dad.

"Not there. Keep going." Jonathan reached the last step and curled around the bannister to walk to the back of the first-floor hallway. Parallel to the stairs from the first floor to the second, a stairway at the back of the hallway led down to the basement. The two walked down into the cool darkness.

The three-story building sat on a solid, stone-block foundation that formed the basement's subterranean walls. The full basement was divided by wooden slat walls into six storage areas, one for each apartment. The Clays laid claim to the storage area in the southeast corner of the basement. While they stored very little in the fenced-off section they secured with a padlock, they kept a washer and dryer there for laundry. Both machines were older than Simon, but they remained useful with only occasional maintenance by Jonathan.

Tap, tap, tap. There it was again, much louder down here. Jonathan led the way, following the sounds to their corner. Jonathan shined the flashlight around the storage area. All was as it should be—

"Dad, look."

—except for the small hill of dust that used to be mortar in the stone wall. Two feet above the floor, between two stones, a hole the diameter of Simon's thumb glowed with artificial light. Simon drew near, but the hole went dark. Jonathan approached from behind and placed a wary hand on Simon's shoulder. Simon obediently took a step back, making room for his dad.

"Hey! Simon? Jonathan?" The hoarse whisper was unidentifiable, but Jonathan took another step forward.

"Who is it?"

Simon couldn't see a thing through the tiny hole, but he could easily picture the goofy grin behind the next words:

"Hey, guys! We're busting you out." After a satisfied chuckle, Jack added, "Welcome back to the Darkness."

Chapter Two

Simon's alarm buzzed an irritating warning that his sleep would fall victim to the call of the Bots. It had been two weeks since he'd made an appearance at Recreation Time. Last Saturday, Jonathan had agreed to call in Simon's absence due to health issues. It was true enough. There was no challenge to Jonathan's report—evidently, the powers of New Morgan weren't in a hurry to have Simon revisit the Arena so soon either. But two weeks in a row would undoubtedly challenge the illusion of routine, and Simon knew he would have to face the duels again someday.

Simon and his mattress groaned simultaneously as he fought to pull himself out of bed. It wouldn't be long before the streets of the city filled with hundreds of kids his age making their way to the western outskirts of town—toward the Plaza and its huge competition building, the Arena.

Simon's feet dragged him toward the bathroom, where he readied himself and took some headache medicine. This was his Saturday tradition, as the Bot duels drained him of both patience and energy, but he was also treating a dull throbbing at his temples that already existed. His mind still reeled as he thought back to the night before.

He hadn't known what to think when he heard the familiar teasing of his partner in crime, Jack, from the other side of the foundation wall.

"Did you guys just dig a tunnel from the City?" Simon had asked.

The condescending laugh in response ended abruptly at the scolding of someone else on Jack's side of the barrier.

"How fast do you think we are, man? No, we're just extending your front door is all. Side door? Supply closet. Whatever." Jack never failed to get on his nerves, but Simon was relieved to hear evidence that his other world still existed—and hadn't forgotten about him.

Another voice joined the conversation. "Jonathan. It's me, Judah. I'm here with this knucklehead."

Simon caught Jonathan's smile as his dad nevertheless ignored the jab Judah gave Jack.

"I'm here," Jonathan answered. "Good to hear from you, Judah. But what are you doing? Coming here is too dangerous. You should be staying away from us."

Simon felt a twinge of panic at the suggestion, and he wanted to shush his dad. But he knew there was truth in what Jonathan said.

"That's not entirely up to you, Jonathan. Anyway, we're going to need your help. We'll be making a mess, and we'll need a cleanup crew on your end. Glad you came down."

Judah and Jack couldn't see the frown Simon did, but they likely heard it in Jonathan's voice: "Well, we heard you. We've heard you for two nights now, it seems; the sound traveled up the air ducts to our apartment."

The silence on the other end was eerie. Jonathan continued, maybe as a concession.

"I doubt anyone in the west apartments heard anything; that leaves my workshop, our apartment, and the unit above us. The noise was faint, so the damage is likely minimal. Still, it may be safer to work during weekdays, when I'm making noise in the workshop to cover you."

"That may be the way. Well, it's time to call it a night anyway. Let's go, Jack." Simon could picture the lean, strong man who typically stood guard at the City's North Gate slapping his teenage comrade on the shoulder.

"Sweet dreams, Simon!"

Simon knew his eye roll was lost on the Messenger on the other side of the wall, but he couldn't deny the sacrifice Jack was making.

"We'll clean up after you, ya slob. Thanks, Jack."

Now in the bathroom hours later, Simon rolled his eyes again as he spat toothpaste into the sink. How long does it take to quietly remove a portion of a stone wall big enough for a person to squeeze through? He could be sweeping up evidence for days.

In the kitchen, his dad was brewing coffee. Simon inhaled deeply and smiled when he entered the room and saw biscuits on the table. Mrs. Meyers' baked goods were on special ration in the freezer. Simon took this as a sign that his dad was willing to part with them in hopes of a return visit to Grand Station—the City—sooner rather than later.

Midway through the meal, Simon confronted a question that had been haunting him since last night.

"Dad, we don't really know our neighbors, especially the ones on the third floor. I guess I've never paid much attention. Who lives above us?"

"Mr. Stapleton lives above us, but he never comes out. And Mr. Brockson lives in the west unit. His wife died the year you were . . . away. But that's really all I know about them."

Simon chafed at the mention of his eighth-grade year, Life Preparation Year, especially since some memories of that time had recently—and painfully—resurfaced.

"Well, the alarms are about to go off. Time for Forced Fun."

Simon was glad to hear his dad laugh at the mild tension breaker.

Simon made his way out of the building just as the first tone pulsed through the streets. He continued west down Merchant Street. Despite the dreary walk toward an event he dreaded, Simon picked up his step when he remembered one of the hundreds of teens who might be there. He knew it was too soon to look, but he couldn't keep his eyes from searching for a black bob streaked with deep red highlights.

"Hey, Simon."

Simon nearly jumped out of his shoes at the soft voice behind him. He spun around to see nearly white hair and pale blue eyes.

"Ella."

"I imagine you don't like the Arena much anymore." Ella's timid smile and hushed tones indicated that she knew the risk of speaking critically about government affairs in public. They were traveling north, and the crowd of teenagers was growing in number.

"Well, I never have liked it, to be honest." Simon's smirk came more easily than he anticipated, and it felt awkward on his face. If Ella noticed, she didn't show it. She fell into step with him and looked ahead.

"This is your first time back? After . . ."

"Yeah."

"You're brave."

Simon didn't reply. He knew almost nothing about this girl who suddenly noticed him after he had confessed to being a part of a banned organization.

"I'm not alone." He didn't know if Ella caught all that he meant by this response the way that his dad would. The way Jack would. The way Charity . . . yes, Charity. *Focus, man.* Simon shook his head and looked around. "Here we go." It was an obvious filler, but Simon was suddenly tired from trying to think of what to say or not say to Ella. The effort was wearing him down. The pair veered left with the rest of the crowd into the central street of town. Just a few more blocks to go until they reached the edge of Westbend.

"Taking the conveyor belt?" Ella asked.

Simon looked up and saw that they were getting close to the end of the paved road. Hundreds of first- and second-year preparatory students migrated from the concrete surface onto the dusty ground. The last time Simon was at the Arena, he'd spent about thirty-six hours there. And he had been unconscious on his way in.

Ella moved toward the long and decrepit people mover Westbend used to maintain for the convenience of sports fans. She looked over her shoulder at Simon to see if he would come along.

"I usually take the dirt. See ya."

Ella nodded at the farewell and followed the crowd taking the metallic trail to the Plaza. Simon watched for a few moments as her fair head disappeared into the mass. He kicked up the dirt with his shoes as he began to travel the barren field for the two-mile trek. The horizon ahead was a straight line interrupted only by the silhouette of the Arena. Simon's knee began to ache as he trudged on.

The Arena loomed large as Simon approached the Plaza, a spacious plot of concrete dotted with statues. Simon rarely gave notice to the homage paid to the heroes of New Morgan; usually he kept his head bowed and avoided any posture that allowed eye contact. But today, as he passed one statue in particular, he was struck by the familiarity of the proud woman. The plaque at the base, which rose about four feet off the ground, proclaimed the noteworthy individual as Mrs. Matilda Druck. It dawned on Simon that he might have more connection to these idle figures than he had ever realized. The woman looking out above him with a bronzed face was his great-grandmother. Simon recalled from library trips this semester that this woman had been devoted to politics. He imagined she would be proud to have her likeness standing among other New Morgan "heroes." He thought of his grandmother, Louise Baden-Druck, with a small shudder. He wondered if she would ever have a statue with her likeness standing guard with the other impassive figures.

"Identification?"

The crowd had carried Simon to the gates, and he once again was unprepared for inspection. As he dug for his ID, he let his hair drop in front of his face—his usual move that allowed him to avoid eye contact. In his world of standard dress and even hairstyles, however, such a move only helped him stand out.

"Simon. Simon Clay, eh?" The guard practically spat his name as he looked at the ID Simon handed over. "You'll need to step aside. Your peers need to get in while we check to see if you have Security clearance."

Simon stood near the exterior wall of the building and kept his face down, as if he could avoid additional attention. Not that it mattered. He glanced up to see that he was deliberately ignored, just like the past two weeks at school, as teen after teen passed into the Arena. A tall guard came forward for what Simon assumed would be an inspection for weapons or other contraband items.

Looking for art supplies? Simon thought dryly. He recalled the last time he held such evidence in his hand, red streaks covering his palm and fingers.

"Hands up."

Simon complied, expecting a fairly routine pat down.

"OOOPH!" A hard blow to his gut left Simon gasping for air. The guard's grim smile challenged Simon to retaliate. Simon doubled over in pain and stared, unseeing, at the concrete. A sharp jab to his left shoulder was next, and Simon's knees buckled. Those nearby in line must have begun to notice the commotion as he knelt on all fours. Simon heard a few guys snicker and a girl gasp, but the crowd just kept moving, content to leave him alone.

"All right, get up. But don't be expecting any sympathy, *Simon Clay.*" The tall guard hurled his name as he jerked Simon up by the arm and shoved him toward the gate.

Once inside the Arena, Simon limped to a bench along the corridor that wrapped around the entire perimeter of the building. He bent over, pretending to tie his shoe, and exhaled relief that he could be invisible for a moment. Anyone passing by now would not have seen the ordeal.

This was too much too soon. The smells, the shouts, the pain. Simon's déjà vu was too real; nausea and tears began to well up. *No. Pull yourself together.* Simon recalled that even through the worst moments two weeks ago, he wasn't alone. *Though I walk through the valley . . .*

Walk. That's the trick. Despite the pain, Simon pushed himself up and onward, willing himself to shake off the aches and move into the crowd. He looked around, taking in the faces of first- and second-year students around him. Some were laughing. Some were fighting. Two girls smiled knowingly while a red-faced boy approached their friend, whose arms were crossed self-consciously.

Simon straightened up as an idea came to him; he walked with renewed vigor, and his search suddenly became more focused. Less aware of the dull ache in his muscles, Simon picked up his pace and began to look for any narrow passageway that would lead from this main corridor to the lower level, below all the revelry of the upcoming battles.

Chapter Three

The boy had taken a beating; it was remarkable how quickly he recuperated. The silent observer waited safely in the shadows, watching as the dark-haired member of the Darkness sought and found a hideaway. *Like a mouse*, mused the onlooker. It was tempting to follow, to dig deeper into the life of this now-famous teenager named Simon. But patience was the tactic for now. It had taken patience two weeks ago when this teenage boy and his father slipped into the shadows and into their apartment late at night. There was no point in acting too early; patience was essential for the end result.

"Long time no see." Logically, Simon knew it hadn't really been that long. But every day of not knowing—not knowing his future, not knowing how the Messengers were, not knowing when they'd meet again—made two weeks seem like an eternity. And as soon as he saw the small figure sitting on one of the horizontal beams that supported the huge building above them, his last conversation with the Messenger ahead of him felt overwhelmingly far away.

The two and a half seconds it took for his addressee to look up with a mixture of relief and happiness made up for the time. Even as the familiar guarded veil fell over her face, Simon knew he would remember that smile as long as he was able to say her name.

"Charity. You look good. Healthy and all, I mean."

"Well, you look terrible." Her smirk betrayed that she was pleased with her recovery. Strands of black and red hair fell back from her face as she lifted her chin proudly.

"Yeah, well. They don't like me much around here."

"Simon, look. I've told you before. You shouldn't be seen around here with the likes of me. I'm an outcast, remember?" Charity's green eyes were earnest with concern, and Simon couldn't help but draw closer to where she was sitting—the same place, he remembered, he sat a few Saturdays before.

"Hey, no big deal, right?" He advanced. "I don't know if you've heard, but I'm an outcast too."

"Right. A really famous one."

Famous. Simon knew Charity's light taunt was meant in good fun, but the truth hit him harder than the punch he endured at the gate. He had become a liability. The burden of this fact caused Simon to lean on a support to his left.

"You're right. Charity, it's me who's dangerous. You shouldn't be seen with *me.*"

As the truth dawned on her, Charity's shoulders fell in regret.

"I didn't mean that, you know; I don't care—"

"I know, but it's true. I can't put you in danger. I already have before." Simon winced as he remembered a late-night chase and not knowing where Charity had gone. "Oh man. Charity. I was so stupid. I'm sorry." What if she had been caught instead of him? What if they had kept searching for another pastel-stained hand like his own?

Charity's aloof demeanor had disappeared. Her head shook stubbornly. "'How are they to believe in Him of whom they have never heard?'" Her voice cracked, raw but sincere.

Simon barked a laugh full of pain. He had used those very words before, and Charity knew it. But in this moment, he had no words to say. He turned around and forced himself to walk toward the main corridors above.

"Simon—"

"I'll see you around. Just . . . not here." Simon choked as he thought of the hope—the small hope—of a one-inch hole in a stone wall.

Simon's painful trek was more difficult than ever. He moved through the crowds and up the ramps until the pain in his abdomen forced him to pause so he could catch his breath. He wasn't far from his usual spot in the stands, but he debated whether he could manage another battle this morning. Ben would no doubt be in his typical row. Would he acknowledge Simon or ignore him?

"Simon? Is that you?"

Simon couldn't believe it. He just happened to be in the same place as his early morning walking companion.

"Hey, Ella. Did I miss anything?"

"Same old, same old," she shrugged. Then she looked closely and took a step nearer. "Hey, you don't look so hot. You okay?"

Simon was grateful the bruises that were no doubt forming were hidden under his shirt. Still, his rumpled clothes and grimace showed that he'd been through something between the time they had parted earlier and now. And the rough altercation with an Arena guard was only part of it.

"Yeah. Well, you know. Not particularly in the mood to be here." He figured this bit of confiding was safe, based on Ella's interest and sympathy regarding his last trip to this venue.

"I suppose not. Still, maybe you should take the conveyor next time. Easier terrain and all." Her mild scolding made Simon wonder if he had offended her by parting ways toward the Plaza.

"I guess it couldn't hurt."

Ella took a step closer, but maneuvered to almost pass him by. "You coming in?"

He shrugged and followed her into the enormous space filled with stands that surrounded a field below. Simon's head began to throb a little, but he forced himself to focus and follow Ella up the steps toward some seats. To his relief, Simon saw the back of Ben's head several rows in front of them. His friend's sandy-colored hair peeked over a seat past the entryway; it was unlikely Ben had seen them come in.

"The first duel is over already," she told him. "It went fast."

"Who won?" Simon feigned interest for Ella's benefit, but secretly hoped she wasn't a huge fan of the games he dreaded every week.

Ella shrugged. "Maximalus played. He won, of course."

Simon could picture the scorpion-like tank of a Bot that held infamy for rarely losing a duel. He just began to settle in when he started with a jolt. A series of screeching wails and pops filled the air, and Simon turned his head to see bright flashes of light at all four corners of the round, covered field.

"Fireworks?"

"Yeah, they added them last week. I dunno." Ella shrugged and offered a clap in sync with the fans around them. Smoke invaded Simon's nostrils as he blinked back the glare of the white-hot fire.

"Residents of Westbend!" The announcer called the participants in the stands to attention, and Simon noticed that the enthusiasm of the speaker had increased from times past. "It is our pleasure to introduce to you the next two challengers in this morning's duels!"

Cheers erupted from the restless masses. Simon fought back memories of the crowd whom he had watched from the field two Saturdays prior. The beat of the stomps and claps quickened his pulse, and Simon forced his eyes to focus on the field in an attempt to ground himself in the present. The machines, each about fifteen feet tall, rose to attention and moved to the center of the field. The Bot farthest from Simon plodded on two large feet. Its legs were long, and they struggled to keep the rotund body from tilting and toppling onto the gravel surface. The other Bot used four wheels to navigate the terrain. The rumble of the motor took Simon back to the sounds he heard when he had been only a matter of feet from the contraptions. The skin on the back of his neck tingled with apprehension.

"Who do you think will win?"

"Huh?"

Ella tried again. "Which Bot do you want to win?"

Simon knew this was typical banter for the event, but he never considered which lifelike creature he would rather see demolished into scrap metal.

"I don't know. I don't care a whole lot, to be honest." He sensed this would cross the boundary of polite conversation, but he could only handle so many challenges at once, balancing past and present in his mind. Bots. Ella. Mobs. Charity. Mr. Burroughs. Noise. Security. Pain.

Screeeeech. Metallic squeals pierced Simon's ears, and the smell of grease invaded his nose. Cheers from the mob called out for murder—no, that wasn't right. Judgment? Arrest? Entertainment. The roar of the crowd grew. "Get rid of him!" *Where did that come from?*

The Bot with wheels spun backward fiercely to pull away from the viselike grip of the tall Bot's two arms. To no avail—the top-heavy Bot exposed a gleaming hatchet and wielded it high in the air before bringing the blade crashing down.

Simon's head hit the concrete floor as two victims succumbed to the duel.

Chapter Four

Weak afternoon rays managed to reach the center of the bedroom through the east-wall window. Simon had spent five minutes silently taking in the dim quietude of his surroundings. Instead of a peaceful calm, however, a growing unease took over Simon's being, and he suddenly itched to move, to get up, to do something—anything. But as soon as he landed on his feet, Simon remembered that he was trapped. There was nothing he could do. Not on a Saturday afternoon and most certainly not on this Saturday in April, weeks after he became the infamous face of the Darkness.

He hadn't even been able to make it through a single Bot duel during this morning's Recreation Time at the Arena. How on earth had he been able to make it through his own duel in front of Mr. Burroughs, Mr. Druck, and a decent percentage of Westbend's residents?

Simon tossed himself back on his bed and stared at the ceiling. Familiar words drifted into his mind. *I lift up my eyes to the hills. From where does my help come?* The words took him further back, to a very different duel—one he had nearly forgotten, either due to evil tricks or his own willful desire to forget. Stone walls and a small window came into view in his mind's eye. Simon suddenly became weary. In his almost sixteen years of life, he'd had his share of struggles. Instead of overcoming these hardships once and for all, it occurred to Simon that he'd only begun what would likely be an entire campaign of conflict.

A heavy groan was all Simon could communicate as his memory led him down a spiral stone staircase into a yearlong nightmare that slowly drew him into the darkness. *I lift up my eyes to the hills.* Yes, he had said those words during his descent nearly two years ago. *From where does my help come?*

"'My help comes from the LORD, who made heaven and earth.'" Simon surprised himself with an audible response, but the words of truth brought comfort.

"Simon? You awake?" The voice came from the other side of the closed bedroom door.

"Hey, Dad. Yeah, I guess so." Simon shook his head free of the daydreams and memories that had been attacking him all morning. The door opened, and Jonathan looked in with poorly concealed concern.

"Mrs. Pharen just called to see how you were doing. Ben apparently saw what happened."

Simon hadn't yet divulged many details to his dad of the duels that morning. After regaining consciousness in the Arena, he escaped the stands with much protest from Ella. Insisting that he needed some fresh air and a bathroom break, he finally was able to evade the attention of his companion. After waiting out the rest of the event in the corridors, Simon regained enough strength and composure to walk back to town with the rest of the crowd. He made it home in time to reach his apartment and crash on his bed. His face now burned at the embarrassment he'd brought on himself.

"I passed out during the Bot duels today. I only lasted about five minutes, Dad."

Simon's dad pushed the door open more, crossed his arms, and leaned against the doorframe. A slow nod took the place of immediate words, but a furrowed brow made it clear that Jonathan Clay had been listening. Finally, he was ready to speak.

"Oh, I imagine you endured a lot more than five minutes."

Still lying on his bed, Simon let his head fall back on the mattress. He nodded at the ceiling. No words came. After a few moments, the hinges of the door creaked as his dad pulled it closed.

"Dad?"

"Yes, Simon?" The door paused.

"Charity. I really put her in danger. And Jack. You too. Everybody, I guess."

Simon turned his head when he heard footsteps come his way. He propped himself on his elbow and made room for his dad to sit on the corner of the bed.

"I don't know if I have the answers you want, Simon. But I can tell you that I've been there. I'm there right now: at what point does my help become a hindrance?"

"Is it worth the trouble?" Simon quoted.

"Exactly." Jonathan Clay slapped his son's leg. "But you know what else? There's the other question."

"What did I learn?" Simon knew both questions by heart after years of hearing them from his father.

Simon's dad laughed. "That's not the one I was thinking of this time. The other risk is not doing anything at all—when does that become more dangerous? Put another way: What is there to lose?"

Simon thought back over the past year. His second year of Preparatory School was almost over, and he had learned more than he could have imagined. He remembered how fearful his dad had seemed when Simon learned about the Darkness.

"Dad, you're not so worried about me anymore when I go—when I used to go—out at night. Are you just impressed with my stealth and mad Messenger skills?" Simon knew his joke wouldn't get very far, but he didn't care. He wasn't sure how else to ask what was on his mind.

"Simon, I don't ever want to lose you. But if that Saturday went—if it went the way I thought it would, I knew I'd see you again." Silence fell on the room for a few minutes.

Simon ventured into the truth. "But this fall—if I'd been caught . . ." No more explanation was necessary. If he had been caught with the Darkness before knowing the light of the truth . . . "I guess it goes back to your newest question. What did you have to lose?"

The evening dragged painfully on. Simon did not get dressed for a nighttime trip. He did not nap in anticipation of a late night. He did not watch the window for clear skies. When Security knows you're part of a banned organization, there's no way an excursion past curfew would go unnoticed. It was all Simon could do to make it through dinner, busy himself with a few chores, and get ready to turn in for the night. Normally, they'd be preparing to visit Grand Station—the City, the underground world they belonged to—in order to join others for their weekly gathering. The knowledge that they would meet without him gnawed at Simon relentlessly.

"Simon? Want to help me with something?" Jonathan called from his bedroom. Simon walked in, wondering what would need his attention.

"Hand me the crowbar, would you?" Simon found his dad kneeling on the floor, pulling at the corners of the floorboard just in front of his wooden dresser. The crowbar in question was resting on the quilt of his dad's double-mattress bed. Simon rarely set foot in this room, and as he observed the quilt's intricate pattern, he wondered who had made it. But he was too curious about his dad's odd behavior to ask.

"Thanks. Now, put the end of the crowbar in the slot right there—that's it." His dad lifted the floorboard, slid it back along a groove, and pivoted it away from the floor, opening a narrow hole about two feet long.

Simon thought back to his birthday gift and marveled at the ways his dad could use wood to conceal messages. Jonathan briefly sorted through the contents below and pulled out a box, which he opened to reveal squares of folded paper and a vial. Simon beamed at the sight of the red wax imprinted with the λόγος symbol.

Before getting up, Jonathan carefully fed the board back into the track he must have worked into the neighboring floorboards long ago. The lid of the hidden compartment slid carefully into place with no sign of a secret below.

"Let's get started, shall we? I don't have the vial for this one, but I copied the text from the marketplace not long ago. Psalm 121. 'I lift my eyes to the hills . . .'"

The large windows that lined the north wall of the apartment offered only bleak clouds and a somber outlook for the day. Sunday promised little more than routine quiet, something Simon was beginning to resent. He resorted to turning on the television, only to change it every few minutes in disgust. "Dad, please tell me there's a place in this world where people have more than five shows to choose from."

Jonathan looked up from the game of solitaire he laid out on the kitchen table.

"Probably. There used to be. But I can't guarantee they would be of much more value."

"No, don't tell me that. Tell me there's a good place somewhere with—what's it called? Wireless something or other?" Simon tried to think back to the pamphlet he had recently given to Spence, the gadget guy in the City.

Simon knew his dad was often eager to talk about how life was better decades before, but his stories rarely got far before he ended them in frustration. Today, it didn't seem his dad was going to play along at all. Simon watched as his dad laid another card down in a careful line.

Knock, knock, knock. Both Simon and Jonathan startled at the unexpected sound. Jonathan slowly walked toward the door, but not before hearing an impatient reproach coming from the hall.

"Now, Jonathan, stop your dilly-dallying in there. An old man needs to sit down his tired bones after a long walk."

Jonathan hurried to unlock the door and swing it wide to welcome a short gentleman with ill-mannered white hair that contorted into a haphazard crown atop his beaming face.

"Zeke! What a surprise!" The joy in Jonathan's voice was unmistakable, but a scolding tone quickly took its place. "But what are you doing here! There's no reason why you should have risked a visit."

Zeke brushed past Jonathan and seated himself at the kitchen table, feet propped on the rungs under his wooden chair. His swift entrance provided doubt about any weary bones needing rest.

"Poppycock, Jonathan! I'm just here to visit friends. Sunday's the day for that, isn't it? No harm in that. Besides, what do I have to lose?"

Simon and Jonathan exchanged amused looks. Jonathan proceeded to lock the door again while Simon began to make coffee.

"Solitaire?" Zeke looked at the cards laid out on the kitchen table. "Which one of you left the other alone with solitaire? Nonsense! Set up the game for King's Corners, Jonathan."

The dreary afternoon suddenly became brighter, and the hours passed quickly. Simon spent the first few rounds of the game wondering when Zeke would get to the point of the visit, but he eventually relaxed and enjoyed the company of a trusted friend.

One curious nuance to Zeke's playing occurred whenever he would lay down a king card. He couldn't resist reciting quotes that Simon assumed were from the Word.

"'These will be the ways of the king who will reign over you: he will take your sons and appoint them to his chariots and to be his horsemen and to run before his chariots.'"

"'Put not your trust in princes, in a son of man, in whom there is no salvation.'"

After a while, Jonathan joined in. "'Therefore render to Caesar the things that are Caesar's, and to God the things that are God's.'"

Simon was curious, but focused mainly on trying to beat his competition. The clouds lifted slightly, but the day began to darken with time.

"Best be on my way. Thank you, gentlemen, for passing the time with me today." Zeke's signature grin accompanied his farewell. "But before I forget, a delivery."

Simon's heart skipped a beat when he imagined Zeke's hand pulling out a vial from his pocket, hoping for a newly verified Message. Instead, Zeke placed a smooth stone in Simon's hand.

"A gift for the birthday boy. Don't know if I'll be able to visit tomorrow, but I didn't want to miss the occasion."

"Thank you, Zeke." Simon's confusion didn't lessen his sincere gratitude for the odd present. Simon had nearly forgotten that he would turn sixteen the next day; his focus had centered solely on the recent past rather than the near future.

"Oh, don't thank me. I'm just the messenger." His laughter bounced off the walls of the apartment. "The gift is from a friend."

Jonathan showed Zeke out while Simon opened his hand to inspect the token. The smooth stone looked as if it could be from the walls of the City. He yearned to be within those walls again. On one side, a tiny but detailed painting portrayed a crowned lamb with a brilliant banner. He had to hold it close to read the intricate letters on the banner, but he laughed when he made out the words: "How are they to believe in Him of whom they have never heard?"

Chapter Five

I am growing mad with the pestilence that is plaguing our people. A new covenant. The Way. The Messiah has come. Fools! Do they not know that if the Anointed has come, I would be among the first to know? And whom do they worship? A man who sat with sinners. A rebel who publicly harassed the authorities. A man who lies dead in a—well, who knows where. But who cares? He's rotting with the worms, and His followers won't be far behind. The time to end this has come.

■ ■ ■

Monday passed with a predictable number of problems. A folded note waited on his desk in the morning. The cartoonist had drawn a stick figure but had taken care in making Simon's likeness undeniable: straight, dark hair;

a lightly shaded face; Xs for eyes and his tongue hanging out as the figure lay sprawled on the arena floor. Simon's years of practiced nonchalance did well to hide facial reaction, but his neck tingled at the muted laughter that surrounded him.

In the cafeteria, Ella joined the line at the counter behind him and whispered a quick hello as she reached for a bowl of soup, but they both caught Ben's eye at the drink counter and silently parted ways to sit at separate tables. No one joined Simon at his corner spot today.

At the end of the school day, Simon leaped from his desk at the sound of the low pulse and hurried home, eager to try a plan that had been taking shape in his mind. Five minutes later, he was halfway home. *Perfect.* His pace slowed to a crawl. When he heard approaching footsteps, he glanced to be sure that a familiar frame was behind him.

It was Ben all right. When he noticed Simon a few seconds later, he froze in place. Simon took a few steps forward, and Ben slowly continued his trek. Simon stopped again, and Ben halted about fifteen feet away. Simon didn't hide his snort of laughter as he began to jog. Ben projected a growl of frustration and picked up a brisk walk. Simon stopped. Nearby, a corner clock ticked the passing time. *Tick, tock.* Time was running out to get home. Ben darted into the street to cross to the other sidewalk.

"Ben, this is stupid."

"Simon! You jerk!" Ben was in the middle of the street, glaring at him. "We're going to be late. And caught. And they're gonna think . . ."

"That you're my friend?"

"THAT I'M PART OF THE DARKNESS!" Ben's reddened face suddenly blanched as he realized what he'd confessed for all who might be listening. "Because I'm NOT a criminal." Ben looked up and around to the windows, checking for faces, cameras, microphones.

"I know, Ben. I KNOW." Simon carried his volume as a gesture of a public alibi, which Ben rewarded with a grudging pivot toward his neighbor. "But can we talk? You can't avoid me forever. And we only have five minutes left to get home. Just give me that much."

A car turned onto the road, and Ben crossed back onto the sidewalk to Simon. The two walked the next block in silence.

"Ben, I made a big mistake. I've put people in danger, and that's not fair."

"Simon, you think you're so cool because of all the stuff you get to do." Ben focused on the sidewalk as he spat his words. "But some of us? We just—it's just—it's not worth it, is it? We're good people and all, ya know? Everyone acts like—the Messen—believ—you know—they act like we're evil or something. It's not like I don't agree with, you know, with you. But don't you think it's better to stay out of trouble?"

Simon was tired of having no answers. He looked up between the rows of buildings and saw gray clouds gather in the sky. Rain might be coming. Simon had grown so accustomed to evaluating his night plans based on the weather, he had momentarily forgotten that storms were moot to his schedule lately.

Ben must have taken his silence as an apology. "Simon, I'm with you. You know that. But can you at least promise that you won't get me arrested? that you won't get my family arrested?"

The two turned right at the next corner and walked down Merchant Street.

"Ben, I'm sorry. I don't think I can promise anything anymore. But I'll stay out of your way. I won't get you into trouble."

Ben climbed a few steps toward an apartment building, and Simon realized they had reached their block. Simon crossed the street to 2350 Merchant Street, his building.

"Oh, hey. Happy birthday." And with that, Ben opened his building's front door and disappeared from view.

As Simon opened the door to his dad's workshop, old bells on a leather strap jingled in mild protest. Jonathan didn't look up immediately; he must not have heard the entrance over the sound of his handsaw. The coffee table enduring the procedure groaned in protest at the modification.

"Hey, Dad." Simon set his backpack on a worktable and sat on a nearby stool, thankful to ease some of the weight of his day.

"It's the birthday boy! Or is that too childish? You're sixteen, after all. Provisional Adult Status, eh?"

Simon snorted. "Like that'll do me any good." For two years, teens of New Morgan experienced slightly more relaxed curfews and controls. Then, as long as no serious infractions occurred during this probationary period, eighteen-year-olds were granted full adult citizenship status, which included more freedom of movement throughout their designated communities during daytime hours. Sixteen-year-olds, for example, could run errands for their parents after school and before a seven o'clock curfew. Simon had forgotten that this new luxury could have bought him more time already this afternoon, but it was of little consequence. As New Morgan's most infamous teen, Simon doubted he'd be able to enjoy this meager governmental concession. He rubbed his ribs, which were still sore from Saturday.

"Have fun at school?"

Simon fought back another scornful snort; the past few weeks were an adjustment for both of them, after all. Allowing sullen silence instead, he subtly reminded his father that criminals don't get to enjoy their birthdays.

"Time for me to close up shop for today. I ran some laundry downstairs during my lunch break; want to . . . straighten up down there?"

The pause was enough to remind Simon of both chores that would need his attention in the basement. Suddenly energized, he grabbed his backpack and headed downstairs.

"I'll meet you in the apartment when you're done," his dad called out as the workshop door closed behind Simon.

Racing down the stairs to the southeast corner of the basement, Simon paused at the most beautiful pile of dust he had ever seen. Grabbing the broom and dustpan he used Friday night, he made quick work of the crumbled mortar on the floor. The hole in the wall had grown to an eight-inch, horizontal line along the top edge of a stone. Not wanting to think how many days it would take to make the hole large enough for human passage, Simon lifted the small metal cabinet that held cleaning supplies and laundry soap and set it in front of the tiny portal to the outside world. He was halfway up the basement stairs when he remembered to transfer the wet laundry to the old but faithful dryer.

The first thing Simon noticed in the kitchen was the aroma of ham slices sizzling in a pan. The second was the sight of a pair of cupcakes on the counter.

"Have you taken up baking, Dad?"

"I marvel at the forethought of Mrs. Meyer," Jonathan explained over his shoulder while opening a can of green beans. "When she stuffed our pockets with baked goods last time, she slipped these in with my load. They've been in the freezer ever since."

The dinner was salty and satisfying, and Simon enjoyed the sweet dessert from the woman who never ceased to extend the right kind of comfort at just the right time.

"Happy birthday, Simon." Jonathan pulled a small package wrapped in a dish towel out of his pocket. Simon unwrapped the gift—a watch with a thick wooden face.

The straps were aged leather, and Simon wondered what had been repurposed for this new item.

"Dad, this is really cool. Thanks!" He examined the wooden design that was clearly accomplished through the meticulous work of his father's hands.

"There's more to it." Jonathan pulled off a ring, which Simon hadn't realized he'd been wearing during dinner. It was his dad's own λόγος ring, a sign that its owner was a Messenger. As a Postmaster, Jonathan had little opportunity or reason to wear it outside the house, but he must have been preparing for a demonstration. Simon thought about his own ring and gave thanks for Malachi for finding it and Jack for returning it the night of Simon's battle. He still needed to ask Spence to help him fix his broken chain.

Jonathan took the watch and turned it over, exposing a curious carving. Jonathan set his ring against the back and twisted it slowly. The base rotated like the lid of a jar. Simon realized that even though the carving was not exactly a relief of the word λόγος, the ring's pattern hooked into specific places of the wood. The ring was a key. Inside the back of the watch was a shallow hollow space—just large enough to accommodate the watch mechanics but deep enough to hold a small note.

"I've always found it handy to have plenty of places to stash information," Jonathan explained.

"It's perfect. Did you make the watch too?"

"The watch mechanism itself was my dad's. It was a wedding gift from him to me."

Simon had never met his dad's side of the family; there were those from his mom's side he'd rather not have.

"Is Grandpa Clay alive?" Simon had never used that phrase before, and it felt strange to say.

Simon's dad adjusted to the question too, furrowing his brow in thought. His gray-green eyes peered through the north windows. "I guess I'm not sure. I've never heard otherwise. Actually, I haven't heard from my parents in years. They live in a very different country. Or at least they did. I pray that they still do."

"Dad, you said things started getting really bad when I was young. Do they know about me?"

A slow roll of thunder punctuated the conversation, reminding Simon of the clouds he saw on his way home.

"They do. Your mother had written to them back when you were very young. She would give them updates about how you were growing up." Simon watched his dad slip deeper into nostalgia, but it brought a pained expression to Jonathan's pale face.

"Hey, Dad, wanna watch some TV?"

The surprise of the question worked to bring his dad out of his thoughts. "Really? I guess so; it's your birthday. You pick the agenda."

The TV fizzled and spat to life as static mixed with the opening chimes of the news program. A middle-aged man with dark features, a crisp white shirt, and silver glasses smiled at the camera. "Good evening, citizens of New Morgan. Today is the twenty-third day of Quarter Two."

Jonathan's low growl interrupted the news anchor. "April eleventh."

The government's decision to divide the year into four seasonal quarters was little more than a superficial mandate on time itself. Even the most compliant citizens still used the "old calendar."

"I'm Robert Strap, and this is the evening news. Rod Benson will have the weather report after the weekend Bot recaps. But first, an announcement from the Tribune." Robert lowered his glasses and held a yellow half-sheet of paper. His image on the screen wavered for a moment as lightning flashed in the north windows.

"Citizens of New Morgan, it is with great satisfaction that we have decided to implement a new measure to further improve your security, specifically after curfew."

Simon leaned forward from his place on the couch and glanced at his dad, who brought a hand to his chin.

"Recent violations have moved your government to consider additional opportunities to ensure your safety, which is our key priority."

Simon was now sitting on the edge of his seat. Shocked that they decided to mention what was clearly a reference to his infamous capture and trial, Simon wondered at the newest implication of his actions.

A visual of Maximalus appeared behind the anchor, and Simon assumed for a split second that the Bot report was cued prematurely. His heart dropped as he heard the next sentences.

"Each night, we will utilize redesigned Bots to patrol the streets of Port Lest, Centra, and Westbend. We are certain that we have rogue groups such as the Darkness well under control, but we will never cease to be sure that you and your loved ones are protected from the criminal action of any rebels who choose to disregard the laws we have set in place. Do not be alarmed by the sight of these machines from your windows. As you know, we make every decision with your best interest in mind. Proceed, citizens, in teamwork, obedience, loyalty, honesty, and order."

As the picture of Maximalus expanded to fill the entire screen, the television went instantly black. *Crack!* And the entire apartment was filled with darkness. Simon's mind went dark as well, until his father's voice called out calmly.

"We'll need to check the fuses."

Simon reached into the cupboard above the stove and felt the metal handle of a flashlight. The beam pierced the kitchen with a glowing circle as the two made their way to the basement. The storm was in full force; lightning flashed, pouring white light onto the stairs through the large window at the landing between the second and first floors. Thunder roared around them, and wind howled against the panes of glass. The sounds diminished as they made their way down into the lowest level, the stone foundation a buffer against the noise aboveground.

Pop. Thud. Crash!

Jonathan and Simon instinctively ran toward a sound that clearly came from within their building. They reached the southeast corner and were met with a spray of rubble and dust.

Despite the tiny particles of debris that still hung in the air, Simon's flashlight beam found a face staring out from the darkness. Simon was so startled he couldn't suppress a gasp. The eerie face was visible through a two-foot square hole that had been the stone wall of the building's foundation. The stones that had been in place that afternoon now lay in large chunks on the ground. The face glowed with equal parts surprise, guilt, and pride. When the figure removed his goggles and knit cap, Simon recognized Spence as the culprit of the invasion.

"That was a bit more of an impact than I had planned."

A second face peered behind Spence, and Simon assumed it amounted to the fifth time ever that its opened mouth was speechless—which didn't last for long.

"Um, well. Happy birthday. . . . Surprise?"

Simon couldn't help but look back at Jack and laugh.

Chapter Six

Despite the noisy cover of the storm, no one wanted to waste time. The rubble was hastily placed in an empty storage box, and the floor was swept clean. Jonathan and Simon positioned a dusty trunk underneath the hole and set two plastic bags of older sheets and clothes on top. After climbing through the new portal, Jonathan shifted the bags into place. Simon knew that the impromptu camouflage was far from foolproof, but it would have to do for now. He couldn't squelch the adrenaline that surged through him. *Freedom!*

Simon stared excitedly at the three figures in the tunnel. Spence peered through dusty lenses and shook his knit cap free of dust and debris. Jack pulled off his hood and beamed at their victory. Jonathan lifted an electric lantern that was sitting on the ground and peered at the handiwork of their fellow Messengers. Simon noticed two shovels, a pick, and a crate full of wires and odds and ends that he imagined contributed to the explosion that liberated him from his imprisonment. The space itself was barely large enough to fit them all, and the narrow tunnel behind Spence made it clear that the next stretch of the escape would require all four to duck and walk in single file.

"You guys dug us a tunnel to the City?" Simon couldn't imagine a better birthday present.

"Um, yeah. In two weeks, we blazed an underground trail halfway across the city. With our bare hands, in fact!"

Simon didn't need to see Jack's dimly lit face to sense his scorn; the sarcasm dripped from his voice. He wished his own look of disgust was more visible in the dark space. So much for liking the guy.

The lantern light mimicked Jonathan's movement as he stepped toward the passageway. Spence shifted out of the way and provided background information.

"This tunnel is only about twenty feet long, and the dirt made things more manageable. The infrastructure underneath your back alley allowed us to tunnel up to the building without much fear of collapse. Still, we typically had a pair of volunteers take shifts nonstop throughout the two-week period."

Simon hoped there was a list of volunteers somewhere; a lot of people were going to get bear hugs.

"After you, Clay."

Simon felt a hard slap on the back of his shoulder that nearly caused him to fall into his dad. And there was at least one person who was going to get clobbered.

Spence took the lantern back and led them into the tunnel. Simon followed his dad, wary of the Messenger who trailed behind. The dirt walls brushed up against his sleeves, and Simon remembered the first time he journeyed through a dark, constricting tunnel. At least then he was able to reach out his hands a little to feel the cool concrete. He willed himself to imagine a tall ceiling above him to force back the tension threatening to clench his muscles into uselessness. The lantern light ahead did little to help him navigate beyond following the shadow of his dad's head, but it was better than a sudden plunge into darkness. With each step, he took a slow, steadying breath.

"Rounding a corner." Jonathan's voice didn't rise above a monotone report of Spence's action ahead, for which Simon was extremely grateful. A consoling encouragement from his dad in front of Jack and Spence would have been horrifying for his first day as a sixteen-year-old.

"You'll have to jump down here." This time, the voice came from Spence, but it was muffled by the corner and short amount of distance between them. Simon took note, even though the direction was to Jonathan. He watched his dad lower himself to the ground and sit on what looked like a ledge. Simon could see the jagged edges of an opening as Jonathan passed the lantern through it to Spence and leaped down.

Simon took his turn, sitting on the rough ledge. He leaned over his knees to see how far his feet were from the ground, but the shadows were no help. Spence and Jonathan stood below, their heads almost in line with Simon's knees. Simon scooted forward, pushed off with his hands, and dropped.

The sound of his shoes on wet gravel signaled that the opening had led to a new kind of passageway. He stepped aside and looked up to watch Jack crouch in the hole. To the side, a panel of corroded metal had been pulled back at the corner. They were in a storm drain, and the opening to Simon's dirt-packed tunnel of freedom was through the top half of the rounded wall.

"This particular drain is more or less derelict," Spence informed them. "Still, you'll have to look before you leap in the future. Wouldn't want to get washed away."

Simon mused at the matter-of-fact warning of doom and wondered if much fazed his spectacled rescuer.

The four followed the drain to the left, which Simon guessed might be south, but he couldn't be sure. The sound of eight shoes crunching on a thin layer of gravel somehow made the journey feel more like a casual stroll than an illegal pursuit. The massive drainpipe felt spacious compared to the dirt tunnel they left behind, and Simon relaxed a bit as they followed the lantern glow.

"You couldn't have waited to get caught in the summer, eh, Simon?" Jack ambled next to Simon's side. "Some of us have exit exams coming up. If I fail fourth year due to sleep deprivation, I'll have you to thank for it."

Simon knew Jack wasn't much older than he was, but he seldom thought of him as a student in Preparatory School.

"What sector do you live in, Jack?"

"Awww, never knew you cared, Clay." Jack's attempt to muss Simon's hair in an exaggerated show of affection was only partially successful. Simon ducked and deflected the attack as best he could. "I live in the East Sector, so I wasn't affected by your reckless antics."

Despite the theatrical scolding, both knew this was not true. A few moments of silence passed, and Simon couldn't help but appreciate the pain in the neck walking a few feet away.

"All I can say," Jack continued after a few minutes, "is that you'd better be thankful for this storm. Without the noise, there's no way we'd have been able to break through your wall so fast. It'd have been days, weeks, months . . ."

"The storm." Spence had stopped short, and it took Simon a minute to realize that a ladder was the reason for the pause. Descending from a circle above and bolted to the ceiling, a metal ladder ended a few feet from the ground. Still, Simon wondered at Spence's stoic face and random comment. Spence seemed to come to a similar conclusion and shook himself out of his thoughts. "No matter. Up we go."

Simon maintained his spot as the third in line. The metal was cold and clammy, and he wondered for a moment if this would become his regular entrance into the world of the Darkness. *The world of the light*, he reminded himself.

"Any time, birthday boy."

Simon looked down at Jack and tried to think of a clever retort, but a roar from further down the tunnel interrupted him. Suddenly, both teens realized the threat and Simon scrambled up the ladder to make room.

"Climb!"

Jack obeyed and began clawing at each new rung of the ladder as a wave of water crashed around a corner and plunged toward them. Simon created space for Jack to climb higher, but the rush of swirling water foamed and grabbed at his legs. Jack cried out in shock, and his right hand slipped. His chin hit a rung, and Simon could see pain and confusion streak across his face.

"I got ya. Hang on!"

Simon couldn't remember climbing down, but he was bracing Jack's left wrist against the side bar of the ladder.

"Climb the ladder, Jack."

Obediently, Jack focused his eyes and uncurled his right arm from the ladder below the water and maneuvered to regain his footing. As Jack planted his right hand on a new rung, Simon shifted his weight to brace that arm instead. He realized he was on the back side of the ladder, hunched almost into a ball to keep from getting wet. It seemed an eternity, but Jack made his way up the ladder, one slippery step at a time. Simon moved around to the front and climbed up after him.

The four were in a narrow alleyway, and Jack was bent over, heaving to catch his breath. Spence surveyed the surroundings, and Jonathan surveyed Jack.

"You're welcome," Simon said, mimicking his best goofy Jack grin. "You know, for saving your life."

Still gasping for breath, Jack coughed a chuckle that sounded more like a cry. "You . . . slowpoke."

"You dripped all over me, by the way. I'll survive, though." Simon enjoyed the role reversal, adopting an air of mock resignation.

Spence interrupted the faux quarrel by peering into the hole. "The water only came up about halfway. The tunnel is high enough that it should still be intact; our work shouldn't be lost. Looks like the water is already receding."

"Glad to know we might still find our way home tonight." Jonathan's grim tone was familiar. Simon knew what must be running through his mind. Simon wondered it too. *Is it worth the trouble?*

"Simon. Your shirt."

It took Simon a moment to realize why Spence was pointing at him. He was wearing a light gray shirt that stood out in the night. His dad's navy clothes would pass in the darkness, but Simon was stuck.

"Allow me." Jack, with regained composure, pulled off his hooded jacket to expose another dark shirt underneath.

Simon didn't bother to grumble as he pulled on the half-soaked garment and zipped it up. The four began to walk toward a residential street, so Simon took his last chance to whisper one more jab toward Jack.

"Man. Your jacket reeks."

The group paired off and angled through the night streets with practiced precision. The smell of the night air hit Simon; he didn't realize it was a scent he missed until that moment. Excitement surged through him, and it took an extra amount of energy to keep focused and on pace with the others.

The alley was in a neighborhood that Simon didn't know well, so he looked around and made careful note of his surroundings. He remembered the advice of another Messenger, Malachi: "Look for the cues. Tall buildings, familiar towers. And the stars. Follow the stars." Simon realized it would be good to spend some time studying astronomy this summer.

Thud. Thud. Thud. Cruuuunch.

All four Messengers froze at the horrible noise coming from what seemed to be a few blocks away. They had been traveling the center of a narrow alley, and after a paralyzing second, they all dashed toward the wall on their left. Crouching down, Simon heard the thudding of his heart as loudly as he heard the steady pounding of massive footsteps.

He saw the smoke first as it obscured the streetlight at the end of the alley. A huge machine the size of a tank filled the view of the street as it moved from left to right. Six legs slammed the concrete as it continued its prowl down the road and out of view.

A hand lifted from Simon's shoulder, and he realized someone had been clenching it as they hid. He looked up to see his dad stand and motion forward.

"Maximalus," Simon informed in a whisper.

"Nice that they give us warning now," Jack whispered.

"It's just for show, for the town." Simon's stomach turned as he reflected how he was the threat they feared, not the larger-than-life weapon on legs that patrolled the streets.

"We'll have to watch for any Security guards that follow behind," Spence cautioned.

The four stayed close to the wall as they crept along the side of the alley toward the street recently occupied by the Bot. Simon could see in the harsh streetlight that the pavement suffered shallow but significant surface damage where Maximalus had stepped. Judging by the marks, one of the Bot's feet was larger than two of his own. With a deep breath, Simon fought back memories of the Bots coming to life around him while he stood defenseless in the Arena. *Wake up, Simon.* He saw Jack jog toward a corner and slip into another alley, and he scolded himself for losing ground. Simon couldn't lose focus every time he thought of the Bots, the Arena, or Druck. Too much was at stake. *You're on my turf now, Metalhead.* He ran toward the others, toward the City.

Chapter Seven

The door of the South Gate had intimidated Simon the first time he saw its foreboding front and sliding panel, but it was a welcome sight to him now. The sentiment on the other side of the barrier must have been mutual; the four-inch-wide panel slid a crack as they approached, and the door opened before Spence had a chance to press the small black button to announce their arrival. Michael stood watch tonight. Though his face conveyed no emotion, he nodded at each Messenger as they passed through the open portal. Simon felt a brief but firm pat on his shoulder as he stepped into the dark entryway, the first form of communication Michael had ever offered him. Once all four were inside, the door closed firmly and quietly against the world outside.

Simon shivered as the group descended through the cool, concrete tunnel. The bottom of Jack's damp jacket hung just a few inches above his knees, and the moisture had slowly permeated his jeans. He unzipped the borrowed garment and tied its sleeves around his waist. The skin on his arms prickled at the cool underground air, but he somehow felt less constricted by the sagging clothing. Almost without thinking, Simon let his fingers brush either side of the tunnel walls, and he was suddenly appreciative of the spaciousness of the pathway compared to the one that waited for him on his return home.

The way became darker until they reached the stretch with lanterns flanking the walls. It had been a while since Simon took notice of the symbols that were illuminated above each flame, but he smiled at the shapes that had at one time seemed so mysterious. He now recognized three interlinking circles as a depiction of the triune God. He knew that the P and the X combination stood for Christ. When he drew near the λόγος symbol, he paused and traced its lines.

"In the beginning was the Word . . ." Simon whispered to himself. In this same chapter of John, Simon had quoted a message on the street for all to see. Three weeks ago. If he could turn back time, would he still do it?

Darkness gave way to light, and the group entered a small marketplace with fire pits, a mural, and a particularly bubbly baker.

"You come here, birthday boy!"

Simon turned red as a woman in her late forties hustled her way across the room to give him a warm hug. Not all women in the City wore long skirts, but Mrs. Meyer always did. Simon wondered how she could manage to move so quickly with all the fabric that swirled around her.

"Did you save those cupcakes for today?" she asked mid-hug.

"It was a delicious birthday dessert; thank you."

When Mrs. Meyer released him, Simon noticed a new tiredness in her face. His dad noticed it too.

"Martha, you don't look well. Are you feeling okay?"

The reaction was terrible for Simon to watch as her cheery countenance fell to sorrow for a few moments, and Mrs. Meyer struggled to maintain her composure.

"Oh, Jonathan, it's George. I just know—" her voice broke off as she shook her head determinedly.

"Where is he? At home?"

Tears welled in Mrs. Meyer's eyes, and she clasped her right hand over her mouth. She managed to nod but lost a few teardrops in the process. Simon had heard Mrs. Meyer speak of her husband before, but they'd never met.

"Let's go now." Jonathan spoke with a voice that Simon had grown to know over the past few months. It conveyed tones of calm in the worst situations and a deep care for others.

Mrs. Meyer shook her head and found her voice. "No, not yet. You've got others to see first. Besides, he was sleeping when I left him an hour ago. He needs his rest."

Simon watched his dad concede begrudgingly, which allowed Mrs. Meyer to regain the rest of her composure.

"Simon! Jonathan!" The voice came from the doorway that led to the rest of the City. Micah's slim frame moved into the room, and Simon grinned at the twenty-something Carrier who had trained him to navigate the streets of Westbend without being detected.

"Glad to see the two of you out and about again. They broke you free, eh?" Micah's calm confidence stood out in contrast to Jack's mischief. The group walked toward him, passing the fire pits and the mural to their right.

"The trick will be getting them back safely," Spence admitted. "We found more adventure than we were bargaining for."

"That reminds me," Jack interjected. "Anybody got spare pants around here? Preferably not soaked with floodwater?"

Micah's bewildered face broke into a wary smile. "I'm not gonna ask. But yeah, I'm sure we can come up with something. Zeke's looking for the two of you, though," Micah said, pointing to Simon and Jonathan.

Jonathan turned back to Mrs. Meyer, who had returned to her table of baked goods. "We'll come back this way before we leave, and we'll pay a visit to George then."

Mrs. Meyer didn't protest; she gave a simple, silent smile as she rearranged a few loaves of bread at one corner of her station.

The group followed Micah toward the heart of the City. Simon grinned broadly as the hallways widened and greetings were tossed back and forth between busy Messengers passing one another on their way to their next errand.

"Joseph! Thanks for the hinges. I was able to make the repairs to our apartment door with no trouble."

"Susan, it's been a while!"

"Matt, we'll have to meet soon and catch up."

The hall opened to the left with open archways, giving view to the activity in the main marketplace. The mixture of smells reminded him of the first day he became acquainted with the aroma, with an accidental collision in a busy hallway.

"Ooph!"

Are you kidding me? Simon looked to his right, in the direction of a hard blow to his arm. His instinct to apologize to whomever he bumped into was quickly replaced with an incredulous grin.

Green eyes peered from under black hair, and a small smirk punctuated an otherwise blank face.

"Seriously. You've gotta stop bumping into people." Charity's smile widened, betraying that the shove was in no way accidental. "Happy birthday, Clay."

Simon struggled to play it cool. He bit the insides of his cheeks to prevent a ridiculous smile from breaking out over his face. "Thanks for the present."

Charity shrugged. "I wasn't expecting to see you so soon."

"Come on, Charity," Jack interjected, impatient with the lack of attention. "Never underestimate our ingenuity, our bravery, our—"

"Batteries," Spence slipped in. "Grabbed a few from the cellar to use in my little explosion. Didn't want to use our good ones in storage, but an old one from the castoffs was perfect. Probably one you brought in, Charity."

It took Simon a minute to realize that "cellar" was the name Spence gave to his workshop in the City. Charity was a frequent contributor to the odds and ends Spence stored there for future contraptions and inventions.

"I rescued you, Clay," Charity said proudly, with only a touch of added drama.

"I'm forever grateful."

"One thing, though. You kinda stink."

Simon gave a mixture of reactions—shock, indignation, embarrassment, realization, frustration. There wasn't much he could do about his jeans and shoes, but he grabbed the soggy jacket from around his waist and hurled it at Jack, who had already begun laughing at him.

"Hey, maverick, you coming or what?"

Jack, Charity, and Simon looked ahead to see that Micah and Jonathan were nearing the end of the marketplace's side corridor.

Jonathan stood at ease near Micah, whose crossed arms conveyed the message that they had waited long enough. Jack gave a deep, solemn bow to his companions and walked down a few open stairs toward the marketplace. "I come naked and hungry," he announced to no one in particular. Simon made a mental note to figure out which Bible passage Jack must be referencing.

Charity rolled her eyes at the not-so-humble beggar. "Well, off to work. Judas is next." She turned to cross the marketplace toward the Room of the Twelve; her artistry in painting the disciples commanded much of her time and attention. Simon wanted to follow and check on her recent progress, but a loudly cleared throat down the way reminded him that others were waiting for him already.

"Catch ya later. And thanks again for the gift!"

Charity waved over her head without turning around and swiftly weaved her way through the people perusing merchandise, exchanging news, and straightening displays. Simon jogged toward Micah and his dad so they could continue on their way to see Zeke.

Simon was expecting to end in the Elders' room, passing the intricate garden mosaic on the way, so he was disappointed when Micah veered left past the marketplace and led Jonathan and Simon to a space full of tables that had a view of the side of the marketplace. Convenient for those who wanted to eat a recent purchase, this common area called the Courtyard also provided a somewhat natural—albeit noisy—meeting place. Simon and Zeke had met here several times throughout the school year as Simon learned his most important lessons of the year. The three walked toward Zeke, who sat at a middle table, munching on a raw green bean.

"The Clay gentlemen! Welcome." Zeke motioned for them to have a seat opposite him and nudged a small open box of green beans their way. Simon had rarely seen these vegetables fresh and readily accepted one. Micah waved good-bye and headed into a nearby tunnel.

"First of all, Simon, happy birthday! If I'd known you'd come so soon, I might not have risked a trip yesterday!" His hearty laugh brought his white, bushy eyebrows into two surprised arcs. His amusement at his own words made it clear that Zeke was purely in jest. He would have come regardless.

"But no, there's more to discuss now, isn't there." Zeke's abrupt rhetorical question changed the tone quickly. "Have you heard the news?"

"About the Bots? Yes. In fact, we saw one on our way here. It was . . . which one was it, Simon?"

"Maximalus." Simon's skin crawled with the word. The indentation in the pavement left an imprint in his memory. "He almost always wins."

Zeke grunted for an answer and shook his head. Simon didn't like to see his face without a smile. Often, he looked joyful even when scolding with a "Poppycock!" or "Nonsense!" but Zeke gave no impression of happiness now. In fact, it grew darker.

"And George Meyer . . ."

"I haven't seen him yet. Martha insisted I wait until later tonight."

"It's no good, Jonathan. It won't be long now."

"Any word from the doctors?"

"They've used up all their health credits this year. Martha gave up her own as well. We have a few doctors here in the City, as you know, but medication is sparse, and there's little that can be done anyway."

Silence fell on the table as Simon observed the two men before him. Both were leaders, pastors who still led and cared for others despite the fact that they had no official churches of people to lead. The people of the City were under their keeping, whether the city of Westbend knew it or not.

"Evil surrounds us, Jonathan." For the first time, Zeke looked old to Simon. The unruly white hair never betrayed the vivacious Elder, but world-weariness set into the wrinkles of his face, and his concerned frown brought years to his appearance.

"Yes," Jonathan conceded. "It always has."

"Amen. Come, Lord Jesus!"

"What do you think they'll do next?" Simon asked.

"Who can say? But we have nothing to fear. 'We are afflicted in every way, but not crushed; perplexed, but not driven to despair; persecuted, but not forsaken; struck down, but not destroyed.'"

"Where's that from?" Simon could tell this was a portion of the Message. Zeke smiled proudly.

"Second Corinthians. Fourth chapter."

Simon made a mental note to copy that one down when he had a chance to visit the main marketplace.

Zeke focused on Jonathan. "Things are going to get worse, Jonathan. We're going to need all the help you're able to give."

Jonathan's face struggled against some silent pain, but he smiled through it. "It's my privilege. What is there to lose?"

Simon wrestled with gratitude, pride in his father, and fear that things were worsening.

"Time to visit George."

Jonathan and Simon said their good-byes to Zeke and headed toward the south entrance, where Mrs. Meyer would be tending her table of muffins and rolls. Simon looked to his right when they passed the main market-place and lamented that there would be no chance for him to cross into the far archways to the Room of the

Twelve to see how much progress Charity had made on the mural in his absence.

When Mrs. Meyer saw the two approach, she bit her lips and gave a quick nod. She removed her apron and set it at her booth, leaving everything behind to guide the way. The three walked toward an elaborate mural that Simon couldn't bring himself to examine today. In the corner near the first panel of the mural was a narrow door Simon had not noticed before. With his attention riveted on the fire pits, dramatic artwork, and effervescent Mrs. Meyer, he had never paid much attention to this subtle corner of the Room of the Martyrs.

Mrs. Meyer led them through the doorway and into a twisting maze of tunnels that were brand new to Simon. Just when he thought he was gaining ground in learning the City, there was a whole new web of passages for him to explore.

After wandering for longer than Simon expected, they came to a steep staircase and still another door. Mrs. Meyer leaned against the door to push it open and welcomed the two to a basement.

"Up we go," Mrs. Meyer said. The three journeyed two more flights and entered a small bedroom on the second floor of a tall and narrow house. Simon wasn't sure if the dim light of night was creating an illusion, but everything seemed small and worn. A hacking cough on the far side of the bedroom greeted them.

"Martha?" The voice was low and raspy. The effort of speech caused the man in the dim light to succumb to another fit of coughs.

"Yes, George," Martha said gently after the coughing stopped, "and Jonathan Clay. And his son, Simon."

"Brave boy," the man whispered, nodding slowly. "May God use you as He wills."

Simon wanted to say any number of things—to argue with the dying man, to thank him, to say a prayer for him. He couldn't. He stood silent.

"George, it's good to see you again." Jonathan interrupted the painful quiet and focused on Mr. Meyer.

"I can't see much of anything, I'm afraid," George said quietly. The effort of the conversation was beginning to tax him again. George's breaths began to wheeze.

"How about this, then? You rest your eyes—and your voice—and I'll share some things with you."

Simon listened to his dad recite Psalm 23, and he felt his own body relax. The words had been a lifeline for him in years past. His dad continued with parts of Psalm 51, Ephesians 2, and John 3. Mrs. Meyer began to cry, and she sat on a wide cushioned stool near the foot of the bed. Her left hand rested on her husband's ankle. Simon's dad was kneeling close to George and speaking clearly so that all could hear. Simon felt strange standing on the fringe of the scene, so he sat next to Mrs. Meyer. He wanted to do something to help, but he could only sit and listen to the spoken Word. She leaned against him, allowing him to share some of her burden.

"Our Father, who art in heaven." Jonathan began the prayer, and Mrs. Meyer and Simon joined in. Simon could see George's lips moving slightly in cadence with the prayer. It was almost time to go.

After the *amen,* Jonathan cleared his throat and began to sing. "Around the throne of David, The saints, from care released, Raise loud their songs of triumph To celebrate the feast."

Mrs. Meyer joined in with a shaky but warm voice, "They sing to Christ their leader, Who conquered in the fight, Who won for them forever Their gleaming robes of white."

Chapter Eight

In the shadows of the alley behind 2350 Merchant Street, a silhouette pulled closer to a wall as a shield against the chill of the evening. For two weeks, all had been quiet. No nighttime exits from the side portal of the building. No visitors dropping in for a visit. It was Monday now, and the onlooker could only guess at the tension Westbend's most recent infamous rebel would be enduring by waiting within the brick walls of the building night after night. It began to wear on the shadowed visitor as well. Watching, waiting every single night took its toll on a person. Would he never leave again? Maybe he had run out in the storm, and it was already too late; too much time had passed. Another wasted night. The figure shook off the frustration and settled in for a longer watch. If he managed to leave undetected, he would have to return eventually. There was a second opportunity to catch someone breaking curfew regulations.

"Do you think it's time to head back?" Simon couldn't believe the words coming out of his mouth. He and his dad had already said their good-nights and good-byes to the Meyers, and they stood with Spence and Jack in the south marketplace, also known as the Room of the Martyrs. Simon was never ready to leave the City, and his first outing since his Arena appearance had been the perfect birthday gift. But his birthday was technically over, and the increased risks that came with being outside their apartment after dark felt strange and uncertain. What if he or his dad were caught? What if his friends were caught? *What is there to lose?* Simon shuddered at the thought.

"The tunnel should be empty by now, I would think," Spence offered.

"Don't go outside without your coat, dear," Jack mimicked in his best maternal voice, proffering a dry black pullover. Simon realized that Jack was wearing a new outfit. Evidently, someone had had mercy on the young man. Simon took the hoodie and pulled it over his head.

"Smells better, anyway."

The four began their trek toward the tunnel of the South Gate, but Simon paused for just a few seconds to say good-bye to one last face: the image of a courageous woman that looked out from the last panel of the mural. *Bye, Mom.* He turned toward the group and followed them out.

The night air was fresh after the earlier rainfall, and all was calm. Spence, Jonathan, Jack, and Simon assumed normal travel strategies throughout the dark city streets, and Simon felt as if he were stretching eager muscles after a brief hiatus from an exercise he knew well. As the four figures moved in and out of the shadows, Simon was grateful that the trip out had been a success. *So far.* They were nearing the alley where the manhole would lead them to the basement of 2350 Merchant Street. In a few steps, they would be crossing the street where Maximalus prowled.

From behind, Simon watched as Spence and Jack crouched low and looked up and down the street several times. They turned to nod at one another; Simon guessed it was just as much an encouragement to be courageous as it was an "all-clear" affirmation. Two crossed the way, then two more. All was clear. Spence moved to the manhole cover and began to pull and pivot it away from the opening. Jack moved in to help.

"So, Spence, is this tunnel gonna try to kill me again?" Jack questioned. "It'd be nice to finish Preparatory School, seeing as I'm so close and all."

Spence lay on the ground with his right arm and lantern dangling below the street's surface.

"No trace of floodwaters. Like I said, this is supposed to be derelict. Must have been a strange coincidence. The storm was worse than usual, after all."

Jack sniffed. "Well. Let's hope we have no more strange coincidences."

"You could stay here, or go home. No reason for you to follow." Spence's response came simply, with no nuance of challenge or scorn, but Jack bristled at the suggestion to leave early.

"And leave Simon on his final stretch home? What kind of Messenger do you think I am?"

Simon followed Jack and Spence down the ladder into the drainpipe, and Jonathan brought the cover over the hole after lowering himself down last. A low, thudding sound began to shake the ground above them as he pulled it in place. In the lantern light, Simon exchanged looks with Jack; they'd both heard it. Maximalus was coming around again.

"Honestly, Spence," Jack insisted, "who gave you the idea of this tunnel? Let's get out of here before it caves in."

Once back in the narrow passageway, Simon felt his everyday life closing in on him too. He dreaded facing the morning, with its new struggles.

They approached the end of the tunnel and the new entrance through the stone wall. Simon noticed the soot-blackened periphery of the hole the explosion made and a brittle black string leading from it and down into the tunnel.

"A fuse?" Simon guessed.

Spence nodded. "Batteries are a bit unpredictable. We might have needed to apply heat a few times, or we might have been part of the explosion the first time around. I figured some distance would help with the latter. Oh! That reminds me." Spence began gathering some of the extra demolition materials on the ground, but he left the shovel and a few digging tools. Simon wondered if he'd have a chance to make the passageway a bit larger.

"A message for you." Jack presented two folded pieces of paper, one to Simon and one to Jonathan. Simon thrilled with anticipation, hoping it might be a verified Message. Instead, there were dates and locations listed.

"You're a Carrier now, Simon. Time for an official schedule. Don't share it with your pops, except to get permission to go out and play." Jack clearly couldn't handle giving Simon added responsibility without including a touch of belittling.

Simon figured his dad's message was his Postmaster schedule. Both pocketed their notes; then Jonathan carefully pushed the plastic bags of sheets away from the new portal.

"Oh!" Spence called quietly from the other side once Jonathan and Simon had climbed back into the basement. "Charity wants a chunk of one of the stones. Don't ask me why."

"G'night, guys," Simon whispered as he handed a stone the size of a soup can into the tunnel. "And thanks for all you've done."

Jonathan and Simon arranged things back in front of the hole.

"A carpenter would be pretty likely to keep plywood in his basement storage, I would think," Jonathan mused. "I can bring some down tomorrow."

Back upstairs in his bedroom, Simon looked at his alarm clock and instantly felt the fatigue he knew he would suffer in a few short hours. Though exhausted, he lay in bed wide awake for a few moments, his thoughts swirling. He pictured Zeke's aging face and Martha's burdened shoulders. He thought of Ben's worried brow and Charity's unguarded smile. The day had been full.

He closed his eyes with a prayer of thanks for the many gifts of the day and for help in the year to come.

Chapter Nine

The first week of being a sixteen-year-old wasn't too terrible. On the surface, not much had changed. Curfew, in theory, was more lax, but Simon hadn't tested it out yet. Aside from that, there were the same classroom pranks, the same Ms. Stetter, and the same homework. Ben was a little different though. Not as friendly as before, but not so hostile either. Simon was still unsuccessful at getting Ben's attention in class to roll his eyes or smirk. But despite Ben's continued attempts to ignore him, he always seemed to be watching.

Ella was different too. She seemed increasingly eager to talk with him. Simon didn't know whether to be flattered or afraid. Did she like him? Was she spying on him? Could he trust her?

The biggest difference from one week ago, of course, came in the form of a hole just large enough for a person to crawl through. Simon was still in danger, but he was no longer trapped. The beautiful truth of his freedom was enough to carry him through the most stifling of school days.

"Mr. Clay."

"Ms. Stetter?"

"Find something amusing in my geography lesson?"

"I'm sorry?" *Honestly?* Was this a trick question?

"Care to explain why you were smiling so broadly at the description of Port Lest's coastal boundary?"

"I just appreciate the eloquence you bring to our lessons, Ms. Stetter."

A faint ripple of amusement coursed throughout the room, and Simon appreciated that the laughter was not at his expense. Ms. Stetter sneered but left it at that before turning to the map of New Morgan she had pulled down from its roll above the chalkboard.

Simon allowed himself one more smile before pulling a guarded shield over his face. His peers, if looking, might have assumed he was celebrating his minor victory. But his grin was the result of something else entirely. He had plans tonight. His schedule, safely hidden under the face of his watch, listed tonight as his first official assignment as a full-fledged Carrier.

He was going to spread the Message tonight.

The Westbend West Sector Preparatory School droned its afternoon tone and emitted several hundred students onto its front steps. Simon watched Ben make his way down the street and paused to give him a bit more space. No sense to rush things. As he began his own trek down the stairs, he felt a tug on his left sleeve.

"Mind a little company?"

Simon looked back into the blue eyes and fair face of Ella. He tried to swallow the sudden lump that grew in his throat.

"I—uh—didn't know you went this way. Do you live by me? I mean, you don't come this way often, do you?"

Ella's steps slowed a fraction, and she looked a little hurt. Simon wondered if he had failed to see her his entire time at Preparatory School and wondered what caused him to be so dense.

"I don't have to go this way if you don't want me to. My family and I were moved to a house on Smith Street a few months ago. Just south of Merchant Street."

Simon didn't know how he felt about the fact that Ella knew what street he lived on.

"Of course there are a couple of ways to get there. I sometimes go a block over, but I've been trying different routes. I noticed you taking this one a few days ago."

"So which way is fastest?"

"Oh, I don't know. So far, I just look for the way that's most interesting."

"Okay, so which one wins that award so far?"

Ella shrugged and gave a small smile. "We'll see."

The lump grew larger in Simon's throat.

They were a block away from the school now, and the crowd thinned considerably as students veered off in all directions toward their own homes. It took one more block before Ella spoke again.

"So that thing you said. In the Arena."

Is it worth it? What will I learn? What is there to lose? After a moment, a new question came to Simon. *What is there to gain?*

"We call it the Creed. All the Messen—all those who believe what I believe, we say it when we want to confess our faith."

"So what do you believe?"

The question stung, but only for a moment. Those words were a reminder of the pain he endured the last time he was asked this question. Then, with conviction, Simon began—

"I believe in God, the Father Almighty, maker of heaven and earth. And in Jesus Christ, His only Son—"

"Yes! That was it. His *Son*."

Startled by the interruption, Simon looked at Ella, who was lost in concentration. After two seconds, she realized she had stopped him.

"Oh, sorry. Okay, look." She wore the earnest expression of one who had a confession of her own to make. "We were watching the television when you were on trial. I guess they wanted to scare us all away from acting like you, but it backfired, right? That's why they stopped your trial and distracted us with Bots?"

Simon shrugged. "Your guess is as good as mine."

"Anyway," she continued. "Lots of people joined in. Like a whole lot. And you know what? My parents. Sitting right there on the couch and watching everything—they joined in too. They knew the words! The Father. The Son."

"The Holy Spirit."

"Sure. Whatever. But they'd never said those words before. At least, *I'd* never heard them before that day. But my parents knew them by memory."

"Are you sure you never heard them? Did they sound familiar at all?" Simon's stomach churned as he recalled his own blindness to the truth his father had been subtly teaching him.

Ella shook her head. "No, they admitted it. They said it was something they both knew from long ago, but that it had been forever since they'd thought about it. Simon, you could have *died* for those words. Why? And why did my parents just forget whatever it was you were saying?"

Simon's head was swimming with questions he couldn't begin to consider in the next few minutes. They were crossing a corner, and the clocks ticked their warning in his ears that time was running out.

"Are you sixteen?"

"What?"

"Sorry, I mean—do you have Provisional Adult Status yet?"

"Oh, no. Not until July."

"Okay, so we have half a block left." Simon gestured just ahead toward the corner where Smith Street intersected their path.

"Right." Ella's voice took on a critical tone. "So here I spill that my parents might be *illegal* or something and you tell me pretty much nothing."

"Hey. The Son is not *nothing*." Simon wasn't sure where his response came from, but he was thankful for it. *True enough.*

"Fine, but you owe me more than that."

Did he? Did he owe her anything? Then again, *how are they to believe in Him of whom they have never heard?* "Okay. I do. I guess I'll see you tomorrow then," Simon conceded.

"It's a date." She grinned and made a sharp turn down Smith.

"Guess who."

The timing was perfect. Simon had used the North Gate tonight, which fed right into the Room of the Twelve. The creator of the masterpiece unfolding before the eyes of the Messengers had just descended from her ladder, allowing Simon to sneak up from behind and cover her eyes.

"Are we four?"

Simon didn't let the insult to his maturity cause him to drop his hands.

"Wrong."

"Well, you don't smell as bad as last week, but I'd venture to guess this is the Carrier who is way too excited for his big night on the town."

Simon dropped his hands. "Close enough. But too excited? Impossible. Charity, we're saving the world, you know."

Charity crossed her arms and raised her eyebrows. "I dunno about you, but I do art."

"I've seen some pretty important artwork lately." That won a genuine smile, so Simon progressed with more confidence. "And freaky artwork," he mused, looking up at the half-painted figure towering over them. The face of the disciple next to the ladder looked calm, confident, even a little friendly. His smile looked amused at the colleagues around him. His eyes danced in the torchlight along the walls, but they were black and indiscernible. Simon felt a chill run up his spine.

"Are you calling me a freak?" Charity protested mildly.

He dragged his gaze away from Judas and looked at Charity. "Never."

"Yeah, well. Go do your important work, Carrier."

Simon shrugged. "Come with us."

"Me? With you? What?"

Simon smiled at the flustered look Charity struggled to hide.

"Sure, why not? I'm on a mission with Micah tonight. Join in the fun."

"There you are! I thought the schedule said to meet in the Archive." Micah strode into the room from the south wall of archways.

"I—uh, yeah. I was on my way."

Micah looked at him and Charity and smirked. Simon inwardly kicked himself for getting flustered as well.

"Whatever. Let's go, man." Micah nodded a greeting and farewell to Charity and turned toward the tunnel out.

"Yeah, about that. What if we bring along a mentee? You know, a Carrier in training? Like I was?" Simon had no idea why Charity hadn't been tapped for the job before, but it suddenly made perfect sense to him that she'd make a great partner for missions and—

"That's not really your call to make, Simon. Besides, the last time Charity went along on one of your little excursions, it led to some trouble, no?"

Charity's eyes went wide with indignation but she quickly lowered her gaze in what Simon recognized as resentful resignation.

"He's right," she said. "I'll stay. Besides, I work better alone."

"What? That's dumb. Come on, Micah. What's one trip?"

Micah, clearly in a hurry, had already taken several steps toward the North Gate. He turned and glared at them. "We don't have time for this!" He shook his head, then gave in. "Fine. If anything happens to her, it's your fault."

Simon didn't know whether to punch his self-confident mentor or to hug him. He nudged Charity's shoulder instead and trotted toward the exit.

"Let's go!"

Simon felt the adrenaline rush as the trio hit the streets and ducked through the alleyways of Westbend. Since they had left through the North Gate, Simon's senses were heightened with Westbend City Hall looming so near. Micah led the way through the concrete maze to a destination known by precious few people. Simon trailed the group, keeping watch from behind and measuring the progress of the other two. Charity's stealth in the Arena was no different from her stealth on the streets; she moved almost silently with quick yet calculated precision. Simon knew her life had been riddled with struggle. He wondered if her trials were what had trained her to move through life unseen.

In almost no time, they reached their post. Since the Message they carried had come from Grand Station, this was only one of many stops before it reached its final destination at an Archive, one of the strategically safe locations to preserve the Word throughout Westbend.

The alley where they stopped was especially dark; one of the streetlights was out. Charity and then Simon followed Micah's silhouette as it rounded a corner into the alley between two buildings. Simon froze. The setup was so similar to his own apartment that, for a second, he thought they'd be greeting his dad in a matter of moments. Except, of course, their portal was compromised. Micah drew close to a heavy metal door only large enough for one person to crawl through. After two quick knocks, a dim ray of light spilled into the alley. Simon glanced up; there was a window similar to his own bedroom window. Was anyone looking down from above, as he used to when shadowy figures would visit at night?

Micah and Simon pulled out their rings to show the λόγος seal while Charity pressed back into the shadows behind them. The man inside gave a quick nod of his shaved head. "Verified or pending?"

Simon spoke. "Verified."

The hand reached out through the portal and waited for the parcel. Micah reached into the inside pocket of his jacket and pulled out a vial, sealed with red wax. Simon couldn't see it in the dark, but he knew there would be three λόγος seals imprinted. The hand took Micah's delivery and closed the portal.

"That's it?" Charity whispered.

Simon felt obligated to satisfy Charity on her first trip of this kind. "Well, most trips are a lot more exciting. I guess this guy—"

"You didn't have to come," Micah interrupted. He slipped past them back toward the way they came.

The return trip to the City felt anticlimactic, like there should be something more to the evening. Simon looked up at the stars to commit more of the sky to memory. There was little sound other than the soft scratch of their shoes on loose gravel or a piece of trash.

Thud. Thud. Thud.

And the march of Maximalus.

The pounding sound came out of nowhere, as if the Bot had been lying in wait for the element of surprise. If so, it worked. Simon sprang forward and caught Charity's arm. Both chased after Micah, who had begun running down the alley toward a wall. Veering immediately left, the Messengers ran into a narrow passageway where a building on their left ended with only a few feet to spare before a tall wall took its own stand on their right. Simon knew Maximalus would have no way to reach them in such tight quarters, but he was glad that Micah kept moving. If he had to sit and wait here, he didn't know how he'd handle the cramped conditions, just hoping Security wouldn't arrive.

"Gotcha!"

"Oooph!"

Simon watched in horror as Micah took a blow to the head from a Security guard waiting at the end of the narrow space. Micah took a step back and rubbed his head instinctively, but then charged full force at the uniformed adversary.

"Gaaah!" The Security guard cried out in pain. Micah shoved him out of the way, and Charity and Simon pushed into the end of this new alley.

"We're trapped," Charity assessed.

Another Security guard ran toward them, catching them in the beam of his flashlight and wielding a club. Simon suddenly wished self-defense had been part of his training as a Carrier. Lunging at the first guard, who was still reeling, Simon pushed him hard against a trash receptacle. Micah and Simon both turned toward the second guard, who stood with legs braced wide for impact.

"If we all three run, he can't get us all," Micah tossed behind his shoulder.

There was no time to contemplate the logic of running past a member of Security in an alleyway, so they all three burst past the man in uniform. Simon had made it through and prepared to round the corner when he heard a scream.

"Charity!"

Simon spun around to find the Security guard holding Charity by her hair, trying to find a way to hold her still. He ran back, ready to barrel into the man when he felt a hand yank him backward and an arm wrap around his neck.

"Char—" Simon lost his voice, choked by the Security guard who had come to. Simon reared back, kicking and swinging at anything he could. Darkness clouded his vision.

Suddenly, he was on the ground, gasping for breath. He looked up to see Micah run back into view from around a corner. Gasping for breath, he clutched a piece of lumber in his hand.

"Where's Charity?" Micah asked.

The question filled Simon with dread. Coughing, he gestured in the direction he saw her last. Simon's vision cleared, but his confusion flooded in. There was no one there.

Chapter Ten

He looked so pious. You know, as if he knew something I didn't. His self-righteous indignation caused my blood to boil as I watched him stand there. Who was he to think he could teach us? Who was he to ask God to forgive us? That miserable cur? Forgive us?! Heresy. Blasphemy! He deserved to be drug out into the streets. He deserved every stone as it was hurled at his body. "Behold," he said. "Behold, I see the heavens opened, and the Son of Man standing at the right hand of God." Outrageous! This sinner would see God before me? I watched. I watched as they shouted over his words. I watched as they carried him out of the city. I watched with every stone they threw. And as I saw this man receive his punishment, I had one thought: there will be more prosecutions. There must be more. This is just the beginning.

■ ■ ■

The deluge was unlike anything Westbend had experienced in recent time. For three nights, rain coursed down the windows, into the streets, and into the storm sewers, even—most likely—the one Spence deemed derelict. Simon was submerged in his emotions with little will to lift his head above water. Tuesday, Simon used one of his excused absences. Wednesday, he attended school in a fog. Today, Thursday, so many streets were flooded that schools were closed.

Water drove like sheets against the north wall of their apartment building, and the wind howled. Simon welcomed the wailing as a testament to the storm raging inside him.

"Simon?"

His dad's hand came into view and Simon watched as he placed a cup of coffee on the low table in front him. But Simon didn't move from his spot on the couch.

"I know you don't want to talk. I don't blame you. You probably don't want to listen either."

Simon didn't know what he wanted. Except to go back in time and change its course three days ago. He wanted desperately to do something, to help, to find Charity. Guilt and powerlessness gnawed at his gut. He couldn't provide his own escape, much less Charity's.

Jonathan turned and walked into his bedroom. Simon heard some shuffling from the hall behind him. He slowly pushed himself into a sitting position and took the mug of coffee in his hands. The first gulp was satisfyingly terrible; the bitter liquid scalded his tongue and burned all the way down. He blew into the cup, watching the black beverage ripple. His fingers began to warm from holding the ceramic sides, and he took another, slower drink. Gradually, he realized he heard music—humming—drifting from his dad's bedroom. Simon took one more swallow and forced his body to stand. He followed the sound of the tune, mug still clutched in his hand.

"What's that one? I don't recognize it," Simon asked as he leaned in the open doorway.

"The tune? It's called Finlandia. It's still famous in many parts of the world."

Jonathan appeared to be sorting through papers on his bed. The wooden box that Simon had first seen over a week ago lay next to him; the board, pried up from its space in the floor, now rested against the dresser. Simon recalled that his dad seemed to need help the last time they liberated the box from its place of confinement.

"Are there words? You know, to the song?"

Jonathan pursed his lips in thought. "I guess that depends on who you ask. The lyrics I know are older than the tune. Somehow, the words and music found each other."

Simon could tell his dad was baiting him a little, but he didn't resist. "So what are the words?"

His dad looked back down at his work and began sorting out some squares of paper. As he did, he sang.

"Be still, my soul; your God will undertake To guide the future as He has the past. Your hope, your confidence let nothing shake; All now mysterious shall be bright at last. Be still, my soul; the waves and winds still know His voice who ruled them while He dwelt below."

As Jonathan sang the last few words, the wind groaned against the south wall. A small window above the bed whimpered against the force.

"Mysterious. That's for sure. Why is this happening, Dad? Maximalus, the storm, Char—all of it?"

Jonathan shook his head. "In some ways, we'll never know. Of course, in one way, we always know. We live in a fallen world. Evil exists. Bad things happen. There's no denying it."

Simon thought back to the mosaic in the city where the serpent lurked in the tree. He thought back to the stoic angel of light in the heavenly mosaic nearby. Lucifer. Satan. The devil. Yes, there was evil in the world; no doubt about it.

"But the details?" his dad continued. "The 'why' behind one thing or the other? Much of that we may never know. Trying to give those answers can tempt us to answer for God Himself."

Simon walked into the room and placed his coffee on the dresser before sitting on the nearest corner of the bed. It felt good to talk, but he wasn't getting the answers he was hoping for.

"You're not alone, Simon. Believers from the beginning of time have wondered these questions."

His dad picked up a square of paper and handed it to Simon. The words were in his dad's handwriting. Simon read them aloud.

" 'The secret things belong to the LORD our God, but the things that are revealed belong to us and to our children forever.' Deuteronomy chapter twenty-nine, verse twenty-nine." Simon set the paper down. "Secret things, huh?"

Jonathan looked directly at Simon. "We don't get to know all we want to know, but we do know all we need to know." He passed another piece of paper to Simon. As Simon read it silently, Jonathan spoke it by memory.

" 'Now Jesus did many other signs in the presence of the disciples, which are not written in this book; but these are written so that you may believe that Jesus is the Christ, the Son of God, and that by believing you may have life in His name.' John chapter twenty, verses thirty and thirty-one."

It was strange; just as Simon started to feel comforted, his frustration swung back, almost in a fight against the calm. He felt in turmoil, and his mind was clouded with a flurry of thoughts.

"Dad? That 'be still' part of your song? I'm not so sure about it." Simon looked out the window and watched rivulets of water stream down the glass pane.

"Well, Simon, at the moment, it doesn't look like you have much of a choice."

The floodwater receded just enough in Westbend for routine to resume on Friday. Simon sat at his desk and stared straight ahead all morning. He didn't care much about the chemistry or language syntax lessons for the day, but the history class jolted him from his stupor. Forcing his exterior to appear apathetic, Simon gripped the back legs of his desk and soaked in every word he heard.

"Slavery was an abomination in Morganland. Entire families were separated, and children were often exploited for the basest tasks in factories. The government did nothing at the time to stop it, spending too much time catering to the people who would decide the length of their stay in office."

Ms. Stetter was in peak form today, pacing the front of the classroom and wielding a ruler with her right hand. At opportune moments, she would smack it against her left hand for emphasis.

"Special interest groups and those who believed in religion—in *fairy tales*—were so consumed with their cause that they neglected to participate in civic duties." Ms. Stetter paused to take a breath and to send a meaningful glare his way. "They caused division and spoke out against the rising forces of New Morgan. They claimed this utopia would not be possible on earth! It took a great deal of effort for supporters of New Morgan to squelch such dissent."

Breathe, Simon, he told himself. Slowly, in and out. In. Out. In.

"Meanwhile, other groups were being neglected, marginalized. To think we lived in such barbarous times only a few decades ago!" Ms. Stetter pulled down a map of New Morgan. The mountainous western border hugged the edge of the unrolled image. Simon tried to make out the name of the country on the west; the letters were faded, but still clearer than his old map at home. R-e-m- . . . R-e-v-e- . . .

"Revemond, our neighbors to the west, were notorious for attempting to enter our borders by selling themselves into human labor. Revemondians, quite backward in their thinking, became a harmful influence on our people."

Ms. Stetter rarely talked about anything beyond the borders of New Morgan, and Simon hung on every word. It was likely that he should believe exactly the opposite of her lecture, as far as he was concerned, but at least he could see into the mind of a true New Morganian when it came to the world outside. Ms. Stetter picked up a poster from her desk and taped the top two corners to the chalkboard. The illustration was of a family—all with pale skin and dark hair—with a large X drawn across it. The title written across the top was "Undesirables." As Simon trained his eye on the family, he noticed with a sinking feeling that the man looked much like his dad—similar jawline, skin tone, even eye color.

"Ever since New Morgan has become the place it is today, however, we have prevented the influx from Revemond and, with it, blights upon society such as slave trade."

Simon considered for a moment what rights a person might have without any identification—save for a branded scar on a left forearm. If you don't exist in the first place, what happens to you when you're in the hands of the government? The thought began to swallow Simon whole as he imagined Charity captive in the hands of Security, and he was grateful for the tone that announced a break for lunch.

"Hey, Simon, anyone sitting there?"

At the familiar voice, Simon looked up from his noodles and red sauce, knowing he would see the light brown hair and freckled face of Ben Pharen.

"I was thinking." Ben sat down and stirred his noodles. "You wanna go to the library sometime next week? It's, umm, my birthday on Tuesday. So we won't need passes anymore."

"Provisional Adult Status gives you a free pass to the library? I didn't know that." Simon hadn't been to the library for a while, and he knew Ms. Stetter wouldn't write him a pass to go even if Ben asked for the two of them.

Ben nodded. "You know. If you want to go. You don't have to."

"No, that sounds great, Ben. Thanks."

"Hi, guys. Mind if I join you?"

Both teens looked up to see Ella approaching.

"Um. Sure, that's fine," Simon replied. "Right, Ben?"

Ben stuffed a forkful of pasta into his mouth and slowly nodded. As Ella seated herself next to Ben, Simon realized that the last time they spoke was Monday, hours before one of his closest friends had disappeared into the night. It didn't feel right to be chatting in a school cafeteria as if nothing was wrong, but what else could he do?

"So you two are friends, right?" Ella asked. "Do you . . . have a lot in common?"

Simon and Ben looked at each other in confusion. Ella tried again.

"So, like, do you agree on a lot of things?" After more silence, Ella tried even harder, her pursed lips conveying a loss in patience. "Ben, do you know things like Simon does?"

Ben turned bright red, and his eyes were wide and fearful. He stared at Simon, using another mouthful of noodles as an excuse to remain silent. Simon knew the implications that any given answer might bring.

"Ben?" Simon practiced his best impression of Jack and smirked. "Look at him. He knows a whole lot of nothing."

Ben swallowed hard and protested, "I do too! I know all about Simon's—I mean, err, what I mean is . . ."

Simon wished his sarcasm had been more obvious to Ben. Now, it was up to Ben to work himself out of this. Ben sighed and dropped his fork onto his tray.

"I know some things. But I'm not, you know, a criminal. Not like—" Ben stopped himself short, but the damage was done. He shot Simon an apologetic look for the indictment. Simon shrugged. The label was fair, and he was getting used to it.

"Yeah, don't let him take all the credit," Simon said with a smile. "I'm the troublemaker."

"Great," Ella said. "Now I have two people I can talk to."

Chapter Eleven

The walk home was strange to Simon in that it was how he imagined most of his peers walked home: walking and talking with friends. Despite Ben's obvious discomfort, he wasn't willing to seem uninformed either. The two talked about the middle part of the Creed, explaining why Jesus is central to their faith. Simon couldn't help but be proud of Ben for confessing his beliefs—even if it was partly to prove his importance to the conversation.

"So if it weren't for Jesus, there'd be no reason to, you know, do anything. We'd have no hope." Ben kicked a small rock as he finished his sentence.

"And you both really believe this?" Ella asked them.

Simon nodded slowly and solemnly. "I do. I've had my moments of weakness, and I will again, I'm sure. But I believe the Message about Jesus is true, and that it's worth dying for."

Ben nodded, but surveyed their surroundings for video cameras for the fourth time on their trip home.

"This is my turn," Ella announced as they came up to Smith. "See you tomorrow."

Simon almost contradicted her that it was Friday, but he then remembered that Saturday offered its own opportunity to meet up again. He gave a quick wave as he and Ben continued north toward Merchant.

Ben waited until Ella was out of sight before he admitted, "Simon, I don't know about her. I mean, can we trust her?"

Simon had no idea. He bounced back and forth between wanting to tell Ella about her Savior and wanting to protect his friends and family from potential danger. Who knew such a threat could come by way of a friendly teenage classmate?

"I'm not sure, Ben. Then again, can you trust me?" The question began as a harmless point, but Simon suddenly found himself keenly interested in Ben's answer. They turned right onto Merchant Street and headed east.

"That depends," Ben answered. There was no evidence of sarcasm in his voice. "Can I trust you as a—as a believer?" Saying the word out loud took obvious effort for Ben, and Simon appreciated the courage Ben was showing today. "No doubt."

Simon felt a wave of gratitude rush through his body.

"Can I trust you not to be stupid?" Ben's voice continued in its sincerity. The *tick, tock, tick* of a corner clock grew louder as they walked forward. His brows furrowed with uncertainty. "I have no clue."

When Simon walked into his apartment building, the workshop was uncharacteristically dark and quiet. He rushed straight up the stairs to the second level and unlocked the door to 2A. His dad was sitting in the living room, giving his full attention to a guest whose wild white hair peeked over the back of the couch he was sitting on. Simon dropped his backpack near the fridge and locked the door behind him. He walked as quickly as he could with dignity to the living room and stared expectantly at Zeke. After no word was spoken for an entire half-second, Simon asked the inevitable first question.

"Where's Charity?"

Zeke stared back, expressionless. His eyes seemed to be trying to read Simon's face, which spread a feeling of unease throughout Simon's core.

"We don't know, Simon. I wish I could tell you, but I haven't been able to find her. No one has. Usually by now, we hear of some form of sentence, but that often comes by way of the captured Messenger's family. Charity, well, we're her family. But the government doesn't know that. They didn't know she existed."

Simon slumped down on the same couch as Zeke, facing the blank TV screen.

"Is there anything more you can tell us about that night?" Zeke asked.

"I don't think so." Simon forced his way back into the Monday-night memory, even though everything inside him fought against reliving the horror of it. "We had just made our delivery and were heading back to the City. One of the Bots—sounded like Maximalus again—seemed super close to us. I had no idea it was coming—it was almost like it had been waiting to sneak up on someone. On us, maybe. I'm not sure it saw us. Er, came close enough for its cameras to find us, I mean. We ducked into an alleyway that looked like a dead end, but there was a narrow path to another alley. That's where the Security guards were. We tried to get away, but everything happened so fast. Before I knew it, everything went dark."

Simon allowed the story to rush out as fast as it would come; he was afraid that reflecting on any part too long would cause him to lose it. Up to this point, he had managed to convince himself that she had gotten away, that his next trip to the City would be like any other trip—Charity would be there, painting Judas or some other twelve-foot-tall disciple. But Zeke's surprise visit and somber news convinced him that things were not okay. Simon bent over and clasped his hands. He stared at the wooden floorboards at his feet and the frayed corner of an area rug a few feet away. He tried to force himself to describe the scene again, but the floor in front of him grew hazy.

"She was just—gone. And Micah knocked out one of the Security guys, but we didn't know for how long. So that's when we came back and reported everything at the City." Simon could barely remember the time between Charity's disappearance and the time he arrived back home that night. Everything was still a blur.

"Zeke—those Bots."

Simon heard his dad speak up, but he kept his eyes trained on the floor.

"They've always been remote-controlled, right? Are there actual drivers inside now?"

Simon looked up at Zeke, who squinted his eyes and shook his head slowly.

"I have no idea. They're big enough, I suppose."

It wasn't until that moment when Simon realized that the next morning would bring another dimension of difficulty: Recreation Time. The Bots created an entirely new memory for him now. This one might be more than he could endure.

"Zeke?" Simon asked after he could focus again. "What was that passage you quoted the other day? The one about being crushed?"

"About *not* being crushed," Zeke answered. "Ah yes. A good one for today. Thank you, Simon. 'We are afflicted in every way, but not crushed; perplexed, but not driven to despair; persecuted, but not forsaken; struck down, but not destroyed.'"

Zeke agreed to stay for dinner but turned down the invitation to play King's Corners and left shortly after the meal. The night was still young, but Simon was exhausted. After helping his dad straighten up, he said goodnight and headed to bed.

Sleep, however, did not come. Image after image passed before Simon like the slide projector Ms. Stetter sometimes used in class. Charity writing the messages on the road. Ben yelling at him from the street. Malachi rescuing him from Security. Mr. Druck staring over him in the dungeon-like room. Zeke's smile as his laugh echoed off the walls of the Elders' room. Mr. Burroughs staring from his podium while the crowd jeered along. The Bots. Charity's scream.

Simon bolted upright, wishing he could jump into action and find her. But he was as helpless as she probably was. There was nothing he could do. Falling back onto his bed, he focused on one more image: a smooth stone with a painted image of the Lamb with His crown and banner of victory. Simon's last thoughts that night were addressed in prayer: "Lamb of God, You take away the sin of the world. Have mercy on us."

Standing right outside his apartment on the second-floor landing, Simon peered through the small window overlooking Merchant Street. The view would have been better from the large windows in his apartment—he would have been able to look in both directions. This view was restricted, but he could see what he needed to see. Simon knew Ben never liked to be late for anything, so the wait wouldn't be long. Sure enough, the door of 2351 opened in no time, and Ben turned to head west.

Simon walked as slowly as possible down the stairs. He knew if any neighbors' doors were to open, he'd have to walk at a normal pace. But it was unlikely that anyone would be out and about at this time on a Saturday morning except for those mandated to attend the Arena event. The others would be spending a sleepy morning in their apartments. *Lucky.*

Before turning north toward the main thoroughfare, he looked through the clusters of teens making their way to Recreation Time. After no sight of a white-blond head of hair, he joined the procession just a few steps behind a group who kindly ignored his presence. The irony of the situation—that he was avoiding friends as soon as he found a few who decided to tolerate him—didn't deter him from his plan of staying as low-key as possible. His agenda for the day wasn't well suited for a couple of companions.

Simon didn't bat an eye as he walked through the dust to the Arena. In no time, he was at the Security checkpoint. He wouldn't have minded a bruise or two so much today; they would have been a testament to the hidden pain he already felt. But the crowd was growing restless, and the guards at the gate seemed to realize that any delay would add to the annoyance of the building crowd.

Unscathed, Simon walked the full length of the Arena. Head at a slight angle so his hair covered his eyes, he scanned the crowd, keeping an eye out for a stealthy female weaving in and out of the groups of teenagers who milled around the outer corridor while grabbing snacks and chatting with friends. He knew the odds were slim, but he held out hope that somehow all would be fine. He would be shoved from behind, insulted for his clumsiness, and forgiven for his failure to be a good friend. After another lap, this time on the upper perimeter, he began his descent. He tingled with anticipation and dread: willing that their unofficial rendezvous point would show her waiting impatiently on a low beam, yet fearing that it would be empty and void of his last hope.

No one was there.

Still, Simon pressed on, forcing himself to keep moving against the despair that chased behind him. His eyes scoured his surroundings, trying to recall a random corner, a telltale doorway—anything that he could recognize from his painful, hazy trek from solitary confinement to the Arena floor. Pushing past his aversion to the terrible memory, Simon strained to see a clue of where he might find Charity. His knee had begun to ache, protesting under the distance he was walking and the emotional fatigue.

It was no use. Every orange flag with its black star looked the same. Every closed door looked unimportant. Every teenager looked unconcerned with the disappearance of a peer. Simon had been so dizzy the morning of his trial, he couldn't find his way to the prison no matter how hard he tried.

The fight inside the stadium raged. Metal clanged, and cheers erupted. Simon's frustration gave way to anger. He wanted to yell at the crowds who eagerly engaged in the manufactured fight. He wanted to find Mr. Druck and give him a dose of his own medicine. He wanted to take a sledgehammer to the Bots until they were pounded to scrap. Scrap metal. *That's it.*

Simon had one more chance of finding Charity perfectly fine, as if nothing had ever happened. He raced down to the ground level and located the out-of-the-way hallway. There, in all its decrepit glory, was a room of dumpsters filled halfway with bits of Bots from previous skirmishes. A scorched wheel. A crumpled mechanical arm. A splintered handle with a hatchet on the end.

Simon shuddered at the sight, but slowly walked closer to see if he could find his friend on a treasure hunt for discarded gadgets. Nothing.

Whizzzzz. Whiirrr. Pop!

The third duel was underway, and Simon noticed that from where he was standing, he had a clear view of the scene over a short wall bordering the field of the Arena. Maximalus belched black smoke into the air as it charged a pitiful creature. The smaller Bot had four tall, thin wheels that could pivot to move in any direction or even rotate its body. Three spindly arms held up ridiculously small weapons: a hammer, a circular saw, and a small flame thrower that spat out fire one foot at a time. The machine wheeled toward the gate where Simon stood—certainly its final resting place in a matter of minutes. As the light shone on the glassy dome, Simon could almost picture eyes of fear within its core as it desperately dashed to evade its inevitable doom.

Maximalus spurted in mechanical mockery as it closed in on its prey. The crowd raised its voice as one to encourage the demise of the unworthy Bot. Maximalus drew out its spinning saw from one leg and attacked one of the lesser opponent's wheels. The victim jolted with a pained squeal as joints popped and the body fell to its side. Maximalus began ramming the heap under the groan of metal and the cheers of the masses. Its hulking body drew back, and the audience moaned with frustration. Maximalus paused then, drawing out its attack in exaggerated restraint. Its engine revved, waiting until the teens joined along. As momentum peaked, it bolted toward the incapacitated Bot, heaving itself into the heap of metal. The glass dome shattered, and something flew out from within, landing ten feet from the metallic carnage, eight feet from the gate where Simon stood.

The entire room gasped. This was new. The projectile was not machine—it was . . . human. The screens around the room flashed a brief image of the crumpled body then faded to black with bold white letters. "The end of the Darkness is near." Immediately, the room went pitch black and the crowd hushed. A few random screams from the stands echoed across the space, but the enormous room was in eerie silence. When the lights came back on, Maximalus had retreated to its corner. The decimated Bot lay lifeless as the grounds crew gathered to clean up its remains.

The human figure, however, was gone. A few shouts for "Maximalus!" lessened the tension, and after a few moments, fans began filing out of the stands.

Simon crouched under the seats, just around the wall behind the dumpsters. It had taken every fiber in his being, every ounce of strength, to suppress his flashbacks and surge onto the stadium floor without vomiting or passing out. It now took all his concentration to keep from screaming out in fury. In his arms, he held the true victim of the Bot duel. He leaned close, checking for breath, for any sign of life. He held the tiny wrist marked with a star and an X. There was a pulse, wasn't there? *There had to be!* He stared at the ivory face, praying for the emerald eyes to open the blank mask.

He would not let a tear fall on Charity's black and red streaked hair. As soon as he would allow it, he knew the floodgates would break into a vengeful roar.

Chapter Twelve

He heard the footsteps he had been expecting. He peered through a small opening and saw the uniformed legs of two Security guards.

"Where is the body?"

"It was right there!"

"People don't just walk away after something like that."

"Well, then, you tell me. Do you see it anywhere?"

"No one goes around stealing corpses."

"Listen, we've gotta tell the boss."

"This is not gonna be good."

Simon clenched his jaw and balled his fists against chasing after them. Their footsteps faded, and Simon stared down at Charity, trying to decide what to do.

"Simon? Hey, Simon! You there?!" The voice was a harsh whisper, barely loud enough to be heard.

No way. There was no *way*.

"He's gotta be here somewhere, right? Do you think it was him on the ground?"

"Couldn't have been. But I bet he knows who it was."

Simon called out in a loud whisper, "Down here."

He was relieved to see Ben and Ella come into view as they followed his voice, but the looks of horror that came across their faces only made Simon despair more for the one he held in his arms.

"It's that girl! Chelsea—Charity, I mean. Oh, Simon." Ben crawled into the space, panic evident as his eyes darted around.

"Simon?"

Another voice. One that gave him hope. The last time Simon heard it was here in the Arena, weeks before.

"Malachi? Here! Down here." *He must have seen Ben and Ella and followed them down.*

The deep brown eyes of Simon's friend took in the scene without showing shock or panic. For that, Simon was incredibly thankful.

"Give her to me."

Simon realized he couldn't move. His arms were numb. It didn't matter; Malachi crouched low and brought Charity up into his arms with the effort it would take others to pick up a small child. He stood and began walking.

"Malachi, wait! Where are you going? You can't take her. She can't die."

Malachi didn't turn around.

"Malachi!"

Simon watched helplessly as his fellow Messenger walked out into the lower corridor; he could only rise and follow. Ben and Ella fell in behind.

Simon's mind raced in anticipation of what would come next. How would they get out of here? Where would they go? Malachi's tall and sturdy frame moved with swift, calm confidence as he navigated the empty corridors of the lower level. Sounds of movement and voices grew as they continued down a hall that Simon had never seen. Huge storage containers dotted the walkway as they approached what he assumed was a loading dock. Malachi edged near the wall and slowed down. Simon followed suit and maneuvered behind the huge boxes as welcome camouflage from the Arena workers.

"These two need to get back to Central Headquarters to get supplies for the next battle this afternoon." The voice must have belonged to a foreman of the loading dock.

Two slams suggested that truck doors were closed and prepared for their trip. Simon watched in awe as Malachi gently cradled Charity in one strong arm while stooping to grab a brick near his feet. Without standing back up, he hurled the projectile above the box they were hiding behind and sent it soaring far beyond the dock and into the corridor. It must have hit some form of inventory, because the resulting crash and echoing aftermath startled Simon, even though he saw the throw. Charity stirred slightly, which gave Simon an even bigger surprise. He was tempted to throw something himself if it would win a similar response.

Footsteps and shadows followed the sound, and Malachi made his move. In a matter of seconds, the back of one truck was suddenly filled with five stowaways.

Ella grabbed the door and eased it closed with as little sound as possible.

"Don't let the latch catch," Malachi warned. "Hold tight."

Holding tight took a great deal of effort. There were a few bolts and brackets on the inside of the truck doors for a tenuous grip, but not much else. Ella braced her feet against the door to her right, which was latched, while clinging to the door as tightly as she could. As soon as the engine roared into life and the journey began, every bump became a battle of will between Ella and momentum.

"Here, let me help." Ben inched closer and found his own grip on the door. Ella let go and shook her hands. The pattern was set to take turns. Simon watched Charity as Malachi held and protected her against the jolts. Her skin was eerily pale in the glow of a small overhead light, and he could see bruises begin to form. A long scrape on her right forearm, a black eye, and a strange look to her right pinky all added to what was clearly bad news for Charity. Simon bent closer to examine a place where her hair seemed knotted and gasped when he touched it.

"Malachi, her head's bleeding!"

"It has stopped. Leave it be."

Simon balled his fists and wanted to hit something—anything. But he could only stare helplessly as her breathing became increasingly shallow.

"We have to hurry."

A few agonizing minutes later, the truck paused. Malachi directed Ella to crack the door open. They were at an intersection in Westbend. Simon couldn't tell which.

"The next time the truck stops, we get out."

Everything Simon knew about daylight, curfews, and Security revolted at the suggestion, but his fear for Charity overwhelmed any doubt. At the next stop, Ella slowly opened the door and all four conscious passengers emptied onto the street.

"Don't move." For a few awkward seconds, they listened to Malachi's direction and froze on the pavement. Simon prayed that the driver would keep his focus forward and ignore the small group suddenly behind him. As soon as the truck pulled away from the intersection, Malachi moved; all followed him and Charity into the nearby alley.

The alley trip should have been familiar, but everything felt surreal to Simon as he followed pathways that he knew only under the cover of night. He began to wonder at the details: a fading sign, discarded boxes, broken glass that he often missed in the darkness. It would have been a fascinating study of the terrain, if he were not consumed with urgency. His impatience to get inside a building grew with each step, but he was surprised when—after a few turns—he saw the edge of an apartment building he knew very well. Traveling past the small metal door in the side of the building, the group looked both ways onto Merchant Street before turning left and walking around the corner through the front door. Malachi climbed the stairs with swift yet careful ease; Simon ran behind him to catch up and unlock the door.

"There you are," his dad's voice called from the hallway. "I began to—"

Simon felt sick again as he watched his dad take in the scene. Without asking, Malachi walked directly into the hallway and turned left, finding Simon's room. He lay Charity's limp frame on the mattress. Simon fell to his knees to see how she had fared on the trip. With the threat of discovery gone, new waves of emotion surged. Simon was relieved that Charity was no longer missing, but if she was gone forever? Simon shook that thought away quickly, and guilt took its place. He shouldn't have asked her to come Monday; Micah had been right. Simon should have been more alert, braver, stronger . . .

"Ben. Go get your dad." Jonathan's calm voice cut through the confusion.

The directive shook Simon from his thoughts and Ben into action.

"Okay. I'll be right back."

Ella had moved out of the way and stood near the window. She seemed distracted with something outside.

"Everything okay?" Simon didn't know how he would respond if he heard a negative answer. If Security guards or another danger lurked outside the building right now, he didn't know how much more strength he could summon.

Ella nodded absently. Simon decided to believe her, temporarily at least. He heard water running in the bathroom and watched his dad come back with a wet cloth in hand. Jonathan began to wash the wounds with gentle care. Malachi stood guard at the bedroom door. When the knock came, he left to allow Dr. Pharen and Ben into the apartment.

No one dared speak, including Dr. Pharen. He examined Charity's hands, limbs, head, neck. Simon realized he had been holding his breath only when he started to feel light-headed. After an agonizing few moments, Dr. Pharen straightened up and sighed.

"It's not good. Broken bones seem likely—it's hard to tell about the ribs. She has suffered many blows to the head; concussion likely. Probably internal bleeding. She needs to go to the hospital. Where are her parents?"

"Dead." Simon choked at the word.

"Does she have papers?"

Simon shook his head no.

They all knew how unlikely it would be for Charity to get care.

Dr. Pharen checked her pulse and breathing again and slowly shook his head. "It's just not good."

Simon fought back in a strangled cry, "That's not good enough! You need to do something!"

Malachi took Simon by the arm and firmly led him into the living room.

"Sit here. She will be fine."

Jonathan walked into the living room with Ella and the Pharens.

"Thank you, all of you. We'll let you know as we learn more."

He escorted the three guests out of the apartment and closed the door quietly. He turned back to Malachi. Wordlessly, the two went back into the bedroom, leaving Simon to sit and stare out the north windows. Without warning, the floodgates opened and Simon wept for a month of mistakes on his part and a lifetime of struggle for one of his closest friends.

He felt someone sit on the couch next to him and put an arm around his shoulder. His dad. Simon wasn't certain, but he thought his dad was crying too. For an unknown length of time, the two sat together in silence.

Finally, footsteps from the bedroom caused Simon to look up; Malachi stood facing them, his expression blank. "She is going to make it. Have patience. Have faith."

Simon believed Malachi, despite Dr. Pharen's grim prognosis. Calmed by his dad's sympathy and Malachi's confidence, he walked into the bedroom to check on his friend.

Charity lay still, eyes closed. Simon thought her breathing seemed stronger, and some color had returned to her face. He marveled at the strength of this Messenger who had little reason to be strong at all. It was as if the trials of her life only brought greater endurance from an otherwise unassuming, innocent-looking girl. Her eyelids twitched, and her face contorted in pain. Simon took the movements as bittersweet progress. Simon turned at a soft sound behind him just as Malachi came back into the room; his face was calm, confident. When Simon turned back toward the bed, he was met with two open green eyes.

"So." Charity's voice was weak and strained, but there. "How were the Bot fights today?"

Chapter Thirteen

"Where is the girl?" The commanding figure sat at the head table of a boardroom; the dim lamps cast more shadows than light, and the two Security guards were disconcerted that the face of the one before them was too concealed to bear a discernible expression.

"She went missing, boss. We were gonna get her body right away, like you said. But she . . . she disappeared. Right, Stan? It was crazy. I'm telling you, it was like she just walked away or something. She disappeared. Vanished. Into thin air—"

"Silence!" The figure in the darkness grew impatient. Lurking in the shadowed alleyways had grown too tiring. It became necessary to enlist help—ineffective as it was.

The two guards looked nervously at each other and then back to their leader.

"You both have failed me. Three times this week, you have failed me. You were supposed to retrieve the boy. You were supposed to gain information from the girl.

You were supposed to dispose of her body. Is it really so difficult to find a dead person?!"

"Boss, umm, well . . . what I mean to say is, theoretically speaking . . ."

"Get on with it."

"What if she isn't dead?"

The silhouette breathed in and paused. The two guards held their breath as well.

"Then you have failed me four times. And that is four times too many."

Simon woke to the smell of pan-fried canned meat. He sat up and looked over the back of the couch to see his dad preparing breakfast. He tossed the sheet aside and walked groggily to the kitchen. Three rolls were thawing on the counter.

"Have you checked on her this morning?"

"Briefly. She seemed to be breathing normally, so I didn't want to wake her."

Tempted as he was to make his own visit, Simon forced himself to be patient. Walking back into the living room, he grabbed some clothes he had set aside the night before and readied himself in the bathroom.

When he came out, three plates were set on the counter. Without a word, Jonathan handed one to Simon, who then walked to his bedroom and lightly knocked. A light moan sounded more tired than pained, and Simon opened the door with hesitation.

"Hey," he said.

Charity's eyes were open and turned toward the door without moving her neck from its straight position.

"Nice room," she answered.

"It's quiet," he said. The situation made him feel awkward. "So, what do you say after your friend goes missing and nearly gets killed?"

"Well, I guess I can speak from experience. No good advice, though."

"I really messed up." Guilt and anger battled through Simon. There was so much to ask, so much to say. "We've gotta stop doing this."

"Let's ask Security to back off."

Simon chuckled and used his free hand to pull his desk chair near the side of the bed.

"I think they're getting the opposite memo. You hungry?"

"No. Yes. But the thought of chewing hurts."

Simon grimaced and set the plate on his desk.

"That bad, huh?"

"Well, there's no reason I shouldn't be dead right now. So all things considered, not so bad. Pretty decent, actually. I can move things, technically. Not that I want to."

Simon's instinct to fight against the enemy surged, but the threat was elusive.

"What do we do, Charity? The Message has been suppressed for years. People are dying without hearing the truth. And now? Laying low isn't good enough. They're coming after us. They—" This was the first time Simon let himself reflect on the morning before. He pushed through the horror to speak. "They put a picture of your body on the jumbo screen. Of *you*. And then they showed a message—a warning. 'The end of the Darkness is near.' This isn't over, Charity. I don't know if it ever will be."

"Well," Charity said slowly, her voice stronger, "in that case, what do we have to lose?"

The words hit Simon full on as he realized she was asking the same question his dad, and he himself, had asked many times. When is the loss worth the gain? When is the sacrifice worth the victory?

A quiet knock interrupted his thoughts. Jonathan came in and noticed the cooling plate of food.

"Not ready for food yet? I had a feeling." He held up a glass of milk, the last of their ration for the week. "You'll need this, then. When you're ready to sit up a bit."

Charity sighed. "Why delay the inevitable?"

Jonathan and Simon stood on either side of the bed, lifting Charity at a painstakingly slow pace. Charity winced at first, but firmly set her jaw as she steeled herself for the task. After Jonathan carefully placed a folded blanket behind her, Charity leaned back onto the makeshift lounge. Simon watched her close her eyes for a moment to regroup, and then open them with determination. He wondered how many times in her life Charity had done just that: regroup, recover, and emerge stronger than before.

"Before Malachi left last night, he said he would ask Mrs. Meyer to come and visit today," Jonathan added. "She can help tend to your needs as well."

A knock came just a few minutes later, but Mrs. Meyer wasn't on the other side of the door. Jonathan opened the door to Dr. Roth and welcomed her in. Simon had never seen her far from the Translation Room; it was surreal to have her in their apartment.

"Would you like to join us for breakfast?" Jonathan asked.

"Thanks, no. Perhaps a cup of coffee later. How is Charity?"

"Unbelievably well," Jonathan answered. "I don't quite understand it."

Dr. Roth nodded and smiled, but her expression fell quickly. "I can't say the same of George Meyer, I'm afraid. I don't believe he'll make it through the day. Martha sends her regrets for not coming herself."

"Is she alone?" Simon noticed that his dad glanced toward the door while asking the question.

"No. Zeke is with her. And Malachi."

Jonathan nodded and led the way to Simon's bedroom.

"Charity, it's good to see you! Grand Station hasn't been the same without you this week. How on earth did you make it?"

Charity's smile graced her face and flashed light into the room. Simon had not seen this smile before. He was both hurt for not seeing it till now and thankful he'd seen it at all. He suddenly yearned to see it every day: unguarded and warm, this must have been the smile Charity's mom and dad saw when she was a girl—before so many sorrows buried it beneath a curtain of hurt.

Dr. Roth was anything but the flurry of activity Mrs. Meyer would have been, but she didn't waste any time either. After raising the window shade, straightening the sheets, and handing Simon the untouched plate of food, she gently guided the two men out of the room.

"I'll tend to her while you two eat breakfast. We won't be too long."

At the kitchen table, Jonathan spoke over his coffee mug. "It's been dry several days; the storm drain should be okay by now. It may be worth trying a visit to the City."

Simon's initial joy was quickly matched with fear. The streets would be more dangerous than ever. But really, was any place safe? *Will I ever feel safe again?* Simon shuddered and took a bite of his cold meal.

"What about Charity?"

His dad pursed his lips and nodded. There was still thinking to do. Simon looked at the clock and was relieved at how late the day was already. Anticipation for a possible trip would only grow as the hours went on.

Jonathan and Simon worked together to clear the dirty dishes and clean up the morning mess, leaving the extra food and a cup of coffee on the table. Dr. Roth came back while they were finishing up and sat down. She took a bite of a roll and accepted the cup of coffee, but turned down the offer of reheated breakfast.

"She's doing very well, all things considered. She didn't have much to eat throughout the week, but she's almost back to sleep again already. I imagine she'll be ready to eat when she wakes again."

"Did she say much about what happened to her? You know, before the battle?" Simon had been too scared to ask her, but he couldn't shake the question from his mind.

"Very little. It sounds as if some Security guards tried to question her. And a Mr. . . . Let's see. A Mr.—"

"Druck." Simon spat out the word.

"Yes, that's right. How did you know?" Dr. Roth must have seen the cloud that crossed over Simon's face as she asked; she let the question go unanswered. "At any rate, I know she's getting good care here, but we'll need to get her home as soon as possible. I imagine that if they decide to search any homes for a Bot victim, they would start by looking where another Arena survivor lives."

She was right, of course. Simon and his dad looked at each other and realized the danger of the situation. The night couldn't come soon enough.

Dr. Roth had left after lunch, after Charity ate soup to her supervisors' satisfaction. Then, just after nightfall, Malachi came. In no time, the four were heading down the stairs to the basement. Malachi carried Charity in his arms, much like he had the day before, only this time she was awake. Simon wondered what they would say if a neighbor would suddenly meet them on the way to the storage area, but all was quiet. Simon cleared the way to the opening, and Malachi carefully passed Charity through it to Jonathan, who waited on the other side. Malachi came through, and Jonathan handed Charity back to him. Once all four were in the tunnel, Simon finished the task of covering the hole while Malachi started leading the way. From behind, Simon marveled how Malachi was able to fit his considerable frame through the tunnel without much trouble, especially while holding Charity.

After setting Charity on the ledge where the tunnel opened into the storm drain, Malachi jumped down and reached for her. Charity, through the pain, did her best to assist, but Simon knew the greatest challenge was still ahead.

"We can't do this," Charity said when they reached the ladder. "How will you carry me up?"

Malachi looked up, undeterred. "I can carry you. Or you can climb."

Charity's mouth dropped in shock at the options; she stared at the one who was holding her. Slowly, she closed her mouth, and her jaw set. Her eyes flashed as she considered the possibilities.

Malachi answered for her. "I will carry you." He set her on her feet on the damp gravel momentarily as he resituated her piggyback style. Simon could see Charity bear down on the pain she felt, but she made no sound. Malachi motioned for Jonathan to go first and lift the lid. Once Malachi was near the opening, he and Jonathan worked to lift Charity through to street level. Simon jumped onto the ladder then and quickly ascended, remembering the adventure Jack faced last time and how rapidly the floodwater came through the storm drain.

The rest of the way was easy by comparison, but Simon remained on high alert for any man or machine that might be hunting for Messengers in the darkness. Malachi led the way to the South Gate, and Michael opened the door. Another guard was standing by to take over the watch, and Michael held out his arms to take over for Malachi. Once at the Room of the Martyrs, the group split up:

Simon followed Michael and Charity toward the main marketplace, and Malachi and Jonathan made their way toward the Meyers' home.

Wordlessly, Michael walked past the main corridor along the edge of the marketplace and passed the Translation Room. Instead of continuing toward the Elders' room, he veered right and led Simon through a maze of tunnels he didn't yet know. The halls soon gave way to doors, one after the other. Eventually, they turned right and headed up a flight of stairs. Another right and down another hallway, Michael finally stopped at the last door on the left. Simon took Michael's nod to mean he should open it. Inside, a small but tidy room held a bed, a dresser, and a shelf full of art supplies. Michael laid a grateful Charity on the bed and lit an oil lamp mounted on the wall near the door. The ceiling of the room was arched, following the curve of a large semicircle window that took up much of the front wall. Michael drew the curtain to the right, exposing a view of the main marketplace below. Simon looked out and saw dozens of people moving throughout the large room. The corridor they had taken was out of sight; when Simon looked down, he could see a short, sloping roof over the area where they so often traveled back and forth throughout the City.

Simon turned back to the room and looked up. Painted on the curved ceiling was a stunning mural. A darkened moon was in the corner near a few stars appearing to fall from the sky. The rest of the mural looked as if the night sky was drawn back, exposing a bright and glorious light. Trumpets and angels filled the expanse surrounding a figure in fiery white robes, a crown with seven points, and eyes bright as flame. His skin was about the same shade as Simon's, and His dark hair and beard seemed to shine in the surrounding glory. Simon was speechless.

"Thank you, Michael," Charity managed. "It's good to be home."

Michael nodded and stood by the doorway.

"You're amazing," Simon said to her. "Is there anything you can't do?"

"Read, for one thing," Charity reminded him. "And at the moment, I'm not too great at walking either."

Simon sat on a chair near the bed, which was pushed up against the wall and under the window.

"Well, we can work on both of those things later. For now, what do you need? Something to drink? Something to eat?"

Charity yawned her answer. "Sleep would be great. Oh! But before you go. Take that with you." She pointed to a board resting in the corner.

Simon walked over to it and turned it around. He couldn't believe it; he was holding a lightweight, to-scale replica of the stones that were once a barrier between him and the rest of the nighttime world.

"You did this from one stone I gave Spence?" The exchange two weeks ago suddenly made sense.

"He helped me with the dimensions. It's supposed to be a little big at the moment; your dad will need to trim and adjust it to fit. I'm sure it's not perfect, but hopefully it will look okay from a distance."

"This is great! Thank you."

Charity smiled. "I was going to give it to you when we came back from the mission that night, but . . ."

Simon grimaced, but caught himself. "It's perfect. Thanks. You should get some rest, though."

Simon followed Michael out into the hallway and began to close the door. "Goodnight."

"See you next time."

Simon thanked God those words were possible.

Chapter Fourteen

"Any plans tonight?" Ella sat next to Ben and Simon at lunch.

"You know, you guys don't have to sit by me. Guilty by association and all that," Simon protested.

Ella shrugged. "What're they going to do to us?"

The awkward silence that followed allowed for all three to consider exactly that. Simon shuddered, thinking of Charity's bloody hair and almost lifeless body.

"Okay, but honestly. Maybe that's the point. Simon, you've braved the Arena. Your friend Charity—she was almost killed. Is this cause worth dying for?"

"My mom thought so," Simon admitted, allowing the truth to sink in for Ella.

Ella's jaw set, and she nodded as she spoke. "So I want to be a part of it too. I talked to my parents yesterday. I asked them why they never taught me the stuff you know. They talked about forgetting, about the government, on and on. And you know what? Then my mom started crying. I can't believe it! I mean, why didn't they think about this before? But here's the point. They're in too. They want to help."

Simon looked to Ben, whose face flushed. But he slowly nodded.

"Simon. From your bedroom window? I saw the back of my house," Ella said. "We're crazy close together, and I had no idea."

Stunned, Simon stared at her and then smiled. "Imagine what you could have seen if you'd only looked out your window at night."

Ella's eyes widened. "So it's true? You run around the alleys at night?"

Simon chuckled. "Sort of. But you won't be seeing me out your window anymore. Too bad we've had so much rain lately . . ."

Simon realized he had totally lost Ben and Ella in his train of thought, but he didn't elaborate. Instead, he considered a completely new idea.

"Ella. What's your basement like?"

That night in the City, Simon paid his first solo visit to Spence. He finally remembered to bring his broken chain to the cellar for inspection.

"Yep. I should be able to fix this with some needle-nose pliers. Might want to reinforce it with a bit of solder."

"Thanks, Spence," Simon replied. "How can I repay you?"

Spence gave the question serious thought before he walked to a shelf full of boxes and baskets of odds and ends. He came back with a part that looked like a broken piece of a robotic arm. Simon instinctively took a step back at the sight of a Bot bit. If he never saw a Bot again . . .

"Wanna see my Bot?"

"What?! You stole a Bot?!"

Spence rolled his eyes. "Of course not. Well, not a whole one, anyway. Let's call it upcycling. I think that's what they used to say. Repurposing, perhaps. Anyway, I'm building one. But see these?" Spence pointed to various parts that held the machine remnant together. "Bolts, nuts, screws, washers. I could use a lot more."

Simon knew the likeliest place to get the parts, and he also knew that it was one of the last places in the world he wanted to go. Two days ago, he'd held his dying friend just feet away from containers full of discarded machinery. She would have been discarded just as easily.

"I'll see what I can do." That was all Simon was willing to promise.

"Thanks. But really, wanna see my Bot?"

"No! Thanks. No thanks, Spence. But maybe later." As Simon left the cellar, he called back, "Thanks again for fixing the chain!"

His next stop was past the marketplace, down and around several corners, up some stairs, and down a hallway. Simon was glad he found the door he was looking for. It was open, and Micah and Dr. Roth were already there.

"Hi, Charity. Hi, everyone."

Dr. Roth greeted Simon with a smile. Micah did not. Charity was propped against several pillows, eating a sandwich. Simon rejoiced over her further progress.

"Hey, Simon. Learn anything at school today?"

More than I thought I would, Simon replied silently. Instead, he offered an apathetic shrug.

"We were just on our way out," Micah informed him. "Coming with?"

Simon didn't know how to stall, so he reluctantly agreed. "Might as well."

This, evidently, was not the response Micah wanted to hear. He sniffed disapproval and edged past Simon into the hallway.

Dr. Roth said good-bye to Charity and patted Simon on the shoulder as she walked out.

"Feeling okay?" Simon asked. He knew he had an audience in the hallway who expected him to leave shortly, but he couldn't help asking—feeble as it sounded.

"Getting there," Charity offered. "Thanks, Simon."

"For what?" Simon's response came out more as a retort, and he regretted the harshness of it.

"For saving my life."

"Huh. Well. Next time, I'll try not to put it in jeopardy in the first place."

"Too late." Charity's smile implied a joke, but Simon knew there was more truth to that than anyone would admit to his face. He'd put her life in danger, and the lives of so many other Messengers too. He waved good-bye and closed the door. Time to follow his companions to the next location.

Simon couldn't resist running his hands along the vivid mosaic of the garden-like paradise that surrounded him as he walked with Micah and Dr. Roth toward the Elders' room. Careful not to touch the sly serpent hidden in the greenery, he imagined the taste of the colorful fruit depicted in abundance along the walls and up to the curved ceiling of the passageway. Then came darkness and ultimately the cross—bold and centered on a bright field with Jesus hanging there in agony. As they crossed into the next garden scene, Simon thought of George. He wondered what the funeral service would be like. He knew his dad was already in the chapel, the place where everyone worshiped, finishing preparations. Where would Mrs. Meyer be sitting? How was she feeling?

If he had been to a funeral before, he couldn't remember it. He was starting to wonder if he had a penchant for burying bad memories. If so, they seemed to resurface eventually anyway. He'd had his share of nightmares this past year, only to realize that many of them were actually memories he had managed to suppress for a time. But as terrible as the past month had been, he was scared to think that he could forget those memories and lose so many good ones too.

The Elders' room was empty, and the three wasted no time moving to the front of the room, where a portion of the wall opened into their worship space. The sanctuary was full. Dr. Roth sat next to a man Simon assumed was her husband. Micah sat near the back. Simon caught his eye, but Micah frowned and looked away, which Simon took to be a warning against trying to sit by him. Mrs.

Meyer was sitting in the very front next to Malachi; Simon's dad was standing near the chancel with Zeke and Cyril, all three wearing white robes.

He saw Jack halfway up the aisle and made his way to the pew.

"Hey, man," Jack whispered. "Glad you're not dead."

"Micah doesn't seem to agree," Simon mumbled. He was glad that Jack didn't mind the company.

"Aw, you know Micah. Classic by-the-book guy. He'll cool off. You're lucky Charity made it, though. Otherwise . . ." Jack gave a meaningful look to imply impending doom at the hands of the clean-cut Carrier.

The scenario caused Simon to feel numb, but it wasn't for fear of Micah. He focused his attention to the front.

His dad began to sing, and others joined in. The hymn was new to Simon, so he listened closely to the words as they conjured images of a paradise beyond description in his mind. "Sing with all the saints in glory, Sing the resurrection song! Death and sorrow, earth's dark story, To the former days belong, All around the clouds are breaking; Soon the storms of time shall cease; In God's likeness we awaken, Knowing everlasting peace."

Simon wondered if George was singing at this very moment. His mind couldn't comprehend how eternity worked, but he knew George was with his Lord, and that brought great comfort. He looked at Mrs. Meyer, who was wiping her tears away with a handkerchief. He thought about his dad. Had his mom's funeral been anything like this? Where did his dad sit? Simon couldn't remember it of course; he had been only three years old.

"They used to have the bodies present at the service," Jack whispered. "That's what I've heard, at least."

"Really? The dead body in front of everybody? Why?"

Jack shrugged. What did anyone know of the outside world? Simon's knowledge of funerals was that the government took the body within twenty-four hours of death. And that was it—no one knew where anyone was buried. A large plot outside the northeast corner of town was designated for a graveyard, but there was no way to know who rested where. All the graves were unmarked. Simon snapped back to attention as his dad spoke.

"A reading from Romans, chapter six. 'Do you not know that all of us who have been baptized into Christ Jesus were baptized into His death? We were buried therefore with Him by baptism into death, in order that, just as Christ was raised from the dead by the glory of the Father, we too might walk in newness of life. For if we have been united with Him in a death like His, we shall certainly be united with Him in a resurrection like His.'"

Simon tried to imagine the surprise those graveyard workers would have if Jesus would return right now. He rested in the confidence that George and his mom would rise up one day, as surely as Jesus rose from the dead.

The final song was one Simon knew well. The first time he heard it this year, memories of the tune had come to him right away. He sang along with fervor, thankful that all in the room had the same assurance he had.

"Go, My children, with My blessing, Never alone. Waking, sleeping, I am with you; You are My own. In

My love's baptismal river, I have made you Mine forever. Go, My children, with My blessing—You are My own."

Later that night, Simon lay awake in bed, thinking of those who were hurting tonight: Mrs. Meyer, sleeping in an empty home; Charity, healing from wounds both seen and unseen; Ella, betrayed by her parents' apathy to the Message; Micah, angry at Simon's recklessness. The list could have gone on, but Simon stopped as he grew burdened with the new cares he considered for each friend. He found peace at last as he cast all those burdens on the Friend who was still listening at this late hour. As Simon prayed to his Savior, he felt relief and sleep come at last.

Chapter Fifteen

House by house, I go. One by one, I take them. Men, women, it makes no difference. Each one is a blight on our people. Each one is an abomination to our God. How dare they worship this Jesus as if He is the Messiah?! Do they not know that I am the authority on truth? My blood boils when I think of the way they mock the promise to Abraham by claiming to know the Son. One by one, I find them and throw them into prison. Theirs will be the same fate as their beloved Stephen, as their beloved Jesus. And yet, this still is not enough. It is time to move beyond this city and into new territory. So help me, I will not rest until I have stamped out any obstacle to God's favor upon His people.

■ ■ ■

"Happy birthday, Ben." Simon sat down to lunch with his noodle broth and slurped a spoonful into his mouth.

"Thanks. Yeah, about that." Ben looked around a moment before continuing. No one was coming their way, to Ben's approval. "Wanna come over for dinner tonight? Mom said I should ask you. I mean, that'd be great and all. But, you know. It's okay with her. If you want."

"Yeah, sure. Sounds good." Simon's Provisional Adult Status meant that he wouldn't need special approval, so he'd only need to stop by the workshop to let his dad know.

"Hey, guys. What's new?" Ella dropped down by Ben, whose face fell slightly.

"It's Ben's birthday," Simon answered. He anticipated the glaring look from his sixteen-year-old friend, but the shade of red Ben was turning was worth it.

"Ben! Happy birthday!" Ella gushed. "Are you going to celebrate somehow?"

"No!" Ben's tact was always lacking, but there was no effort on his part to be kind to their inquisitive friend.

Ella shrugged and moved on without missing a beat. "My mom said kids used to have parties with lots of friends and games and cake with ice cream. It sounds so nice. Don't you wish we could have that?"

Ben grumbled under his breath, and Simon laughed at how easily Ben got irked. It was hard for Simon not to tease his friend about taking himself a little too seriously.

Ella was unfazed as she continued to share all she knew about party hats and pin the tail on the donkey. Simon listened with interest until he remembered something.

"Oh, Ella. I told my dad about you and your parents. You might get a visitor or two soon."

Ella's eyes lit up brighter than before. "Great! I hope I'm home when they come. Oh, this is so exciting!"

A pulsing tone brought them back to the present, and they followed the rest of their classmates out of the cafeteria and into their classrooms.

The end-of-day tone sent Ben rushing out of school. Simon chuckled at the enthusiasm that propelled his friend toward his birthday celebration as quickly as possible. Simon and Ella followed at a slower pace, heading north from the campus.

"You're sure you want to get into this, right? I mean, you've seen what we're up against."

"I've seen what you're up against in New Morgan. And I know what you're up against in reality too—the world that's both seen and unseen. I mean, come on, Simon. If this Message is worth dying for, why don't you want to share it with me?"

The question nailed Simon in the gut. A few weeks ago, he was reciting Romans 10 as his mantra, yearning to share the truth with everyone. Now, he was basically asking a friend—someone who had seen his messages and heard his confession of faith—whether she really wanted to know what he had to share. Shame filled him. In his enthusiasm to spread God's Word, he had forgotten to consider his friends. And now, in his caution to keep the Message and its Messengers safe, he had forgotten to consider his neighbors. *What a balance. Was it worth the trouble? What is there to lose?* Simon grew tired with the burdensome questions.

"Look, based on what I've heard from you and—finally!—my parents, this is a big deal. And as far as I can tell, it's worth fighting for. I'm so tired of having nothing more to think about than what I'll study and clean and eat day after day after day. There's gotta be more to this life. I can't wait to learn more."

Simon observed the determination and earnestness on Ella's face and committed himself to doing whatever it would take to help Ella learn the Word and share the Message.

They had reached Smith Street, and Ella veered right.

"Thanks, Simon," Ella tossed over her left shoulder.

"For what?"

Ella turned and flashed a quick smile. "For saving my life."

Simon took a few seconds to process those words, and he regretted being slow with his response. "That'd be Jesus, Ella," he called after her, hoping it wasn't too loud.

Ella's blond ponytail bobbed as she threw her head back in laughter. She waved a quick good-bye and continued home.

Twice this week, a friend had thanked Simon when he didn't deserve it, and the importance of those moments wasn't lost on him. The balance of sharing eternal life and preserving earthly life wasn't going to be easy. Simon wished he had the evening to mull this over in conversation with his dad. Or to sleep. He was exhausted, and dinner with the Pharens was not likely to be relaxing. Still, he had accepted the invitation and Ben was his friend. With a resigned sigh and a tug on his backpack, he entered 2350 and veered left into the workshop.

An hour later, Simon walked across the street for dinner. He had asked his dad for gift ideas after school. After looking at a few projects his dad had finished over time and set aside in the workshop, he'd found a promising candidate and slipped it into the pocket of his sweatshirt. He tapped it self-consciously while he waited for the Pharens' apartment door to open.

"Simon! So good to see you. I'm just so very pleased to have you visit us tonight. Thank you for coming. Come in, come in!" Mrs. Pharen ushered Simon in during her extended greeting. Simon nodded hello to Ben and his dad. He wanted to thank Dr. Pharen for his visit just a few days ago, but he didn't know the proper etiquette for mentioning a somewhat unsanctioned house call for an orphan, undocumented citizen, and apparent enemy of the state—especially with extra company present. Simon nodded toward a new face: a woman with eyebrows shaped in a frozen look of surprise, the other visitor could only be a younger and slightly thinner sister of Mrs. Pharen.

"Simon, this is my sister, Sarah. You may call her Ms. Rosten."

"Nice to meet you," Simon offered.

"Of course. The same. Now, is this the Simon Clay I've heard so much about? My, you're quite the celebrity, aren't you? And how is your father? It's been so long since I've seen him. And dear George Meyers, may he rest in peace. Do you think Martha will be able to manage without him? I'm just so terribly sick when I think of her. It's been so long. But my Alice. She goes down to fetch me some of those lovely vegetables in the marketplace. Really, you would think New Morgan could grow better ones than the underground village down there, but no matter. Anyhow, when she brings me my produce, she makes sure to tell me all the latest that goes on down there. My, my. It just amazes me how so many people can function in tunnels and holes. Well, now. Did I hear of a young lady who was injured? Chantilly, Chelsea . . ."

"Charity." Simon instantly regretted the misstep. He could tell by Ms. Rosten's exultant smile and Ben's defeated eye roll that he had walked right into her trap. He reacted with a question of his own.

"And is Alice your daughter?" The question seemed to unsettle Ms. Rosten, and Simon celebrated the small victory of a diversion.

"Oh, heavens, no. She lives in my building. A neighbor, my Alice is. Goodness, I simply cannot keep her from doting on me. She's at my apartment nearly night and day; I have no idea how she can possibly get anything done in her own home, but that's not my worry, I suppose."

"Ellen, dinner smells wonderful," Dr. Pharen slipped in during Sarah's tiniest of breaths. Ben's aunt looked annoyed at the interruption, but she reached for the glass of water Mrs. Pharen had just set on the table and took the opportunity to rehydrate.

"All of Ben's favorites," Mrs. Pharen answered. "Not much, of course, considering the times. Not that I'm complaining. We manage, to be sure."

To be sure, Simon echoed in his mind as he eyed the table. A roast chicken—just like the occasional meal he had seen on vintage television sitcoms—adorned the table, surrounded by steamed carrots, brown rice, and a light gravy.

The rest of the dinner progressed with relative ease. Mrs. Pharen and her sister carried most of the conversation, including Dr. Pharen on occasion, but they largely ignored Ben and Simon. The two teenagers ate in grateful silence.

"Now, Simon, you simply must take this parcel of food to your father. I imagine he hasn't even taken a break to eat this evening."

"You may be right, Mrs. Pharen. Thank you," Simon answered. He took a small, warm foil package and headed for the door. "Happy birthday, Ben."

"Thanks for coming," Ben said as he waved from the middle of the living space.

Dr. Pharen held the apartment door open and followed Simon out. "I know you don't need a chaperone," he said with a quick glance toward the women, "but it would be rude of me not to see you to the outer door."

On the way down the steps, Dr. Pharen spoke softly. "Ben told me that Charity is doing better. Quite honestly, I cannot fathom how she improved so quickly, or at all, if you'll pardon me saying so."

Simon forgave the honesty; he liked Dr. Pharen and trusted that his motives were genuine.

"She's doing better each day, I think. I can't believe it either."

"Thanks be to God. Well, don't you hesitate to let me know any time you need help. And Simon?" They were at the building's front door now, and Dr. Pharen paused before he pulled on the handle. "Please be careful out there."

Chapter Sixteen

"Dad, what do you know about the Revemondians?"

"I am one."

Jonathan had just finished Mrs. Pharen's leftovers and brought in a deck of cards from his bedroom.

"Oh, Dad! I forgot to give Ben his birthday present. His aunt Sarah completely distracted me. I guess I'll have to give it to him some other time."

"She's a character, isn't she? We used to see her while visiting the Pharens when you were small. I always had the impression she was sizing me up when we talked."

They prepared a game of King's Corners, but Simon was more interested in other government powers.

"So is Revemond anything like New Morgan?"

Jonathan laughed. "The Revemond I knew is nothing like the New Morgan I know. But Morganland and Revemond were very similar when I grew up. People could travel back and forth without much trouble. I never considered that I wouldn't be able to easily cross a border and visit my parents. In hindsight, we all should have seen it coming. But it didn't seem possible at the time."

Simon laid a queen of hearts on a king of clubs, but he forgot to draw a card first. It was hard to focus on the game with so much on his mind.

"So, did the Morganland and Revemond people like each other?"

Jonathan leaned back in his chair. "For the most part. There was always back and forth banter and all, but growing up, I didn't notice too many problems. Maybe I was naive. When New Morgan came to being, though, the government kept talking about their inferior neighbors. Revemond had pretty healthy churches, which New Morgan scorned. If Revemondians moved to New Morgan but fell on hard times, they were treated very poorly. Some were paid a pittance. Others were paid nothing at all."

"So, New Morgan had slavery."

"Yes, I guess you could say that. It wasn't obvious, so it was hard to know when people were being oppressed, but I'm sure it happened more often than people knew or believed. Pretty soon, anything shy of New Morgan 'perfection' earned a sneer and a condemnation."

"Like the Bible?"

Jonathan set his cards down. The game would have to wait.

"Yes. But all kinds of people have a problem with the Bible, for all kinds of reasons. I suspect the main reason the government hated it was because they feared anything that named a higher power than the state. But plenty of others either didn't believe the Bible or didn't care about it, so there wasn't much of a fight when it disappeared from sight."

"Sounds like the Maxons were that way too—Ella's parents. They just sort of stopped caring. Is that even possible?"

Jonathan chuckled sadly. "More possible than you would think."

"Ella really wants to join us, Dad. She says her parents do too. But we don't really know them, do we? What if they're not serious? What if they tell Security?"

"I don't know, Simon. I guess it comes down to this: What is there to lose?"

Simon slumped in his chair. The answer wasn't easy.

Night fell, and Simon dressed for his mission. Dark hooded jacket and jeans would do the trick. He grabbed his ring, his watch, and a book from his near-empty bookshelves. He longed for the days when the workshop portal was feasible. The tunnel was safer now—assuming a flash flood didn't sweep him away—but Simon still didn't like being so confined.

The days were getting longer, which shortened the time Carriers had to bring Messages from post to post. But restoring the Word to the people piece by piece was of utmost importance, and Simon was more ready than ever to fight against the forces that would stop it. He only hoped he'd be able to make it to the City early enough to pay a visit or two before it was time for his mission.

Michael wasn't at the South Gate that night. Simon nodded at the guard on duty. She cracked a fraction of a smile in return, but immediately focused back on the door. Her long brown hair was held back in a tight braid, and her belt kept several weapons at the ready.

When Simon reached the Room of the Martyrs, he was saddened. No boisterous voice called out his name. No beaming woman in a long skirt ran to give him a hug—not that he really expected it. Instead, a woman about Micah's age tended the table where Mrs. Meyer usually stood. She smiled as Simon approached.

"Hello. Would you like to buy some rolls?"

Simon didn't know how to respond to this change. "Did Mrs. Meyer make them? Where is she?"

The vendor's face fell apologetically. "I made them, I'm afraid. I used her recipes; she lent them to me ages ago. But they're not as good, sorry to say. Some of us are trying to help build up her funds again while she tends to her home right now."

"Funds?"

She nodded. "Many of us would contribute funds so she could buy extra ingredients. She called it the baking pool. And then she would take some of her breads and rolls to families who don't have enough vouchers to get by. Sometimes, though, she would slip some of her own money into the cost. We're trying to return the favor."

"Thanks, umm . . ."

"Rosie."

"Thanks, Rosie. I'm Simon."

Rosie laughed. "Yeah, I know who you are. Most of us do."

Simon suspected that he likely owed his fame to his time in the Arena, but he dared not ask for confirmation.

"Well, Rosie, thanks for helping Mrs. Meyer. I don't have money or vouchers with me this time, but I'll try to remember to bring some next time."

"Thanks, Simon. Here. Have a roll anyway."

"No, I couldn't. Thanks, though."

"Really," Rosie protested while grabbing his wrist and placing a roll in his hand, "I insist."

There was no tactful way to refuse now, so Simon held up the roll and thanked her once more. He knew where he'd take it.

"Hey, Spence."

Spence had a huge metal mask on, which he lifted in greeting. "Simon! I have your chain. Good as new."

"Great! Thanks. Now if I could find the opportunity to thank Malachi for finding it."

"You're welcome."

The deep voice behind him caused Simon to jump to embarrassing heights. Malachi laughed as Simon turned around to see who had snuck up on him.

"What are you trying to do? Kill me?! I might take it back."

Malachi slapped Simon's back, which seemed innocent enough if not for the sheer power behind it. Simon would have been knocked to his knees if he hadn't caught himself on the counter that divided him from most of the cellar.

"Hi, Malachi," Spence said as he handed the repaired chain to Simon from across the counter. "What can I do for you?"

Malachi shrugged. "I'm here to help you. Good-bye, Simon."

"Umm, yeah. I guess I'll go then." Simon realized he was being dismissed. "Later, guys."

Simon encountered another surprise when he reached the end of an increasingly familiar hallway. Charity sat in a chair in her room, carefully painting a small piece of plaster in her lap. Simon noticed that she kept her back straight as she worked, using her hands to make the crucial movements instead of using her entire body to move the color from one place to the other.

"Look at you! How do you feel?"

Charity smiled, but winced as well. "Getting there—not as fast as I'd like. But getting there."

"What hurts most?" Simon didn't really know what prompted him to ask the question, but he wanted to be sure she was recovering completely.

"My pride."

Simon emitted a guffaw in relief. Charity was on the mend. A dark cloud crossed his mind, however.

"Charity . . ." He didn't want to ask, but he had to. "Dr. Roth mentioned that you met a Mr. Druck. Did he hurt you? Or say anything to you? Are you okay?"

Charity frowned at the memory, but Simon judged her expression to be more of concentration than anger or fear.

"I know he was there, and at least two other men too. Guards. Not always at the same time, though. They wanted to know about you. About the Messengers. Mr. Druck—he was the tall guy, right? He noticed my brand. There was some argument about it. I can't quite remember, but I think maybe he wanted to send me back to . . . well, you know."

Simon clenched his fists but remained as calm as he could.

"What did he say to you?"

"Simon, I know this is weird, but I really don't remember very much. I didn't say anything—I'm sure I didn't. I couldn't have. But everything's so foggy. Does that make sense?"

Simon's hunch about the poison must be true; Druck's mind-numbing chemicals were likely a common tool back at Druck-Baden Manor. He nodded, but took a moment to find an even voice. "Yes, it makes sense. Don't worry about it."

"You know, at the end, everyone was really mad. That's when they put me in the Bot. So if they were mad, I for sure didn't say anything, right?"

Simon forced a confident smile. "Without a doubt." It was true; he had no doubt that Charity had stayed firm through it all. It was more than he could say for himself. The thought of Druck hurting Charity caused his blood to boil.

"Simon? You okay?"

"Oh! Yes. But oh no! Look. I ruined this roll." Simon held out the baked good he had intended to deliver to her. Instead, he had crushed it in his anger.

"Thanks, Simon. No big deal. It'll still taste fine."

Simon handed the damaged food to his friend. He had a mission and it was time to go—and he hated that their brief encounter had been filled with painful memories and dumb mistakes.

"I'll come back soon, if that's okay. Keep getting better."

"I'll do my best."

"Oh! Here. I know it's not much. But we can work through it together sometime." He pulled a thin book from inside his coat and handed it to her.

Charity looked at it and back at him, questioning.

"*A Student's First Reader*. It's been on my shelf forever."

Charity smiled as she gently arranged the small book next to her art supplies. The smile was almost as warm as the one she gave Dr. Roth the other day. Simon decided to bring gifts like this more often.

"Simon! I was about to give up on your lazy self. Where've you been? No, don't tell me. Like I need any guess." Jack rolled his eyes and crossed his arms as he stood in the middle of the Room of the Twelve. "Enough delay, man. Time to get a move on."

As Simon followed Jack out of the room and toward the North Gate, he noticed a partially painted Judas staring out into the room with piercing eyes but without any body. Simon shivered not only at the uncompromising figure but also at the fact that its painter had been delayed from her work for so long.

Jack noticed. "Yeah, creepy Judas," he agreed. "And thanks to you, I've had to hang out with him for more time than I care to think about. Micah saw me standing around like a lost sheep or something."

The scolding was enough to bring Simon back to the present, and he followed Jack with the kind of determination that comes after tragedy. He was ready to fight back.

"All right, Jack. You've made your point. Lead the way, boss."

That was all Jack needed. The two sped off on their mission.

Chapter Seventeen

The late April night was warm, and Simon made a mental note to rethink his clothes for his next trip. His go-to Carrier clothes guarded against the chill, so a few wardrobe adaptations would be in order. He also noted that Jack was wasting no time tonight. Simon imagined that he was trying to make up for some lost time. As a last-year student in Preparatory School, Jack would be facing a few weeks of tests. Every spare moment would be precious time that could be used for studying. Simon was happy to oblige with a swifter pace, but he knew better than to be too daring. His ears were trained on the sounds of the night, listening for footsteps, engine rumbles, anything that signaled they were not alone on the streets.

Jack led the duo through the Central Sector, and they eventually neared the corner by the Central Sector Preparatory School. As Jack waited at the end of the alley to cross the street, he flashed a grin. Simon couldn't help but smile back at the shared memory. *The light shines in the darkness* . . .

Farther back behind the school was a large stone building. Simon had no idea what purpose the building had served in the past; he knew only that there was a purpose to visiting it tonight. A small door stood squarely in the center of the back wall of the building along the alley. A dim lamp shone down, creating a small circle of light. Jack reached toward the door, knocked, and pulled himself back into the shadows. The door opened, and an older man with wire-frame glasses and a knowing smile stepped out.

"Verified or pending?" Jack asked.

The man's smile widened. "Verified."

Simon spoke up. "Destination?"

"Archive."

Simon held out his hand for the vial and address, but received a patient reminder instead.

"Present yourselves."

Simon pulled back his hand to bring the ring up from the mended chain that hung underneath his clothing. Both Jack and Simon presented their names and rings, the λόγος symbols shining in the light.

The man handed Simon the vial and a small piece of paper.

"God keep you safe," he said as he closed and locked the door behind him.

Simon held the piece of paper to the light. "It says, 'Archive Two.'"

Jack groaned. "More walking. Here we go."

The moon was full, and the stars were bright. It would be the perfect evening to stand outside and watch the sky—if the nighttime pedestrians were not criminals and if transferring biblical passages was not a punishable offense. The beauty of the light also presented danger as it was harder to hide in the shadows.

After plenty of zigs and zags through the city, they arrived at an alley that was faintly familiar to Simon. It became especially clear to him where they were as Jack bent near a window just a foot above the pavement and knocked. As a dim light began to glow through the panes, Simon knew he could expect a small, older woman to approach—likely in a floral nightgown.

The window opened, and a beaming face peeked from below.

"Verified or pending?"

"Verified," Simon answered, knowing the joy this news would bring.

"Present yourselves," she replied brightly.

"Jack Lane."

"Simon Clay."

"Thank you, boys."

Simon handed the vial to her, and she broke the seal. Simon was thankful that she was willing to share the Word with them.

"Hmm, this is an intriguing one." She cleared her throat and read it out loud. "'So have no fear of them, for nothing is covered that will not be revealed, or hidden that will not be known. What I tell you in the dark, say in the light, and what you hear whispered, proclaim on the housetops. And do not fear those who kill the body but cannot kill the soul. Rather fear him who can destroy both soul and body in hell.' It's from Matthew, chapter ten."

"Thank you, ma'am," Jack said.

As they turned to go, the woman called out her farewell. "Simon? Your mom, Abby, she was a wonderful lady. I miss her."

"Thank you. I do too."

On the way back, all was calm and they made good time. That is, until they neared the South Gate to the City. As they approached one corner, they heard the *step, step, step* of soles on the pavement. A growing light shone on the street, and Simon and Jack ducked into the darkest corner of the alley.

Step, step, step. Two Security guards were no more than twenty feet away.

Simon held his breath until the footsteps faded. Then he and Jack backtracked through the alleys for a few more minutes. Approaching a street again, they suddenly heard a new threat.

Thud, thud, thud.

Jack looked at Simon with a you've-gotta-be-kidding-me expression. Again, they hid in a dark corner, peering out just enough to see a Bot with four long legs pass by. Just as they were about to move forward again, they saw a dim beam of light approach.

Jack jumped up and ran deeper into the alley; Simon followed suit.

"The City's surrounded," Jack whispered. "We'll just have to break up and go home. See you when I see you."

Simon nodded as they both waited for the light and accompanying Security guards to pass. Afterward, they parted ways and headed home.

"I'm in!" Ella set her lunch tray down with such exuberance that half of her vegetable soup sloshed out of the bowl. "Zeke came to our house. He talked to us. We get to help! And learn. Ooooh, this is so great!"

"It's also illegal," Ben reminded her. "I'd be a little more careful before you have a party in the school cafeteria."

Ella's joy diminished for just a moment before her smile bubbled back and she bounced slightly in her seat. "Aaaand," she added, "that's not all. But it's a surprise. You'll have to wait."

Simon was pretty sure he knew the surprise; he'd thought of it before, but he decided to leave it alone for now. Simon noticed Ben perk up at the mention of a surprise, but he didn't press it either. The rest of lunch was fairly quiet as each second-year at the table considered the last few days—and their future.

When the end of the day finally came, Simon was exhausted. The tension of the past week was catching up with him, but he didn't want to waste the opportunity of the afternoon. Ben was waiting for him at the bottom of the school's front steps, and they headed off toward the library together.

"Hey. I forgot to give you this the other night. Happy birthday."

Simon handed Ben a palm-sized wooden block that appeared to be solid.

"It slides," Simon explained. After a few tries, Ben finally was able to slide a panel from the top along nearly invisible grooves. A deck of cards was tucked safely inside.

"Cards? Cool, thanks! Nice box too," Ben commented. "Did your dad make it?"

Simon nodded. "We've been playing cards lately. Helps to pass the time."

"Thanks, Simon." Ben tucked the box into his pocket. "So, what do you plan to research? And don't tell me it's chapter nine of our history book," Ben teased. "That one won't work anymore."

"I want to learn more about Revemond. No one ever talks about our neighboring countries, and Ms. Stetter mentioned them the other day. I want to see what I can find out about that place."

"Your dad looks kind of Revemondian, come to think of it," Ben mused. "You must take after your mom."

The two rounded the corner just as they heard a call behind them.

"Guys! Wait up!"

"Oh, hey, Ella. We're going to the library today," Simon informed her as she trotted up.

"Great! I love the library."

Ben made a huge show of annoyance, but the other two ignored him.

After one block, they were there.

The librarian standing guard at the door raised his eyebrows as they approached.

"Haven't seen you two in a while," he commented—perhaps the first words he had ever spoken to them. "You're that kid, aren't you? The one from the Arena?"

Simon braced himself for what came next.

"That's what you get for reading, eh? Pretty soon, they'll be hauling us all out there for reading books. Not that I condone your reading selection, mind you." The librarian lifted his glasses and peered at them, making it clear he was no criminal like Simon. "But most of my library's gone thanks to all the books New Morgan deemed it necessary to censor." He sniffed with frustration. Ben shuffled his shoes, and the librarian shifted his attention to the freckled teen. "Well, I suppose you're back for a visit too, mmm? Happen to have a pass from your teacher?"

"Actually, sir," Simon interrupted, "we both just turned sixteen." Simon gestured to Ben, and they both presented their identification.

"Well, now. Sure enough. And what about you, miss?" The librarian eyed Ella, who had stood a few steps behind during the exchange.

"I, uh, didn't remember. I forgot I needed a pass."

Ben groaned audibly. Ella looked nervously at the clock above the entrance, realizing her walk home would have to be a rapid one.

"Hmm. Well, you're here to read books too, aren't you?"

"Yes, sir!"

"It seems I happen to have a pass right here, but let me be clear. If anyone stops to check it on your way home, you are to blame for a counterfeit pass, do you understand?"

Ella nodded readily. Simon marveled at the exchange—how easily Ella took to being a rebel and how God had used Simon's time in the Arena to affect even this small interaction with the librarian.

"Thank you, Mr.—" Simon began.

"Leiver. Mr. Leiver."

"Thank you, Mr. Leiver."

The three entered the library. Ben and Simon immediately headed for the curved stairs, but Ella paused a moment to take in the building. Once they were all on the second floor, they sat at a table in the west wing.

"So, where do we start?" Ben asked.

"I'll take the history section. You take geography," Simon suggested.

"And what about me?" Ella asked.

Simon tried to come up with something but was at a loss.

"I don't know. Where else could we learn about our neighboring countries?" Simon asked.

"How about the Internet?"

Both Simon and Ben stared at Ella.

"Umm, Ella," Simon tried to explain patiently, "the Internet is basically useless. I mean, I guess it used to be great. But now the government just uses it to remind us about all the rules. Besides, it tracks and censors everything."

"There are ways around that, you know," Ella countered, rolling her eyes. "My dad works in an office. I'm not even sure what he does, really. But he has a computer at home. An old one, of course. He's taught me a little, but I learned some things on my own too," she admitted proudly.

There was a neglected computer station in the center wing nearby, so Ella stood up from the table and headed in that direction. The other two shrugged and parted ways as well.

Simon walked through the history section, not sure where to begin. He walked by each bookcase, eyeing the covers and titles to see if anything jumped out at him. Idly, he selected one fairly innocuous volume and opened it.

"And what did you learn?"

Simon leaped at the sound of a voice he'd hoped he would never hear again. He wheeled around to see the eyes of Mr. Druck peering between the shelves of the bookcase. He didn't need to see his uncle's mouth to know there was a sinister smile lurking behind the books. In a moment, Mr. Druck curled around the case and slid into the aisle where Simon stood. Simon gripped his book and tried to estimate how much damage it could do as a weapon.

"I've been waiting so long for the chance to see you here. I hoped it was only a matter of time." Mr. Druck took a step closer and towered over his nephew. "It's a pity that I'm bound by my current schedule and other responsibilities. Otherwise, I'd invite you to come with me for the evening."

Mr. Druck's eyes narrowed viciously, and his breath stung Simon's nostrils. Simon remembered the pin his uncle wore the last time they'd met, and fury began to boil within. The symbol on the pin matched the scar Charity bore as a permanent reminder of the slavery of her past life. The connection couldn't be good. Worse yet, he knew Mr. Druck had been there during Charity's weeklong captivity. It took all the willpower Simon had to restrain himself from charging at his uncle in rage.

"Hey, Simon?" Ben's voice drifted from a few aisles away. "I think I found something."

Mr. Druck retreated a few steps. As he turned back around the corner where he'd come, he threatened, "Just remember, Simon. We're watching you. And your dad. And your friends. It's simply a matter of time . . ."

Ben came into the aisle from the other side and stopped dead in his tracks. His mouth gaped open in shock; the book he had been holding fell to the ground with a muted thud. Simon turned back from Ben toward Mr. Druck—but he was gone.

Chapter Eighteen

The boardroom was unchanged except for one thing: the people present. Two new Security guards stood at attention at one end of the long ebony table, flanking a tall man with a somber, pale face.

"I'm disappointed in you, Roderick. Again."

The voice came from the far end of the table and belonged to a figure that was almost entirely hidden in the darkness of the long room.

Mr. Druck wrung his hands and cleared his throat. "I can assure you we have nothing to fear. We know where he is at all times—well, we know where to find him. He knows it too. *That* I can tell you. The look on his face today was priceless!"

"You failed to discover what he was doing. You were unsuccessful in gaining any information whatsoever. And frankly, I doubt you so much as flustered the boy. He's made of better mettle than you, I'm afraid."

Mr. Druck swallowed back frustration and fear. "You'll see. We'll keep prodding. We'll get him right where we want him."

"See to it that you don't botch this up—as you did with the girl."

"The girl was mine! One in my ring. I don't know who had been her direct owner, but she was stolen from me, nonetheless."

"Silence!" The command echoed in the room. "Your own greed prevented you from acquiring the information we need. She was only suitable for the refuse, and you know it."

Mr. Druck opened his mouth to protest, but he reconsidered his strategy. He closed his mouth, smiled, and tried again. "I will not fail you. I have not failed you. Wait and see."

A few moments of silence amplified the tension in the room.

"And our informant? How fares our young companion?"

"Quite well." Mr. Druck smiled broadly, relieved for the conversation to have moved onto a more successful topic. "The arrangement is proving quite fruitful."

"And what of the Darkness? Are they suspicious that we are gaining information from inside?"

Mr. Roderick Druck's grin stretched even wider. "They haven't a clue."

"They don't have a clue," Ella said emphatically on their walk home from school the next day. "I'm telling you. There are safe places on the Internet. Places where the library—the government even—won't know to look."

"How do you know this? What makes you so smart?" Ben asked.

Ella rolled her eyes. Simon admired the way she put up with—and stood up to—Ben. She'd released her hair from the tight school-day ponytail required of all girls, and Simon noted that her hair flew wildly around her face. It was fine and seemed intent on going in as many different directions as possible. But after a few steps, Ella gave up and pulled it back again, this time twisting it into a loose knot.

"Like I said. My dad works for the government—"

"The *what*?! The government?! You told us an office. You said, 'My dad works in an office.' Not the stinking government!" Ben's eyes bulged as he attacked Ella with the loudest whisper he could muster. Simon admired how often Ben could mute his indignation for the purpose of protection.

"Hey! Like I said, I don't really know what he *does*," Ella countered. "But he's taught me some stuff. Like the Internet, and parts of the web that other people can see. You know, the people who aren't kept from the rest of the world by the government.

"Like what?" Ben challenged. "What have you seen?"

Ella pursed her lips, but her eyes glowed with excitement and her answer grew more animated with each word. "There are islands. And books. And music. And beautiful buildings—"

"Will you be quiet?" Ben begged. "I can't believe this."

"And for the past month or so, I've been trying to figure out who this Jesus is."

Simon wanted to throw his hands up in indignation at Ella for asking him so many questions when she could find the answers on her own, but he didn't want to scare her away from telling them more.

"And? What did you learn?"

Ella's earnest smile fell into a confused frown. "All sorts of things. Some people believe in Him, no doubt. But there are plenty of people on the other side of our borders who don't like Him either. That's why I need your help," she explained, answering Simon's unasked question.

"Well," Simon offered, "maybe it's about time you meet some of the others too."

"Really? When? Are you serious?!" The group approached Smith Street, but Ella was slowing down to prolong the conversation.

"If possible, maybe tonight. What do you say, Ben? You in too?"

Ben shook his head through nervous laughter. "You're kidding, right? No. No way. My mom would kill me. I can't risk her finding out. Besides, I'm sure my aunt Sarah would find out somehow. And she'd never let up about it."

"What about you, Ella?"

"Totally. I'm in. Yes."

Simon laughed. "You said you can see your home from my window, right?"

Ella nodded. "I can see my bedroom window, in fact."

Her words unsettled Simon a bit, but he pressed on.

"Okay. Wear dark clothes, and wait for my signal. Two flashes of light means to meet me downstairs. Three means to hold off for the night. Then flash the same back to me so I know you saw. Got it?"

Ella jumped as she nodded and trotted off down her street.

"Simon. You're an idiot."

"Thanks, Ben."

"What if they catch you?"

"Ben, my—Mr. Druck found us in the library. And of course he could. I was dumb to think we were safe there."

Ben's cheeks flamed as they turned down Merchant Street.

"They might catch me no matter what I do, Ben. I'm just tired of doing nothing."

Ben said nothing in response and was silent the rest of the way home, but he waved as they parted for the evening.

Simon was winning the card game, but he kept watch on the clock as well.

"Hey, Dad, wanna watch the news?"

Jonathan looked up from his cards with surprise.

"I don't see why not," he answered slowly. "Increasingly interested in current events, are you?"

Simon shrugged and walked over to the television to turn it on. The two sat on the long couch opposite the television and settled in for it to warm up.

"Good evening, citizens of New Morgan. Today is the twenty-second day of Quarter Two."

Simon couldn't help a smile when he heard his dad groan.

"I'm Robert Strap, and this is the evening news. Rod Benson will have the weather report after the weekend Bot recaps. But first, our headline stories."

The next few minutes were filled with predictable, mundane assertions that all was well in New Morgan, the Bot patrol at night had been met with unanimous approval, and the economy was in better shape than ever.

"And they say *we* believe in fairy tales," Simon quipped.

Rod Benson came up eventually and reported that the next two nights would be stormy. "But don't worry," he insisted. "The rain will only fall at night, and there will be no danger of flash floods; the Infrastructure Council has taken extra steps to ensure that all flood precautions have been taken into account."

"Batten down the hatches," Jonathan mumbled.

There was Simon's answer. And Ella's. Jonathan and Simon returned to the card game, and rain began to fall just as Simon declared victory. An hour later, Simon sent his message through the window and waited for a return light. On the second story, in a window that faced west, a flashlight returned three short flashes.

"Goodnight, Ella," Simon said as he placed his flashlight in his desk drawer and headed to bed. The next adventure would have to wait.

Chapter Nineteen

Saturday morning came with no excursions to the City and no rain, as Rod Benson had predicted. Simon knew Ella would be bursting with anticipation, but it was out of his control. So many things were out of his control—especially mandatory attendance at the Recreation Time in the Arena that morning. He had no idea how he'd endure the next few hours of deafening violence between created mechanical creatures, knowing that at any given time, a real life could be at stake. He would need all the support he could get, and he was glad to see some waiting for him at the corner. Ella and Ben stood together, but were not speaking to each other. When they saw Simon approach, they both walked toward him, step for step, almost in competition. Ella reached him first.

"Hey, Simon, you okay? Ready for this?"

"Simon, will you please tell Ella that you're not going to faint in the middle of a battle today?"

"Heh. No promises. But I'll do my best not to get beaten, arrested, or killed. How's that?"

"Not funny," Ben decided.

Strength in numbers must have helped Simon at the gate. He recognized the guard as the one who had delivered a hearty blow to his gut a few weeks before, but the man just grimaced and proceeded to let all three in the Arena.

Simon's instinct was to veer toward the lowest level, but he quickly checked himself. No one would be waiting for him there. Charity, as far as he knew, was still recovering in her room. Simon mourned for the pain he and she had both suffered in this place. What would happen next? How many more victims would there be? *Was it worth the risk? What was there to lose?* Simon didn't want to consider the impending danger.

"Simon, where are you going?" Ben called behind him. "We always sit this way."

Simon shrugged. "I don't plan on sitting much." He turned to see Ben contemplate his options. Ella determinedly walked toward Simon, which decided things for Ben.

"So what exactly are we going to do?"

"Walk. There are always kids in the hallways. We'll just be three more."

"You realize we have to walk all the way back too, right?"

"You'd make a terrible Carrier, Ben."

"What's a Carrier?" Ella interjected.

"Nothing! Good grief, Simon!" Ben's panic could be entertaining at times, but it was starting to get old. Simon resisted rolling his eyes and kept walking.

The crowds in the corridor began to thin out as most of the teens filtered into the stadium seats. Ben had some refreshment vouchers, so they took a break from walking to stand in line and purchase a pack of peanuts. A nearby table and chairs offered a place for them to sit for a few minutes. No one spoke; Ben warily eyed the remaining people for anyone who might find them guilty of sitting quietly and eating a snack. As Ben threw away the paper bag, they stretched and set out on another circuitous journey.

"So I take it you've done this before. What do you do when you walk all over?" Ella didn't say so, but Simon had a feeling she was getting bored. He pictured a trim, stealthy teen with a dark bob haircut leading the way as she weaved in and out of the crowd, blending in, loading her pockets . . .

"I recycle."

Ben and Ella, flanking him as they walked, both turned toward him for clarification.

"You what?" Ben asked.

"I'll show you." He increased his pace and veered right as soon as he saw a bin filled with the day's trash. A few drink cans were easy to grab, and Simon immediately regretted that he hadn't worn a pair of pants with more pockets.

"Here," Ella said, coming up from behind him. "I have a satchel."

Ella's bag began to fill as the three conducted their own scavenger hunt. A screeching roar spilled out into the corridor, indicating that some Bot had just met with a particularly noisy demise. The crowds reciprocated in kind, shouting in harmony with the groans of the latest victim. Simon suddenly felt dizzy as he pictured Charity's body being flung from the Bot that was intended to be her tomb.

"Simon? Simon. Hang in there." Ella shook his arm and fought to keep Simon coherent.

"I'm here. Sorry. Thanks."

"Anywhere else to go?" Ben asked as he eyed an open hall toward the stadium. His peaked face made it clear he wasn't interested in watching the skirmish either.

"Now that I think of it, I need to do a favor for a friend. But it won't be pleasant."

It took a few minutes to reach the recycling area. Ben and Ella both slowed down as they got closer.

"You sure about this, Simon?" Ella asked.

"No."

Together, the three approached the space where they had met last week, where Charity's limp body had lain silently.

Out of nowhere, Simon heard his own voice in his mind.

Though I walk through the valley of the shadow of death . . .

A wave of comfort overwhelmed him. *Of course*, he scolded himself. When was the last time he'd run through

Scripture during dark times? A month ago, for sure, but not nearly enough since then. He'd been so consumed with preserving the Word that he didn't even think to use it—for himself or for others.

"'We are afflicted in every way, but not crushed; perplexed, but not driven to despair; persecuted, but not forsaken; struck down, but not destroyed.'"

Ella and Ben looked at Simon as he spoke the words at a low volume.

"'Do not be afraid of them, for I am with you to deliver you, declares the LORD,'" Ben said quietly.

Simon smiled at Ben and nodded. It was time to get to work.

"Grab anything, but especially the little parts: bolts, nuts, washers, screws, that kind of stuff."

They made fast work of the dumpsters that held the remains of defeated Bots, filling Ella's bag as they did. Within minutes, they were finished—leaving a new memory in a place they were eager to leave as quickly as possible.

On the way home, Ben rushed ahead, but Ella and Simon walked together.

"How's Charity?"

"Better. I haven't seen her in a couple days, though."

"You two are close, aren't you?"

"Sorry?"

"You're close. Like good friends. You know." Ella's tone hinted at a deeper meaning than her words conveyed, but

Simon was still at a loss for how to respond. "You were really upset when she . . . when she was hurt."

"Well, yeah," Simon said flippantly, but then paused. "Yeah. It was terrible."

Ella nodded as they walked on.

"She seems like a good friend. I hope I get to meet her when she's, you know, awake." She laughed awkwardly, realizing too late that a near-death experience is not the material for a casual joke. She cleared her throat and looked ahead.

"I'm glad you're my friend too, Simon."

"Umm, yeah. You too."

The rest of the trip was a bit awkward, and Simon was glad when they arrived at Merchant Street. "See you tonight, maybe. Don't forget to bring your satchel."

Ella beamed. "Yes! I think I'll be there. Some Messengers took advantage of the storms this week."

Simon wasn't sure what Ella meant, but he had a feeling he would find out soon enough.

Chapter Twenty

The heavens opened. Stephen said he saw the heavens open. "And the Son of Man standing at the right hand of God." That's what he told us. And I stood there and watched as they hurled rocks at his body until he died. Oh, what a fool I've been. Now, the heavens have opened for me. And my eyes have been opened too.

On my way to capture more followers of the Way, there, before me—the Son of God! The heavens open, and God speaks to me. And what does He say? He says, "Why are you persecuting Me?" Persecuting Him. Persecuting my Lord. In my self-righteous ambition to rid those I deemed irredeemable, the Redeemer tells me that I am killing His people.

So now, I wait in darkness because I have seen a bright light. But soon, my waiting becomes action.

Soon, the time will come for me to proclaim the Messiah, the Christ, to all nations. Even if they hurl stones.

■ ■ ■

Saturday afternoon, Simon slept. The sheer tension of the morning always exhausted him, and he crashed on his bed after lunch until dinnertime. He and his dad ate a meal of toasted peanut butter sandwiches and stewed tomatoes and tried to pass the time until nightfall. After some cleaning and a few rounds of cards, the windows were finally dark.

"Time to get ready," Jonathan said as Simon gathered the cards. The two donned dark clothing and headed to the basement. Simon chose a long-sleeve T-shirt and a thin, black knit hat to accommodate for the warmer weather, but he realized he now had fewer pockets. He'd need to think ahead on mission nights, but he didn't have time to do that now.

Jonathan reached toward the plywood facade, prying at the edge to dislodge it and open the way into the tunnel. Simon marveled at Charity's artistic talent and his dad's carpentry skill to fit the cover perfectly, and even mount a hinge in the open space to create a door.

When they pulled the door open, Simon had to check himself before shouting in surprise: four others stood on the other side of the foundation, waiting for them in the tunnel. After the initial shock, however, Simon smiled.

Malachi, a woman and man a little younger than his dad, and Ella greeted the Clays. Simon wondered how long they had been waiting. Ella hopped in excitement, her satchel bouncing against her side.

"Hey, Simon! Wait till you see what everyone did!"

Simon and Jonathan climbed through and closed the panel behind them. The tunnel immediately on the other side was larger than it had been, but was still tight quarters for six people. The biggest change, however, was a second tunnel. Instead of leading right to the storm drain, the new passageway led left, and Simon could guess where it ended.

The new tunnel was quite narrow. Aside from efficiency, Simon suspected that the conservative tunnel was also an attempt to keep the city of Westbend structurally sound. He began to wonder just how many holes and tunnels existed under the infrastructure of the city.

It was a short trip through the new tunnel, which opened into a basement much like the Clays' only without partitions. Simon recalled that Ella had said "house" when she talked about her home.

"Must be nice to have your own basement," Simon mused.

"It helps with things like mobilizing covert operations," Ella teased.

In the private, open space, everyone made quick introductions. Ella's mom, Lori, looked like an older version of Ella except that her blond hair was cut very short. Lucas, Ella's dad, had pale skin like the rest of his family but wore his jet black hair in a perfectly official parted style.

"Well, ready for the next leg?" Ella asked.

Simon began to head toward the stairs to the first floor, but Ella crossed to the opposite corner.

"Sometime in the past, the owners of this house must have worked across the street. Get this—they actually built a *tunnel* from this basement under Smith Street!" Ella's enthusiasm was contagious, but Simon still had questions.

"Do you own that building too, or will we be surprising some couple doing their laundry late at night?" Simon wondered out loud.

"The building belongs to us. It's empty; it would be too expensive to remodel it," Lucas explained. "But it came with the house when we moved a few months ago. Apparently, they've been part of a package for decades. So far, the government has not confiscated the space."

Simon mused that Lucas's job might provide some level of protection from government interference, but he didn't mention it.

"Coming?" Malachi asked.

The six made their way through a full-size door and entered the next passageway. It was lined with brick and, although not spacious, it was less stressful for Simon, who was happy to be out of the narrow dirt tunnel behind him.

The door opened to an area completely consumed in darkness. For a moment, Simon wondered if they had hit a dead end, but the flashlights pierced through the gloom and illuminated the way to the stairs. Boxes stacked along the back walls appeared old and dirty even in the dim light, and Simon couldn't help but notice all the cobwebs that laced their way through the basement.

Once on the first floor, a hallway cut through the center of the building, connecting the front door to the back door. Three pairs of interior doors lined the dusty hallway, but the group didn't take time to explore. Everyone headed to the back.

Malachi cautiously opened the back door to the alley behind the building. He motioned to the Maxons to remain silent, and the caravan began their trek outside. Halfway there, Malachi drew to the side of an alley, and Simon recalled a similar scenario near the beginning of the school year on a trip with Jack.

Malachi held up three blindfolds, and the Maxons all held still as Malachi, Jonathan, and Simon tied the fabric in place. The group paired off so that Malachi guided Lori, Jonathan guided Lucas, and Simon guided Ella. Ella kept her right hand on his left shoulder, which allowed her to follow his lead, but Simon wasn't used to navigating for someone who couldn't see while he maneuvered through dark alleys and avoided Bots and Security.

"Oooph!"

Simon stopped when he felt Ella's hand pull away. He looked behind him to see that she had tripped on a long crack in the concrete.

"Oh, sorry, Ella."

Simon held her arm and helped her back up.

"Watch your step, I guess?"

"I can't," she mumbled.

Sufficiently chastised, Simon proceeded with a bit more caution and a lot more verbal cues. He had to hand it to Jack, who had been able to guide Simon on his first trip to the City relatively unscathed.

The trip took longer than usual, but the group arrived at the South Gate at last.

"Thank you, Jael," Malachi said quietly as they entered through the gate and passed the guard with the long braid. Malachi removed the blindfolds, and they walked through the tunnel and into the Room of the Martyrs.

"This place is amazing!" Ella exclaimed as she looked at the murals to the right.

Simon followed her and pointed. "That's my mom."

Ella studied the picture closely. "I'm so sorry, Simon."

Ella's parents examined the room too; as they stood in awe of the mural and the underground marketplace, Simon wondered what was running through their minds.

"Hi, Rosie."

Simon turned to find his dad heading to the table of baked goods, and he followed.

"Simon mentioned you could use more funds for the baking pool."

Rosie smiled. Her light brown hair was tied in a loose bun, and a smudge of flour crossed her forehead.

"Yes, that would be wonderful. Thank you."

As Jonathan pulled a flour voucher from his pocket, he asked, "How is Mrs. Meyer?"

"Not well, but doing better. She'll be at the service tonight."

"I'm glad to hear that," Jonathan answered. "We still have an errand or two to do before then. Take care."

Rosie waved as all six moved toward the main marketplace. Malachi waved good-bye and parted ways, but the rest moved deeper into the city.

Simon enjoyed watching Ella take in the City for the first time; it allowed him to relive the wonder he had experienced when he was new. Ella pointed and talked excitedly with her mom at each new revelation. Her satchel swung behind her, and Simon reminded himself to add another errand to the list. It would be easier to visit Spence first, but another meeting was more pressing.

After twists and turns through the passageway, they arrived at the garden mosaic hallway. Ella held her arms around her; it was as if she noted every tile as she passed. Her mom and dad pointed to the fruit, the serpent, the cross and told her what they remembered of the stories from long ago.

Jonathan opened the door to the Elders' room and motioned for the Maxons to enter. Simon felt empathy for the Maxons; his own interview had been intense. But at least Ella and her parents would be together as they met this group of leaders. Simon realized now that he had nothing to fear from them, but at the time, he had been terrified.

Simon recognized Cyril, Johann, and Zeke. This evening, there were eight Elders in attendance. The Maxons sat in three of the empty spaces at the table. Simon stood by his dad in the back of the room, against the mahogany wall. Johann sat in the front of the table again, and he spoke first.

"First of all, I would like to thank you, Maxon family, for offering your property as a means for Messenger travel. It will be a great benefit, especially to the Clays."

Ella turned around and smiled at Simon.

"We are pleased that you are so interested in the Messengers, and it sounds as if we have Simon to thank for that."

Ella turned and smiled again.

"But we have concerns. You knew of the Message before, is that correct?"

Simon squirmed for their sake, but Jonathan remained still.

"Lori and I did," Lucas answered. "We had been believers as children, and we called ourselves believers at the time of our marriage."

"But slowly, we just . . . drifted away." Lori picked up the story. "I don't know how else to explain it. We hadn't attended worship since Prep—since high school. There weren't any churches anymore. To be honest, we barely noticed when the Bibles were confiscated. Everything was changing in our country, and it didn't even register what was happening."

"Jonathan," Lucas said as he turned in his seat, "I'm so sorry. We should have been a part of the protesting. That mural—your wife—everything. It was all more than a news story. We understand that now."

Ella looked sorrowfully between her dad and Simon's. Jonathan gave a small, pained smile. Simon felt a pang of anger as he watched.

"Ella was the one who reminded us of what we had abandoned," Lori said. "When she saw Simon—brave like his mother—on television at his trial, she wouldn't stop asking questions. It came down to the painful answer: Jesus is our Savior, and we completely denied Him."

Ella stared at her hands while her mom tried to suppress her tears. Simon reconsidered his notion that their time in the Elders' room would be easier than his.

Lucas spoke again. "We believe, and we want to change. We want to learn again. We want to help."

"You have much to learn," Cyril answered. "And we can help. I will take all of you under my care; I will teach you all."

"Thank you!" Ella responded loudly. "We won't let you down!"

"We'll do our best," Lori edited. "With the help of God."

As the group left the room, Simon stopped to examine the stoic figure in the golden paradise of the next mosaic panel. It had taken time, but he had finally made the connection that this luminous individual was Lucifer, the fallen angel who became Satan himself. There was so little indication that he was a traitor, so few clues that this bright messenger would drag as much of the world into damnation with him as he could. Simon thought about Charity's unfinished painting of Judas. What did the disciples think when they realized what Judas had done? *What do you do with a traitor in your midst?* Simon realized the others were waiting for him at the end of the mosaic hallway, and he hurried after them.

"I'll show Mr. and Mrs. Maxon around," Jonathan said to Simon. "How about you do the same for Ella?"

"Sounds good," Simon agreed. "We have some errands to do anyway. See you at the service."

As they separated, Simon turned to Ella and offered his welcome. "On behalf of the believers of Westbend, welcome to the Messengers. Or as Security would say it, welcome to the Darkness."

Ella chuckled. "It's an honor. I feel like I'm finally seeing the light."

"Tell me about it. Let me show you around Grand Station. We call it the City."

Simon was still unfamiliar with many of the weblike passageways in the underground community, but he took her to a few of his favorite points of interest.

"And here is Spence's cellar," Simon directed as he led Ella down a few steps into the work area Spence used.

"Simon! Hi. Any progress on the scavenger hunt?"

"We've had a good start," Simon admitted, motioning to Ella to empty her satchel of the pieces they gathered at the Arena.

"This is great! Thanks so much. And you are?" Spence asked.

"Ella. Ella Maxon. I'm new here."

"Welcome. And thanks for the help." Spence turned back to Simon. "Say, have you noticed any new—or old, really—pamphlets lately?"

"I haven't been looking, to be honest," Simon told his twenty-something colleague. "Why do you ask?"

"Still thinking about the one you brought about the Internet. There has to be better ways for us to communicate."

"Oh!" Ella inserted. "I know some things about the Internet."

The conversation between Spence and Ella took off, and Simon felt in over his head.

"I'll catch you guys in a minute." He headed out to the passageway and around a few turns to the main marketplace. There was a tent he wanted to visit.

Chapter Twenty-One

Simon couldn't wait to get to the tent and was glad to see it empty, save for the attendant who sat in a chair, ready to assist. In the center of the tent, an album was at the ready, keeping portions of the Word safe and available to the Messengers.

"May I help you?"

"Yes, thank you," Simon replied. "I'm looking for Second Corinthians, chapter four."

The older man nodded and quickly flipped to the correct page; he then stood to the side to give Simon room to read. Simon took a piece of paper from the table and began copying it down. When he finished writing, he read it once out loud.

"'For God, who said, "Let light shine out of darkness," has shone in our hearts to give the light of the knowledge of the glory of God in the face of Jesus Christ. But we have this treasure in jars of clay, to show that the surpassing power belongs to God and not to us. We are afflicted in every way, but not crushed; perplexed, but not driven to despair; persecuted, but not forsaken; struck down, but not destroyed.'"

"That passage reminds me of one of my favorites," the attendant shared.

Simon stepped aside and let the man find the passage he had in mind. He read it out loud:

"'Yes, and I will rejoice, for I know that through your prayers and the help of the Spirit of Jesus Christ this will turn out for my deliverance, as it is my eager expectation and hope that I will not be at all ashamed, but that with full courage now as always Christ will be honored in my body, whether by life or by death. For to me to live is Christ, and to die is gain.'"

Simon wasn't sure he understood this passage, especially the last part. But he didn't want to admit that to the man who looked up from the album with a confident smile.

"Where is that from?"

"The first chapter of Philippians. Paul wrote that one, as well as your Second Corinthians passage. That man sure endured a great deal in his lifetime, but as long as it gave glory to God one way or another, Paul suffered through it willingly."

As the man stepped away from the table to offer Simon a closer look, Simon noticed he had a significant limp. He wondered what this Messenger had endured in his lifetime. Surely he'd seen many changes in his years. Simon took another sheet of paper and copied this portion from Philippians as well. He took both together and folded the sheets into a very narrow strip. He then rolled the strip, creating a short and fat cylinder. Somewhere between the tent and the cellar, Simon would need to unlock his watch for its first concealed message. His watch. *The time!* There would be no chance for any other visits, and Simon grieved the loss of time and opportunity, but he needed to pick up Ella right away.

"Thanks for your help," Simon called over his shoulder as he waved good-bye to the tent attendant.

He found Ella and Spence talking animatedly about something they called "servers."

"Guys? Ready to go?"

"Oh! Is it time for something else? Bye, Spence!"

"I'll see you in a few minutes. Thanks for the help, Ella."

"Any time!" Ella replied as she followed Simon out of the cellar.

After a while, they were back in the garden mosaic hallway.

"So we have another questioning?"

Simon could hear the uncertainty in Ella's voice.

"No. You'll see." It wasn't much longer before Simon demonstrated the secret door to the stone chapel. As they moved forward to find their place among the people sitting in the pews, he was glad to see Ella react to the chapel with the same awe and respect he felt for the place. There were already quite a few Messengers in the room.

Simon stopped short at the sight of one worshiper.

"Charity?! You're up!" Simon ran toward the row in the back where she sat.

"Yes," Charity smiled. "Jack and Micah helped me down. Took some doing, but we did it."

"We're here for you, Charity," Micah assured her while at the same time scowling at Simon.

Jack's face registered the awkward moment, but he shook it off quickly. "That's right, Charity. Good ol' Jack is here whenever you need him. Much more reliable than *some* guys, I might add." Jack's obvious jab wasn't quite as annoying to Simon as usual. Juxtaposed against Micah's overt disdain, Jack's words seemed harmless, even humorous.

"Hi, Charity. I'm Ella." Ella held out her right hand in introduction, which Charity took after a momentary hesitation.

"Hi, Ella. You're new, I take it?"

"Yep! Just met the Elders today. But I've known Simon for a while. We're in the same class at West Sector."

"Oh, sure. Nice. It's nice to meet you."

"I was there, you know, last week. So I guess I kind of met you then. Charity, you looked terrible!" Ella quickly turned a light shade of rose when she realized her mistake. "I mean, Simon was really worried about you. We all were. Even though I didn't know you. It was all so scary."

Ella seemed to realize the growing disaster and stopped there. Jack was failing miserably at suppressing his laughter, but Charity smiled. Simon was a little indignant that Charity was so warm with a stranger—she had snubbed him for so long when they first met—but he was more irritated that Charity was surrounded by Jack and Micah. He and Ella would have to sit elsewhere.

"I guess we should find a seat," Simon said. "See you later."

Simon skimmed the rows of pews. His dad was sitting by Mrs. Meyer and the Maxons, but there was some room in the row directly in front of them.

As they sat, Ella turned to whisper, "Oh, Simon. I've been meaning to ask. What's the big deal about Revemond? Why do you want to research it?"

"Well, lots of reasons, I guess. But for one thing, my grandparents live there. I've never met them though."

Ella looked at him with concern. "That's sad. What are their names?"

"I dunno. I guess I should find that out. Their last name is Clay, of course."

Ella nodded and faced forward as Elder Johann walked to the middle of the front. Simon watched Ella throughout the service to see how she would respond to different parts: confessing that they were sinners, receiving forgiveness, hearing the Word, watching Communion. The way she took it all in reminded Simon of how Ben studied for exams, except Ella had even more joy.

During the Lord's Prayer, Simon had trouble focusing.

"And forgive us our trespasses." His mind traveled down stone stairs, ones he had been led on to face imminent trials in a cold, dark room.

"Lead us not into temptation." Simon pictured the platform where he had stood before Mr. Gerald Burroughs, cochair of the Department of Security. He remembered struggling to stand under the delirium of exhaustion, pain, and poison.

"But deliver us from evil." Simon pictured his uncle, grinning with his sharp, white teeth and towering over him in the stone room. Now in the prison cell. Now in the library. He pictured Mr. Roderick Druck interrogating Charity. Simon's jaw began to hurt, and he realized he'd been clenching it. The prayer was over.

After the service, Simon felt exhausted. Ella, on the other hand, bubbled excitedly with her new friends: Jack, Micah, and Charity.

". . . and they connected to our old building across the street, so that makes things a little safer."

"You guys have two buildings? That's crazy cool," Jack commented. Simon was a little surprised Jack hadn't yet resorted to his usual snark.

"I guess so. But my dad says the government puts all kinds of regulations on everything, so it's better to just leave things alone—not use the building or draw attention to it. Chances are, if you improve it, they'll just take it anyway."

"But your dad works for the government, right?" Micah asked. "Wouldn't he be under some sort of amnesty from all that?"

Ella shrugged. "I don't know. I doubt it. In some ways, working for the government is scarier than working against it."

"Doing both is probably the worst," Charity commented. "That takes some courage." She stayed seated in her pew while the others stood around her.

"Then again, if Simon starts to annoy you, you can just have your dad haul him away!" Jack laughed at his joke loudly, and Simon felt validated that Jack truly could not last an entire conversation without sarcasm.

"Knock it off," Micah chided with a playful slap to the back of Jack's head. His face was serious, though, and he watched Ella for her reaction. Simon looked, too, and saw a look of horror on Ella's face.

"I'm sorry. No, really, I am. Simon and I are partners in crime, right?" Jack must have noticed Ella's expression as well and tried to ameliorate the situation.

"Simon? Ella? Ready to head back?" Simon turned at his dad's voice and found him waiting with the Maxons near the back of the chapel.

"Be right there," Simon called. "G'night, guys. Good to see you up, Charity."

"Don't worry, Simon, we'll take care of her. Run along now." Jack probably knew he was finding a way to annoy at least two people in the group, but he evidently couldn't help himself.

"See you all soon," Ella said as they headed out.

Simon collapsed on his bed once he arrived home. It was a good thing there was plenty of time to rest tomorrow. Still, he couldn't shake a niggling thought that refused to let him go.

"Hey, Dad? You still up?" Simon called from his room. He heard footsteps on their way to his door.

"What is it, Simon?"

"That part about 'as we forgive those who trespass against us'... Think the Lord's Prayer could do without it?"

His dad chuckled at the obvious joke, but sat at the desk chair to address the earnest question.

"Forgiveness isn't the easiest thing Christians are called to do, is it?"

"A lot of people have sinned against you, Dad. How do you do it? How do you forgive them?"

"Well," Jonathan began, "first, I think about the terrible sinner I am. I reflect on all that I've done to God, to others, and I consider what I could have done but didn't. I let all of that pile up in my mind." He paused a moment before continuing. "Then I think about the fact that there are so many other sins I can't even remember, and I let that pile up too. After that, I reflect on how even one of those sins separates me from God and earns my punishment of death and condemnation."

Simon sat up to listen. This was getting involved.

"And then I realize that every single one of those sins has been taken away. I am forgiven. I am considered innocent of every single one. That helps. Who am I to hold back forgiveness?"

"Yeah."

"But even then, it can be hard." Simon's dad looked out into some unseen distance. "Sometimes it takes time. And prayer. I can't do it without the help of God."

"Have you forgiven the people who killed Mom?"

Simon watched his dad take the question to heart, pausing before he responded. "I have. I don't know how, but I have. 'I can do all things through Him who strengthens me.'"

Simon paused too. "Where's that one from?"

"Philippians."

"I'm beginning to like that book."

Jonathan smiled. "It's one of my favorites. We have all of it in the archives now."

Simon made a mental note to take a closer look during his next visit to the City. "But still. If I could get my hands on Mr. Druck—Uncle Roderick—and all those who hurt Charity . . ."

"Then what?"

"I—I don't know, but I'd—"

"Think about this, Simon. If those people died without knowing the truth, who wins?"

Simon knew the answer, but it took him a moment to admit it.

"Satan."

Jonathan leaned his elbows on his knees. "People aren't the enemy, Simon. They're the prize."

Chapter Twenty-Two

"Hey, guys," Ella said casually as she joined Simon and Ben on their way home after school on Monday. "Going to the library anytime soon?"

"No thanks," Simon replied.

"You can't hide from that guy forever, Simon," Ella protested.

"That guy is bad news, Ella. None of us should be in a hurry to see him again."

"Well, how are we supposed to learn more about your family if we don't keep looking around?"

Simon shrugged. "I don't know. But I'll say this. I'm perfectly content to avoid knowing some of my family."

Ella gave up for the moment, but she was clearly disappointed. As a concession, Simon offered a little more information.

"I learned the names of my dad's parents. I asked him last night."

Ella brightened. "And?"

"Caleb and Jane Clay."

Ella nodded with satisfaction and let the conversation drop. When she waved good-bye at her corner, Simon took the opportunity to share more information.

"Here, Ben. This is for you."

"What's this?" Ben accepted two pieces of folded paper.

"The other part of your birthday present. I copied them from my own yesterday."

Ben carefully opened one, but as soon as he saw the words, he closed it and stuffed the paper in his pocket.

"In broad daylight, Simon?!"

"Well, if you'd rather wait till the cover of darkness . . ."

"No, no. Fine. You're right. Is it what I think it is?"

Simon nodded. "Two different passages. Thought you'd want to start your own collection."

Ben smiled at the idea, but he turned serious again in a matter of seconds. "Where should I hide them?"

Simon shrugged. "That's up to you. But the card box I gave you? On the other side is a smaller lid. It can hide a few messages pretty well. And if your collection grows more," Simon added, noting Ben's wide eyes of uncertainty, "you can always put the cards somewhere else."

Ben pondered the implications of possessing concealed words of the illegal truth. Slowly, he smiled.

"Thanks, Simon."

"Don't mention it."

The next few weeks flew by. Simon focused on finishing the school year without bringing trouble on himself. He avoided antagonizing Ms. Stetter and drawing attention from other kids. He came home, did homework, straightened around the house. He endured the Saturday Bot battles as best as he could. At night, he carried the Message from house to house, his small contribution toward spreading the Word. When he could, he helped teach Ella the Word. And when he could, he helped teach Charity to read it.

"Charity, tell me something," he said during one of the lessons. "Why didn't you learn to read before this? You're so smart; you're going to learn in no time. Didn't anyone offer to teach you before this?"

The two were sitting in the Courtyard, where Zeke had often taught Simon the Word. Tables surrounded them, and to Simon's right, the main marketplace was visible and humming. In front of him were several semicircle windows—one of which he knew marked Charity's room. Charity sat opposite him, almost fully healed from the battle that nearly cost her life.

"After Zeke saved me and I moved here, I didn't talk. At all. I'm still not exactly sure why. I was traumatized, I guess. Maybe I was afraid I would say something to mess everything up and make them send me away."

Charity shrugged. She absently stroked the scar on her right forearm, a habit that bothered Simon. He'd rather the scar be somehow healed and gone forever. Instead, there was a new mark: a straight line down the center of the brand, dividing in half the five-point star and its interior X. Instead of healing, Charity seemed to be accumulating scars.

"Some people did offer to help," she continued. "They asked if I wanted to learn, like in school. I barely remembered school, Simon. I just shook my head and stayed quiet. I guess they finally decided to leave me alone about it, and I sort of forgot."

Somehow, the pressures of life had only strengthened her into someone both tough and kind. Simon couldn't believe he could call such a strong, remarkable peer his friend. He didn't miss that this was one of the rare times she spoke his name, and he decided it was something he could get used to.

"I bet Dr. Roth could help, you know, if you asked. Not that I mind helping!" Simon quickly clarified. "It's just that I'm not able to be here as often as I'd like."

"Maybe you should try coming more often," Charity said sincerely.

Simon couldn't believe what he was hearing. He was so used to the sarcasm, teasing, and other mind games the two would toss back and forth with each other. He considered how to proceed. How could he show that he cared without scaring her away?

"I'll do my best." *There.* Maybe that was enough.

The last day of school held the promise of rest, freedom, and adventure. Simon had completed half of his Preparatory School training, and it was time for a much-needed break. The last few days, it almost seemed that his classmates had forgotten about him, but this morning had proven otherwise. Thick letters scrawled across the top of his desk proclaimed, "THE END OF THE DARKNESS IS NEAR!"

"Mr. Clay," Ms. Stetter punctuated with derision the moment he sat. "Are you so without self-control that you must scrawl messages all over public property?" Her voice was cold and angry, but one corner of her mouth twisted upward, enjoying the prank as much as the whispering students around them. "You must clean this desk perfectly during lunch time. I simply will not tolerate your insubordination. I'm inclined to keep you in class one more day for this mockery of our school property, but I couldn't possibly endure one day more with you in my classroom. See to it that I don't need to keep you any longer than the rules say I must."

The monologue was greeted with subtle approval from the class, and Ms. Stetter gloried in her success.

Simon spent his last lunch period of the school year doing exactly as she had commanded. But now, the final tone had pulsed and nothing could keep Simon within those four walls any longer.

"Simon!" Ella ran toward him with unbridled enthusiasm. "You won't believe what I found. It wasn't easy. I tried to go about it one way, but then there was a wall, so then I tried this way, and finally—finally!—I did it."

Simon stared dumbly at her without a clue what she was talking about.

"Caleb and Jane, Simon. I know where they live."

Simon couldn't believe it. He'd put off going to the library to search for them for fear of drawing more attention and danger to his friends—and of running into his uncle again. But this friend had risked danger for him.

"Here. Here's the address."

She took a piece of paper out of her pocket and handed it to him. He took it discreetly and placed it into his pocket without looking. He knew he would have to wait until he was home.

"Thank you, Ella. Really. I can't thank you enough."

Ella beamed, but then frowned. "So it's summertime now. I hope I get to see you sometimes."

"Ella, I'll see you every week."

The Maxons were learning quickly, and they came to the City every weekend to join the others in worship.

Ella turned her head to the side. "Yeah, I know. But I mean more than that. During the day too, maybe. I turn sixteen in July! With my new status, I could meet you at the library sometime."

"I guess maybe. I haven't thought much about the summer, to be honest."

This was only partially true. He had plenty of plans to visit the City and to take on some more tutoring sessions.

"Okay, well." Ella shrugged. "Think about it. You know where you can find me." She smiled again.

This wasn't the first time Ella had suggested using the tunnels to meet. But Simon would not compromise such an essential gateway by using it for anything other than his nighttime assignments as a Carrier. And visits to the City.

"Have you seen Ben?" Simon asked. They were halfway home, and there was no sign of their friend.

"No," Ella answered. "He must have taken off pretty fast to get home."

"Can't blame him, really," Simon confessed. "Besides, being seen with the likes of me has its risks, especially today."

"That trick was just terrible, Simon," Ella chided the absent classmates. "You shouldn't have had to clean it up."

Simon shrugged. "Good exercise, I guess. Anyway, at least it's over. For the next two months, I won't have a worry in the world."

"Well, enjoy," Ella replied as she turned toward her street. Simon couldn't miss the note of disappointment in her voice. "See you sometime, I guess."

Simon flung the workshop door open, and the decrepit bells on the door jingled in protest.

"Done. DONE! I'm done, Dad. Done with Ms. Stetter, done with the pranks, done with everything. I'm going to take a two-month-long nap."

Simon's dad bent low to sweep dust from the floor into a dustpan.

"This calls for a celebration. We had a meat voucher for the butcher shop, so I grabbed some fresh ham for dinner."

Simon savored every bite of dinner and reveled in the fact that he would not have to go to school on Monday. Often, teens would find some menial work to do or simply spend their hours hidden in their apartments. Simon planned to spend much of his time in the workshop, helping his dad. Maybe he could arrange a schedule that would allow him to sleep in late and visit the City almost every night. He considered how he would propose the idea when he suddenly remembered a piece of paper in his pocket.

"Oh! Dad. Ella gave me this today." He unfolded the paper and handed it to his dad.

Jonathan studied the paper and looked back up.

"How did she find this?"

Simon shook his head. "I'm not sure, but she used the Internet."

"There's a phone number and even an email address. The street address is the same as it was last time I was home."

"Do people use email addresses anymore, Dad? I thought those weren't safe."

"Here, they are very risky. In other places of the world, I imagine they can still use them with relative ease. It was a risk for Ella to find this. Did she contact them?"

"Not that I know of."

Jonathan stared at the sheet for a long time in silence.

"Please thank her for me. I don't know if we'll be able to use this, Simon. But somehow, it's enough to have it."

He handed the paper back to Simon and stood up. Patting Simon on the back, Jonathan retreated to his room for a while. Simon studied the information on the page:

Caleb and Jane Clay
425 South Mockingbird Lane
Maple County, Revemond 32451
23.482.6292
ClayCJ316@revem.net

Simon folded the paper into a thin strip, rolled it, and went to his room for his λόγος ring, the key to his watch.

Later, Simon and Jonathan passed the time by watching the news. Since Simon's birthday, it had almost become a habit to watch it a few times a week to stay informed about surveillance updates and the like.

"I was thinking," Jonathan said during the Bot reports, "that we could stop over at Grand Station tonight. Micah said the Translation Room could use my opinion on something."

"Sounds good to me!" Simon said as the news anchor came back on the screen.

"As temperatures rise, the Westbend district of New Morgan Security will increase their vigilance to be sure no criminal activity puts our law-abiding citizens in danger. Security reports that Westbend will see an increase of Bot patrols on the streets at night to keep residents safe."

Simon looked over at Jonathan for a reaction, but there was none. Simon hoped that the news wouldn't affect their plans for the night—or his missions this summer.

Just before nightfall, there was a knock on the apartment door.

"Malachi!" Jonathan announced with surprise. "Good to see you. How can we help?"

"I am here to help you."

"Oh, great. Well, we were just getting ready to take a trip to Grand Station. You're welcome to come with us."

Malachi nodded and stood near the door as the two finished preparing. Simon could rarely read Malachi's face, but he seemed more guarded than usual. Simon felt a twinge of unease creep up his spine, but he pushed it aside with the thought of seeing his friends in the City.

Jonathan led the way through the new tunnels, and Malachi followed Simon. As soon as they left the empty building at the end of the new tunnel and stepped into the alley, Simon smiled at the warm air. It was going to be a beautiful night.

"This way," Jonathan said as he turned a corner into a wide alley.

Simon followed and slammed hard into his dad, who had stopped cold.

There, directly in front of them, stood a Bot.

Fear gripped Simon as he stared at the creation in front of them. He had never seen this Bot before. The legs were thick rubber tires, perfect for stealth. High in the air, two arms spun silently, each rotating in a circle on a pivot like an elbow. One arm ended with a huge block of metal, which the Bot wielded like a hammer. The other arm held a rotating saw. Slowly, the Bot grew in height, taking a battle stance.

"Run!" Jonathan directed. But just as they turned around, they saw flashes of light as two Security guards ran up behind them.

"Stop! You're under arrest!"

Simon watched in horror as the next few seconds unfolded.

A Security guard took a club and smashed it down on Malachi's head. Malachi grabbed the club and pinned the guard against a wall. In the same instant, the second guard came after Simon, but Malachi tossed the club to

Simon, who used it to block the blows that came his way at a rapid pace.

Meanwhile, Jonathan found a rusted pipe on the side of a building and wrenched it free to beat at the front tire of the Bot, which advanced on the fight.

The rest was a blur. While Simon shielded himself against the guard, he saw the Bot's hammer glint in the moonlight as it swung down, aiming for him. The hammer hit the guard instead, cracking against his ribs and knocking him several feet back. Simon looked to see where Malachi and the other guard were when, out of the corner of his eye, he saw the Bot's blade come spinning toward him.

"Simon!" his dad shouted and lunged for him, knocking him out of harm's way. But Simon saw blood fly and knew it wasn't his own. Before he could blink, before he could scream, he saw the hammer connect with his dad's shoulder and head, lifting him up and knocking him off of Simon.

"Daaaaaaaaaaaad!" Simon screamed. Malachi was immediately there, picking up the pipe and launching it like a javelin toward the windshield at the top of the Bot. Glass shattered, and the driver of the machine shouted and leaped from the cockpit, scrambling down the Bot like a terrified rodent. Shadows concealed the attacker within seconds, but not before Simon saw the unmistakable face of his worst nightmares.

"Jonathan. *Jonathan*," Malachi called.

Simon whirled to see that Malachi was already at his dad's side. He was kneeling at a growing dark pool.

Without delay, Malachi picked Jonathan up and swiftly carried him back to the empty building.

Malachi entered the first door on the right in the main hallway. The room had no windows and no furnishings except for a few wooden crates scattered on the floor.

"Get the Maxons."

Simon ran. He flew down the stairs and tripped, falling down the last few. He did not stop moving, ignoring the sharp pains all over his body. In the Maxon's basement, he pounded on the door that led to their home—dead bolted now that there was a passageway that ran through their property.

"Ella. Maxons. Mr. Mrs. Lori. Lucas." Simon shouted every name and repeated them as he hammered at the door.

Clicks of the dead bolt announced progress, and Ella swung the door open.

"Dad. Your building. Help. Go. Oh, help. Please!"

Ella shook her head in confusion, but he pointed emphatically toward the tunnel through which his dad lay.

Simon couldn't think straight. There must be more. More to do. Who could help? *Dr. Pharen!* Simon nodded as Ella grabbed her mom's hand and headed down the correct tunnel. He ran the other direction.

Bursting into the apartment building across from his own, he raced up the steps to the Pharen apartment and pounded on the outer door.

"Doctor! Dr. Pharen! Please!"

The door opened quickly to an alarmed Dr. Pharen. Mrs. Pharen stood ten feet behind him with an equally shocked expression.

"My dad. Now. Please, Dr. Pharen."

"By no means, Arnold. It is nightfall. Simply out of the question. Arnold? Arnold! Really!" Mrs. Pharen continued her protests, but Dr. Pharen immediately grabbed a black bag and headed out the door with Simon.

Simon's lungs burned. Every muscle ached from the run back to his building and through the tunnels, but he could not get back to his dad soon enough. There was no question in his mind that he had to keep moving.

"Malachi. Dr. Pharen. Dad. Where?" Simon heaved breaths between his words as he slid into the room where his dad would be waiting for him.

Simon looked in horror at his dad's swollen face. The cut must be on his back; Simon could not see a wound, but there was a new circle of blood on the floor.

"No, no, no." Dr. Pharen muttered as he examined Jonathan. He stood up and shook his head.

"No, stop," Simon protested. "You said that about Charity too, Dr. Pharen. Look again."

Simon's voice prompted Jonathan's right eye to open, and Simon fell to his knees at his dad's side.

"Dad? It's going to be okay. I love you, Dad. Stay here! Malachi. Malachi! You said Charity would be fine. You knew. Tell me. Tell me Dad's going to be okay."

Jonathan opened his mouth slightly and whispered. Simon knelt down to hear him.

"Simon, oh, Simon. I'm sorry."

"No, Dad—" But Simon stopped; his dad was still speaking.

"Forgive . . . forgive them, Simon."

"No, Dad; I can't. I can't do this. You can't go."

"I love you, son. Your mother and I. We love you."

Jonathan's eye closed again, and his body fell limp. Simon shouted through tears.

"Nooo, Dad! Stay! You have to stay. . . . Malachi . . . tell me he's going to stay."

Dr. Pharen ushered Ella and Mrs. Maxon into the hallway, and Simon shook his head at their giving up.

"No. Malachi. Don't let this happen."

"He will be safe. He will be taken care of." Malachi's low voice rumbled with a strange calm.

"No, Malachi. No, no, no . . ."

Waves of sorrow engulfed Simon as he bowed his head to the ground. He held his dad's hand against his cheek, and he wept. There was nothing but silence and Simon's sobs.

He was alone.

Simon didn't know how long he knelt there. He didn't know who came or left in the moments that passed next. But finally, when his moans subsided into silent streams of tears, he felt a hand on his shoulder. Malachi stood over him.

"He is safe now, Simon."

"No. No, Malachi. What about me?! What will I do now?"

"You will continue to fight."

Simon shook his head in denial, but something else welled up too. He felt rage begin deep in his gut and explode throughout his being.

"No!" He jumped up and shoved Malachi. He hit his fellow Messenger hard in the chest. He threw himself at his stalwart friend and attacked in a frenzy.

"You could have done something. Like with Charity. You could have stopped this."

Malachi shook his head at Simon, unflinching at the violence he endured from his mentee.

"Who do you think I am, Simon?"

Simon shouted back in rage and lunged forward again. He slipped and crashed onto a crate, hitting the very spot on his left shin that he'd hurt before his Arena battle. Blinding pain caused Simon to double over, but the fury continued.

"I hate you. I hate you, Malachi! I don't want to see you anymore. Leave me alone!"

Simon wallowed on the floor, only barely aware as Malachi picked up his father's body and carried him away.

Chapter Twenty-Three

The boardroom contained only two individuals. Roderick Druck stood awkwardly, facing the seated figure at the end of the table.

"The guards?"

"One is in Westbend Hospital, the government wing. I don't know where the other one is."

"Shameful. And the boy?"

Mr. Druck shook his head, knowing the impending wrath that would come his way.

"We don't know."

"Unforgiveable! How dare you even come before me now with this information?! Your sister—what a tragedy. What a waste of intelligence. And *you*. You don't even deserve your name."

Roderick Druck braced himself against the wounding blow. Such deeply personal attacks did not happen often. He sniffed but otherwise remained silent and rigid.

"You are an embarrassment! Westbend must now clean up your failure, your mess. You destroyed a completely new Bot. The first day!"

Druck looked at the floor and waited for the next assault.

"What of the father, then? That miserable cur."

"I can't say for certain. But we believe he may be dead."

"You *believe*?! We must be sure. If he's dead, even now the resistance will be scurrying like ants to gather any information, any evidence, and sweeping their home clean. The Darkness is a plague; they will hide any sign of their existence. And you've given them time and reason to do just that."

Roderick Druck clenched and unclenched his fists, fighting for courage. He took a deep breath and said, "We're waiting to hear from the informant. We'll know soon enough."

"Don't be too sure. But even so. If Jonathan Clay is dead, it's a long time in coming. This changes things."

Simon was numb. He heard people come; he heard people go. Jack led him back to the apartment, where a small army of Messengers worked to clean, to clear, to gather. Furniture was left behind, food remained in the cupboards. But every corner and cranny of every cabinet, drawer, and cushion had been examined for evidence of the Messengers. Everything was stripped away.

Simon sat on the floor and absently watched it all happen.

"Simon," Elder Johann said once. "Your father probably kept hiding places. Do you remember any?"

Somewhere deep within, Simon wanted to scream at everyone, to banish them from his home. But he had no strength to fight.

"Floorboards. Bedroom."

"Thank you, Simon."

The work continued throughout the next few hours of the night, and eventually he was carried out with the rest of the objects and memories that had accumulated in the only home he'd known. He followed a caravan of silent workers down the stairs. Through the door's square window, he noticed that a group was tending to the workshop too.

The secret passageway. The jingle bells. The workbench and jar that used to hold mints. The smell of sawdust. The sound of his dad at work. Simon doubled over, dry heaving at the loss of the safest place in the world. Jack and Dr. Roth led him away.

"Time to say good-bye, Simon," Dr. Roth whispered as they brought him down the stairs and through the basement.

Simon only answered with a stream of tears. He knew others would work behind him to seal the portal back to his home.

Through the tunnels and into the vacant building, Simon's knees buckled as they drew near to the room where his dad had breathed his last. He pushed against their efforts to guide him away. He braced himself inside the doorframe and took a long look at the room. A dark oval remained where his dad had lain. A broken box gave evidence to the pain in his shin and the anger that boiled within.

"Good-bye." His only word. He dropped his arms and allowed them to take him away.

The night had been young when Simon first entered the streets for the evening. Now, the sky was the pitch black darkness that comes before the dawn. Simon remembered his prediction of a beautiful night just a few hours before, eager for an outing with his dad to see their friends. *Fool.* Now what? He walked aimlessly, forgetting all he knew about traveling at night under the threat of Security and Bots. He didn't care. *Let them catch me.* Simon walked forward for no other reason than he didn't know where or when to stop. The group had split into groups; some would go to their homes. Others would enter the City through the South Gate. His group went through the North Gate, and Simon looked up when they passed through the Room of the Twelve. He eyed the unfinished disciple, studying him carefully. *Okay, Judas. Where are you lurking?* He knew there had to be a traitor somewhere. It was a truth he had been trying to ignore, but he couldn't shake the realization any longer. His body suddenly ached everywhere, and Simon became conscious of the fact that he had been limping on his left leg this entire time. He collapsed to the floor, too tired. Some of those in the group paused, at a loss of what to do. Jack handed his cargo to someone else and motioned for the others to keep moving, taking their loads to their destination. Jack sat on the floor and waited.

"Jack, I don't want to face this."

"I'm sure you don't."

"What are we doing? I don't want to do this anymore."

Jack nodded silently.

"I mean, who do we think we are, going up against an entire country? We must be insane."

Jack heaved a sigh and kept quiet.

"Jack? What's next? What do I do now?"

Simon looked at his friend. Jack's eyes were red.

"Now?" Jack said finally. "Now, you get up. And you let me help you."

Jack stood and gave his hand to Simon, pulling him up off the floor. Together they walked through the Room of the Twelve. Even the marketplace felt different to Simon as they passed through to the hallways on the other side. After some twists and turns, familiar to Simon but now oddly distant, they arrived at an open door. It was a small room, similar to Charity's. The photograph from Simon's Baptism sat on a table near the head of a bed, and Simon picked it up to look at his young parents, smiling at the camera and holding their son. Slowly, he set it back down, careful not to hurt the frame in his tense grip. He threw himself on the bed and let go of tears he thought had long run dry. He heard the soft click of the door as Jack left the room.

Simon awoke to silence and darkness. There was no window for him to know the time of day. He looked at his watch. It was past sunrise. The Bots would be on their final round by now. Maybe his dad called to excuse—then the crushing weight of last night came down on him. School was out. And his dad was gone. Simon would never get to ask him another question, get his help with another project, listen to another story. Pain clutched at his chest, and he rolled to his side. The movement triggered sharp pain in his left leg that shot up to his spine. Simon gasped for breath and realized that his ribs were bruised. He let out a deep groan of anger and agony, shouting out his rage.

"Simon?!"

Simon lay motionless, waiting to hear the voice again.

"Simon, is that you?"

Charity.

"I'm not sure."

The door opened, and Charity and Mrs. Meyer looked in from the hallway. Charity held some clean linens, and Mrs. Meyer carried a tray of food.

"Mind if we pay you a visit, son?"

Simon bristled at the word, but he nodded. Sitting up, he felt an urge to straighten things or to find chairs for them, but he had no idea where anything was. A heap of belongings was piled in the corner of the room with no discernible order. Charity sat on a box, and Mrs. Meyer sat on the corner of the bed.

"Simon, I—" Mrs. Meyer's eyes filled with tears. "I just don't know what to say."

Simon didn't want to say so, but seeing her here brought him some relief. Charity picked up a mug of coffee and handed it to him. He stared at it for a moment, then took a drink. The bitter warmth felt good and caused him to relax the muscles in his shoulders. He hadn't realized how tense they had been.

Mrs. Meyer put her arm around Simon, and he let her. Less than a year ago, he'd known nothing about the woman sitting beside him. He didn't know Charity. He had known nothing about this underground city or the reason it existed. In spite of his physical pain and emotional grief, he marveled at how much can change in a year, at how much can change in a day.

"I can never go back, can I?"

The two women in the room looked at him with compassion.

"I'll never be able to live a normal life again, will I?"

Mrs. Meyer gave him a squeeze, but only shook her head in reply. He wanted to say something to get them to answer back. His anger grew, and he was tempted to find some cutting remark to move them from their sickening sweetness. They didn't know what it was like to lose someone. They didn't know how it felt to lose your entire way of life in one day. They didn't—except they did. Of course they did. It was he who hadn't understood them fully until now.

"We'll let you eat and get situated, dear. Michael will come later and show you where you can wash up."

Simon didn't want them to leave, but he didn't know what else to say either. He was too tired, too sore to think.

He thanked them as they left and took a bite of his breakfast. The warm food piqued his appetite, and he devoured the meal with little thought. Slightly less hollow, Simon laid back down to sleep again.

Chapter Twenty-Four

Eat. Sleep. Eat. Sleep. The first day was a haze in which Simon avoided thinking as much as possible. He didn't want to think of the pain in his body. He didn't want to think about the government raiding his apartment and desecrating the home where his dad had created a place of safety and happiness in a world of darkness. He didn't want to think of the fact that for the rest of his life, he wouldn't be able to turn to his dad for help. He ate, he slept, and he endured the hours.

Nightfall came, or so he assumed. Sounds of people amplified as time ticked closer to midnight, when Messengers gathered to worship. Simon lay awake in his bed but refused to move. He heard faint sounds of music drifting up through the halls. He knew they would be praying for him today, just as they prayed for Mrs. Meyer and so many others in years past.

He couldn't hear the words, but he heard the melody, and he knew they were singing "Lord, to whom shall we go? You have the words of eternal life." Simon didn't know where to go. He didn't know what to think. He let the tune wash over him, but he refused to be moved.

He felt a cloud hover over him, and it was strangely familiar. Something in him resisted the fog, but he felt drawn to any place that could shield him from the intense pain he suffered last night. *Was it worth the trouble? What did I learn?* Simon kicked back at these questions with bitterness: *I've learned nothing. All year, I've learned nothing but pain and heartache.* He rolled over to his side, favoring his shin, and turned his back to the door and the music.

Then, it came. Simon knew they were near the end of the service. "Lamb of God, You take away the sin of the world; have mercy on us. Lamb of God, You take away the sin of the world; grant us peace."

Simon gritted his teeth. He wished everyone would just leave him in peace—leave him alone.

The sounds of music faded, and the sounds of chatter grew. The people were coming back into the marketplace and filtering through the mazes of the underground village. A knock on Simon's door came soon after, to Simon's annoyance.

"Who is it?"

Zeke opened the door.

"We missed you, Simon." Zeke came in and sat on the box Charity had used for a chair earlier. Simon noticed Zeke hadn't waited for an invitation, and he allowed his frustration to target one of his closest mentors.

"Didn't feel up to it," Simon said, rotating just enough to see Zeke but without facing him entirely.

Zeke nodded. "It's been a terrible thirty hours."

"I'd say so."

"It probably won't be the worst thirty hours in your life. Maybe so, but you never know."

Simon turned around and faced Zeke with indignation.

"Boy, thanks. You've got a way of cheering a guy up."

"Simon, I've seen a lot of changes in my lifetime, and I've seen a lot of tragedy. There are plenty of times I didn't want to deal with it anymore, and I certainly didn't want to be comforted by phrases like 'things will be better' or 'God works all things for good.' Ultimately, these are true. But I didn't want to hear it. And I didn't really want to hear the Word, either. Precious as it is, I wanted to turn away from it. I chafed when I heard words of peace and rejoicing. So you know what I did?"

Simon thought for a moment before he responded. "Stopped reading it?"

"No. I read the Word more. I filled myself with it. Even when the truths of God's love fell on my hardened heart, I kept reading, listening, repeating them. At times, it felt like nothing was getting through. But I knew the words were true, even when I didn't feel better after hearing them. And God's Word doesn't return empty. So whether I *felt* anything or not, I kept in the Word, because it was all I had."

"Did it help?"

Zeke looked directly at Simon. "There was a sower, and he spread seed on the ground."

Something inside Simon broke. He pictured his dad, saying those words on a Sunday afternoon in their living room. Simon realized he was a seed being choked by the weeds of pain, the thorns of anger, the thistles of oppression, and the briars of his own sinful self, and these weeds were squeezing out his joy, threatening to suffocate him to death.

"Simon, when Charity was captured, I was devastated. You'd think by now I'd be immune to pain, but I'm not. Then, last night, a part of me died with your father. This will be difficult, but I'm going to hold you accountable, and you do the same for me. We will not neglect the Word."

Simon was wary of making any promises; he felt too fragile to be strong enough for anyone. But if Zeke would help him, he would try to do the same. He slowly nodded.

"You missed your father this evening," Zeke said as he stood to leave.

Simon couldn't believe his ears. What did Zeke mean by that? The comment stabbed at his heart. "What?" he gasped. "What are you talking about?"

"Think about it," Zeke said. A glimmer of compassion in his eye shone through the sadness. "'The angels and archangels and all the company of heaven.'"

Simon had missed Communion. He had missed the forgiveness of sins, the strength to endure, and the fellowship with saints in the City as well as the saints with the Lord—including his parents.

"More than that, you missed time with your heavenly Father."

Simon felt a pang of guilt. He knew it was true, but he resented Zeke for the jab.

"Why are you picking on me?"

Zeke opened the door and let himself out. Before he left, he answered, "Because I love you, Simon." And with that, the door closed.

Simon had lived in his new home for less than seventy-two hours when he started noticing the ebb and flow of life in Grand Station. It was one thing to come and visit the City regularly. It was another thing altogether to live there.

The residents all had jobs that kept the place running: sweeping floors, tending to the lights and lanterns, serving food in the Courtyard area with the tables where Simon had often studied. The weekends were alive with dozens of visiting Messengers, but the weekdays brought a busy quiet to the community. Mondays, Simon learned, were when residents cleaned their rooms, handled trash disposal, and otherwise recuperated from the crowds of the days before. Mr. Samuel Roth, husband to Dr. Elizabeth Roth, served as supervisor over the inner workings of Grand Station. He oversaw food, maintenance, and every detail that kept the community working in good order. After washing up on Monday morning, Simon passed Mr. Roth changing an electric lantern bulb in the hallway.

"Do the Roths live in the City too?" Simon asked Charity in the afternoon.

"Sort of. Their home is connected to the City, like Mrs. Meyer's home. But they don't have government-approved jobs; their skill sets are considered obsolete. Mr. Roth is listed as a part-time maintenance worker for government officials' housing, but they rarely give him any work. Their home belongs to Mr. Roth's mother, who lives with them. So they get to keep their house, but they receive very few vouchers for food and goods. On the bright side, it frees them up for work here, and they receive help like the rest of us who work."

Physically, Simon had begun to mend from Friday night's injuries. He ached here and there from the fight in the alley, his tumble down the stairs, and other bumps he gained without him realizing it at the time. His ribs were sore, but his left shin was the worst, and each time he tried to put pressure on it, he suffered a flashback of his fight with Malachi. Anger would then gnaw at him, and he would have to push the memory aside to keep focused on the task at hand. At present, he was sitting in the kitchen next to the Courtyard, drying dishes with Charity.

"So, we work here, and we get food and lodging. Is that how it works?" Simon asked.

Charity shrugged. "More or less. I like to think that I receive food and lodging, and so I get to work here."

"You're unique, Charity."

The smirk that used to be so prevalent flashed across her face. "I've heard that a time or two."

"And now that I'm here, I get to figure you out better."

"Good luck with that."

Simon chuckled for the first time in days. But a nagging thought finally came to the surface, and Simon couldn't wait any longer.

"I'm an orphan now, Charity. How . . . how does this work? How can I do this?"

Charity set down the glass she was drying and folded her hands, letting them fall in her lap. After a moment, she admitted, "It's been so long, I guess I don't really know how *not* to do it."

Simon took Charity's glass, the last one to dry, and wiped it with his towel. He placed it in the storage crate. "Charity, you're so much stronger than I am."

"I'm not so sure about that," she said, a softness glowing in her green eyes. "But I know we're stronger together. We all are."

With that, Charity stood up, gave Simon's left hand a squeeze, and walked away.

When Simon returned to his room, he was surprised to find the door open. Inside, Mrs. Meyer was busily dusting some furniture. The boxes were completely gone, and a new quilt lay on his bed.

"Surprise!" Mrs. Meyer chirped. "It's time you settled in, dear. And no one wants to go through everything right away, if they can help it."

Simon knew what she meant: unpacking boxes would have meant unpacking memories and all the sorrow that would come with it. That's why he had left his room as it was thus far. He realized how keenly Mrs. Meyer knew this fact.

"Now, your clothes are here. Your toiletries are over here. I set your books on this shelf here, and see this chest?" Mrs. Meyer touched a large wooden chest sitting at the foot of his bed. "Your father made it; George and I bought it years ago. I asked Judah and Michael to carry it down today. It holds special things, for whenever you're ready to look."

Simon didn't know what to say, so he said nothing. He responded by giving Mrs. Meyer a huge hug.

"I'll come back later this week to see what else you need. I'll get out of your way now." Mrs. Meyer saw herself out and closed the door behind her.

Simon sat on the bed and took in his new living space. It was shaped like an L, with his bed on one side and the door at the corner of another. The brick walls felt cozy, but the room was bare. The clutter was gone, though, and the room looked more spacious than before. Grateful, Simon leaned back on his bed for a nap. He knew he would need it for tonight.

Chapter Twenty-Five

My life is near the end; of that I am certain. And what is there to say? I have been brought low; I have been raised high. Stones have been hurled at me, even as they were hurled at Stephen, that first martyr, whom I happily watched die. But did the Word die with him? By no means! In fact, it has flourished all the more as the devil and the world have tried to suppress it. If I have learned one thing, it is that the truth spreads with more fervor when it is under pressure. And so it is with me. Whether I preach in public or in chains, the Word is spread. Whether others speak with boldness in my footsteps or to spite my work, the Word is spread. Whether I live on earth or live with my Lord, He is glorified and the Word is spread. To live is Christ; to die is gain.

■ ■ ■

Simon sat in the pew. It had taken nearly all his energy to walk from his room to the chapel. It was taking all the energy he had left to remain seated there. Mrs. Meyer arrived and sat next to him. Simon remembered that she'd sat in his place five weeks ago today. Charity came next and sat on his other side. Jack came up and sat directly behind him, giving him a brotherly pat on the shoulder.

The Maxons were next, then the Roths, then Micah, then Spence. The congregation began to grow, and Simon admitted to himself that it was good to have family surrounding him.

Yet the cloud that hovered over him was never far away, and he felt it thicken as the service began. He allowed the haze to keep him from reeling into despair as the words of the hymns and readings came toward him. He felt as if they were arrows trying to pierce something inside him, and he fought against losing control.

Zeke stood to speak.

"None of us want to be here."

Shocked, Simon looked up at the jarring confession.

"If we could, we would be going on with our lives this evening, not gathering here together."

Simon didn't know whether to laugh or yell at the man who stood before him and the rest of the people. How dare he, a pastor—an Elder!—complain about this service? If anyone wanted to leave, they should be more than welcome to get up and go. He'd be the first.

"Gathering together is always a good thing, of course," Zeke continued. "But if it were up to us, we would have no reason to gather tonight. We would have no reason to mourn. We would continue in our daily routines, Jonathan especially."

The arrow hit its mark, and Simon bit his lip against the grief that threatened to overwhelm him.

"We live in a world of sin. And because of that, we live in a world of death. We live in a world where children are orphaned and the Word is suppressed and people are killed for their faith."

Zeke had broken something inside of Simon on Saturday night, and he was doing it again tonight. Simon wanted to pull the cloud down around him as a shield against the pain he was feeling, but light was piercing through the darkness, and Simon was at a loss for what to do. So he listened.

"If it had been up to Jonathan, he would not have suffered through more than a decade without his wife by his side. He would have been able to proclaim the Word in all its truth and love from the rooftops with all the boldness he could muster. But my brothers and sisters, we live in a world of sin. We live in a battleground. Truth and deception are at war. Heaven and earth are at odds. Goodness and evil vie for every foothold in every heart."

Simon felt at war with himself. He was being pulled in different directions. He wanted desperately to shut everything out, to close himself off from any chance of more tragedy. But he was so tired of fighting. Something inside broke and even softened. Pain was there—burning inside. But as the agony smoldered, a balm made its way in too, seeking out the hurt and providing healing.

"There will be times when we want to give up," Zeke went on. "There will be times when we want to attack one another or those who work against us. But I pray that we never forget what Jonathan knew: the Message is worth dying for, because it gives life beyond this fallen world. Jonathan is alive and in the presence of his Savior, who did not give up. He is with his Savior, who has already won the war. He is with his Savior, who died for all, even those who cost Jonathan his life on earth. We continue to fight, but not against a government that comes and goes. We continue to fight, but not against those whom Jesus would welcome with forgiveness. We continue to fight against sin, death, and Satan himself, and we know that in Jesus, the victory is won."

Simon felt open and vulnerable, completely powerless to protect himself against the grief that swept over him. He remembered his dad's words: "People aren't the enemy, Simon. They're the prize." And Simon lost it. Zeke continued to preach, and the words sank deep into his heart. All Simon could do was cry.

By the end of the service, Simon had internalized Zeke's sermon and resolved to continue his mission—his parents' mission. He had begun a mental checklist to accomplish during his summer break. Astronomy might still be on the agenda, despite the fact that Malachi was the one to suggest it. Carpentry was definitely not. But his resolve toward his new plan of action gave Simon enough energy to express his thanks to those who came to the funeral service.

"Hey, Jack,'" Simon mumbled to his friend. "Busy tomorrow night?"

"Well, I passed Preparatory School, no thanks to you." Jack visibly appreciated the fact that Simon seemed stable enough for a joke or two. "Looking to start more trouble?"

"The way I see it," Simon countered, "what do I have to lose?"

Tuesday evening, Simon knocked on Charity's door. "Have any art supplies I can borrow?"

"One condition. I come with you."

Simon had prepared for this. "You're still hurt. I don't want to keep dragging you into my ideas. You've been caught once; I don't think I could handle it again."

Simon threw all his reasons at once in hopes that it would help his case. Plus, the last admission crossed a new line of honesty with Charity, and he didn't know if he'd get it out otherwise.

Charity paused, set her jaw, and fired a response. "You're hurt too. I'm volunteering my services. And right back at ya; we're in this together."

Simon conceded defeat.

The two met up with Jack in the Room of the Twelve. Charity's work on Judas had slowly picked up over the past week or so, and he was nearly complete. Simon examined her additions and remembered another line on his mental checklist.

"Where to this time, Simon?"

Simon motioned for them to head toward the tunnel of the North Gate, and he spoke quietly. "School's out, so there's no point stopping there. The bus stop near South Sector Preparatory School was risky last time."

"To say the least," Charity added.

"What if we try City Hall? Right in front of them?" Simon asked.

"And right in front of us too," Jack cautioned. "I like to live dangerously, but that might just be crazy."

"I guess we'll have to settle on another bus stop, then," Simon concluded. "Let's go north."

The three wound in and out of alleys, more alert than ever for threats both big and small. Jack took the lead, and Simon was grateful to simply follow. One block into the journey, Simon wondered if he was wise to go out so soon after Friday night. He shook the fear from his mind; it was too late now.

All was calm one block from the bus stop, so they decided that a few pedestrians missing the words was not worth the risk of getting closer.

"I'll stand watch," Jack offered.

"I'll take half of the message," Charity said proudly. They all knew that she would likely need some help, but she was much faster now that she had learned so much. The passage had a clean break, and Simon easily divided the paper in two.

There was no time to spare, and the two worked silently. In a matter of minutes, they were finished.

"Let's get back," Jack suggested, and the three disappeared back into the night.

CHAPTER TWENTY-FIVE

Behind them, in bright yellow letters, early risers would find the following:

> AND EVEN IF OUR GOSPEL IS VEILED, IT IS VEILED TO THOSE WHO ARE PERISHING. . . .
>
> FOR GOD, WHO SAID, "LET LIGHT SHINE OUT OF DARKNESS," HAS SHONE IN OUR HEARTS TO GIVE THE LIGHT OF THE KNOWLEDGE OF THE GLORY OF GOD IN THE FACE OF JESUS CHRIST.
>
> 2 CORINTHIANS 4:3, 6

As the three entered the north tunnel safe and sound, Simon breathed a sigh of relief. One part of his checklist was well underway: continue to get the Message out. The passage came just before the one Zeke had quoted on his sixteenth birthday. Seven weeks had passed since then, and Simon felt ages older.

"That'll show 'em," Simon breathed with satisfaction.

"Uh, Simon?" Jack questioned. "We're doing this to share the Message, right? Not just out of spite?"

Simon brushed the question aside. "Does it really matter?"

Jack shrugged. "For them, it doesn't. For you, it does."

"You don't have to help, you know," Simon snapped.

"Hey, easy. Just, you know. Think about it."

"Yeah, thanks," Simon threw back. He eyed Charity to check her reaction, but her thoughts were concealed. Her default expressionless facade was set firmly in place.

Jack waved as he turned to head home. "Goodnight, you two. Until next time . . ."

Chapter Twenty-Six

One advantage to being driven to an underground civilization was not needing to be excused from Recreation Time. Even if Charity decided to head over for more recyclables, she would have to be careful that she wouldn't be recognized by Security. That was even more the case with Simon. He had no chance of blending in with the crowd. Not that he minded; he was perfectly content to delegate the Bot-bit task to Ella and Ben. Every Saturday night before worship, Ella would deposit that day's findings at Spence's cellar, which suited Spence just fine. The two conversed about the Internet and collaborated over Bot plans, and Spence even began giving Ella a customized shopping list. As for Simon, he had plenty of opportunities to encounter various Bots on the streets—he had no desire to watch their destruction or their construction.

"Simon! You need to come see our progress."

Ella had come up behind Simon and sat next to him in the pew.

"Say you'll stop by after worship to see what we've done."

Simon gave her a pained expression.

"I'm sure you're doing great work and all, Ella, but—"

"Pleeease!" Ella pleaded.

"What can I say?" Simon gave in. "Fine."

The service followed the familiar pattern, and Simon was content to slip into the clouded haze. He'd sit there, as Zeke told him to. But he was ashamed of losing control of his emotions during his dad's funeral, so going through the motions tonight seemed the best way to survive without feeling attacked with grief and pain. He didn't exactly know why, but he didn't even go up for the Lord's Supper. Something held him back; whether it was fear of a breakdown or what, he wasn't sure. He just remained in his seat until the end of the service.

Ella gave Simon a strange look, but she was still new and would be observing anyway. At the end of the service, Simon wasted no time leaving and heading toward Spence's workshop in the cellar. He would wait for Ella there.

"I lost you," she said as she walked up to him.

Simon shrugged and followed her in. He was not prepared for what he saw.

On the other side of the counter sat a larger-than-life Bot, partially constructed and organized into main pieces.

The chassis was sleek, like an egg with a flat undercarriage. At the nose of the machine, a rectangular prism protruded halfway out, underneath the front point. Spence was testing this piece, rotating it to see if it would balance smoothly when it was eventually powered.

Spence looked up as the two entered and nodded a hello. "You were right, Ella. This titanium will be perfect for the armor. It's both light and strong."

Ella hopped up and over the counter to take a closer look.

"Yeah, I'd heard a lot of medical equipment uses it. Glad you found some scraps near the hospital."

"And what exactly do you plan to do with this Bot?" Simon asked.

The two looked at him, bewildered.

Ella shrugged. "We'll see, I guess."

Simon shook his head and turned to go.

"Wait! One more thing," Ella called.

She ran up and jumped back over the counter to whisper, "I've learned more about Revemond. And I think I found a way to contact your grandparents."

"Ella—"

"Listen!" Ella's patience was gone. So was her capacity for speaking softly. Spence jumped at Ella's shout and hit his head on a protrusion on the Bot. "You help your friends when they need it, and you risk your life on a regular basis. Well, guess what. Your friends want to help *you* sometimes. I'm tired of being treated as if I'm not a help. Let me help you!"

Spence and Simon stared at Ella.

"Fine," Simon said.

"Good," Ella confirmed. "Stop by my house Monday night."

She flew up the stairs out of the cellar and was gone.

Nightfall used to mean excitement and purpose for Simon. It meant an escape from the mundane apartment building and an adventure into the unknown. Now, however, Simon felt trepidation at the thought of entering someone's home. Alleyways were filled with more danger than ever, and he would give just about anything for another quiet evening in his apartment with his dad.

He drew near the empty building that led to Ella's basement, and his heart clenched in panic. Why had he come alone? How would he be able to walk through the building, past the room? Just as he reached for the doorknob, the door swung open. He bit back a shout just in time: it was only Ella.

"Good timing! Thought you'd want some company," she explained.

She led the way through the hall, and Simon was relieved that the first door on the right was closed. Still, his imagination pictured what had been on the other side of the door—his father's body, lifeless on the floor. Simon felt the cloud come near again, and he welcomed it. The fog would numb his fear. They descended into the tunnel and proceeded to Ella's home.

Ella led him into the first floor of her house and pointed him toward a small room. In it, there was a desk, a chair, a computer—and Ben.

"Ben! What are you doing here?" Flustered at the surprise, Simon didn't quite know what to think about Ben's presence.

"I invited him. He doesn't get enough excitement, and my house is easier and safer to get to than the City, so his parents agreed to let him come over."

Simon recalled Mrs. Pharen's protests that Friday night and instantly grew suspicious. But then he remembered that Dr. Pharen hadn't hesitated to help. Ben sat in a chair toward a corner of the room, arms crossed tightly around himself. He was clearly nervous about being there.

"Okay." Ella was all business. "This is what I've figured out. Revemond is still pretty free as far as the government goes. They can travel easily—to places with open borders, that is—and censorship seems fairly low. Turns out, there was a faction that rose up about five years after Morganland became New Morgan, but everyone there realized that New Morgan was already pretty awful, and the effort failed."

Simon devoured the words. It felt good to be learning something new again.

"Plus, I think I've been able to create an email address using an open domain that'll be tough for Security to track." Ella pulled up a window on her monitor and clicked a few buttons.

Simon looked where she was pointing and saw an email addressed to ClayCJ316@revem.net.

"Okay, Simon. You're up. What do you want to say?"

Simon's mind went everywhere at once. Were these the right people? Were they like his dad? Would they answer back?

"What am I supposed to write? 'Hi, Grandma and Grandpa. Hope you're not spies. I'm writing this email illegally, so hopefully our government doesn't find us and hunt us down any more than they already are'?" Simon had been halfway kidding, but the word "spies" triggered something in him that set him on a trajectory he could not escape.

"Wait a second. Maybe that's it." Simon whipped toward Ella, his face hot with anger. "Ella. Ever since you came to me about the Messengers, bad stuff has been happening."

"Wait. What?"

Ben sat up in his chair. "Simon, hold on."

"No, it's making sense, the more I think about it. The past week, I've been thinking. Maybe there's a Judas in our midst. What if there's a spy among the Messengers?"

"Simon—" Ella protested.

"And think about it. You've been asking me question after question for weeks. You've been begging to join the Messengers. You tracked down my family. You even roped your parents into this. Wait! No. Your dad. He put you up to this, didn't he!"

"Simon!" Ella started to cry.

"It's a good thing you didn't know which room was my bedroom until near the very end, eh? Otherwise, you could have just tattled to your daddy every time my light went on at night. What a perfect view to be able to betray me." Simon moved toward Ella; his heart pounded at the thought of how he had been duped.

Ben stood up now. "Simon, you're wrong—"

"And that Bot! It was right next to the empty building. Perfect! You would just wait inside your safe little home until I ran to you and told you what you already knew—my dad was murdered! And you were behind it all! They knew exactly where to find us, didn't they? It was an easy kill. Now, you want me to write some sort of confession on your government-issued machine so I can be hauled away for good!"

Simon could barely keep his voice low enough to avoid interference from the Maxons. Everything inside him wanted to lash out in revenge for his dad. It took two seconds to realize the stinging in his face was because Ben had punched him.

"Simon!" Ben said with as much constraint as he could. "Ella never betrayed you. How could she? She never knew enough. Besides, I know who did." Ben's eyes filled with fear and anger and regret. "I did."

"What?"

Simon took a step back to regroup, but he was dizzy. Too many thoughts circled in his head, and the fog he welcomed earlier that evening just made things worse.

"Simon. Sit down. You have to listen to me."

Simon refused to sit, but Ben kept talking anyway.

"When you started getting involved with the Messengers, I was glad. You know? I mean, I knew you wouldn't turn me in for being a believer, at least." Ben laughed, but his joke fell helplessly flat. "Life Preparation Year, no one knew I was a believer, so everything was okay. They never bothered me the way they did you, and I had no idea what was really going on with you. All I knew was that by the end of the year, you weren't the same."

Simon didn't know where this was going, but the rage inside him grew impatient and begged for a chance to attack.

"But then, as a Messenger, you started acting risky. You were always tired, so I knew you were going on missions at night—and potentially leading Security right across the street from me! Then, you started hanging out with Charity. And it was stupid of me to get mad, but I was jealous. I wanted to be a part of the Messengers, but I was forced to be careful. And you were reckless. And, and . . . ooooooh!" he moaned.

Ben had been standing between Simon and Ella since the moment he punched Simon, but now he stepped aside and sat on the chair near the desk. His face was red and his eyes were wild with panic.

"After that one time in the Arena, when you left the duel to go with Charity? That creepy guy, Mr. Druck? He showed up all of a sudden and asked about you. He said he wanted to talk with us both at the library on Monday. I didn't know who he was—not really—but I didn't care either. If you were in trouble, I wasn't going to cover for you."

Ben's words came out in a rush; this story had been pent up for long enough.

"And then you ditched me! You said you couldn't go to the library that day. I felt so stupid. What if Mr. Druck was mad and came and found me?! I was scared, I felt alone, and I definitely felt betrayed." Ben's jaw set.

Simon was seeing a new side to Ben tonight. All the masks were gone.

CHAPTER TWENTY-SIX

"And what did you do that night? Do you remember?" Ben asked.

Simon did. He'd relived that day often, questioning his actions.

"You vandalized the city!"

"I spread the Word."

"You brought attention from the government and danger to all the Messengers." Ben rushed these words. "So you know what? I went back to the library that Thursday, after you attacked our own school. Sure enough, Mr. Druck was waiting."

This is where Ben's tone changed. The anger was gone, and his face contorted into one of regret. "I told him. I told him that you were probably behind the words. I told him I had a feeling you would do it again soon, though I didn't know when or where. I didn't tell him about Charity. I don't know why I didn't, but I'm glad now."

Simon was in shock. He wanted to strangle Ben, but he was trying to connect all the dots in his head.

"Simon, I am so sorry. I had no idea Mr. Druck was so cruel. I thought he'd just stop you, that's all. I had no idea. And then at the Arena, I realized that exactly the opposite of what I had hoped for happened. You were infamous, and everyone knew about the Messengers. I blamed you for it all. It wasn't until Ella started to push her way in and talk about Jesus that I realized . . . what happened to you in the Arena was my fault. But at least God used it to reach Ella."

Ben stopped his rant and stared at them both. "Simon. Ella. I am so sorry. But I'm telling you, Simon. I had nothing, *nothing* to do with your dad. When Mr. Druck found us that time in the library, I knew I'd made a huge mistake when I talked to him before. And I knew I'd never do it again."

Simon wanted to yell. He wanted to attack. He wanted to tell them, just as he had with Malachi, that they could remove themselves from his life forever, as far as he was concerned. But the only thing he could manage was to walk straight out the Maxons' front door and into the dark night.

Chapter Twenty-Seven

Simon threw open the door to his room and slammed it shut. He wanted to scream at the top of his lungs. He punched his pillow twice and paced the floor. Nothing could keep him from the unbearable pain inside. He'd tried so hard to keep it all in, but it was erupting out of control. Restless, he burst out of his room and started walking. Tunnel after tunnel, turn after turn, Simon wound down and around again until he was completely disoriented. He turned down unfamiliar halls and through foreign archways, and still he would not stop.

What was wrong with him? Why did life have to be this hard? Where were his friends when he needed them the most? Where was his dad? Question after question, Simon fired through them all with frustration. He thought about all the evil he had endured in the past: the evil that took his mother away, the evil that tortured him in a dank stone room, the evil that left him in a yearlong cloud. *A cloud.* Suddenly, Simon realized a terrible truth.

The fog that felt so familiar when it came a week ago was the same fog he had allowed to cover him near the end of Life Preparation Year. Giving in to despair, he had welcomed a haze that promised to protect him from the pain but only suppressed it, hardening him against true healing. And it was happening all over again. In an effort to avoid the damage, he was refusing the balm. In an effort to avoid the darkness, he was ignoring the light. In an effort to guard against upheaval, he was denying the realities of grieving. Worst of all, he was numbing himself against anything that could touch his heart—even the saving truth of the Word.

Simon fell to his knees. He'd been trying to do everything alone, and he pushed away everyone who loved him. *Forgive. Forgive them.* They had been the words of Jesus. They had been the words of Stephen. They had been the words of his dad.

"And forgive us our trespasses, as we forgive those who trespass against us."

Simon shook his head. *But how?* He remembered his dad's answer.

"'I can do all things through Him who strengthens me.'"

Simon lay flat on the cold stones of the tunnel and prayed.

"Simon? Is that you?"

Simon looked up and saw a pair of shoes, a short man, and wild, white tufts of hair.

"Hi, Zeke."

Zeke stared at Simon for a moment and erupted into laughter.

"What are you doing down there, boy?"

"Praying."

"Ah, yes. I've been down there myself a few times—not right here, mind you. Well, it just so happens I stopped by your room to pay you a visit, but you weren't there, as you know." He chuckled again. "Glad I bumped into you after all." Zeke sat on the floor next to Simon.

"Zeke, I'm a terrible person."

"Hmmm, well. I suppose so. We all are, you know. You are, by nature, sinful and unclean."

"And I'm all alone."

"Poppycock!" Zeke argued. "Now that, I refuse to agree with. Think of your friends."

"That's the problem."

"Think of this community of Grand Station."

"Yeah, okay."

"Think of your Savior. Seems to me you've turned your back on Him on more than one occasion. But—don't you forget this—He has never turned His back on you."

Simon sat up and dusted off the front of his shirt.

"And He forgives you for being a terrible person too."

"Zeke, could you say that again?"

"About forgiveness?"

"Well, sure. But I was thinking 'poppycock.'"

Zeke chuckled once more, and Simon was glad to see Zeke was more himself again after months of a less jovial version of the Elder who taught him so much. Simon felt a tiny bit better too.

"Come, Simon. Let's get you back to your room."

"Great. Because I have no idea where I'm going."

Simon woke Tuesday morning sore and drained, but with a greater sense of peace. The absence of fog left him with a clear head and a realization that he had a hole in his heart that needed filling.

He walked down to the marketplace, which was quiet and calm. A few Messengers straightened some tables and readied the area for a new day, but it was mostly deserted. Simon walked toward the tent where the album of Bible passages was kept and said hello to the older man, who was reading a passage. He saw Simon coming and read aloud.

"'It is the glory of God to conceal things, but the glory of kings is to search things out.' From the twenty-fifth chapter of Proverbs."

Simon walked up to the table. "I don't get it."

The man chuckled. "Exactly."

Simon shook his head. "Feels like a whole lot of things are concealed right now: God's Word, His will, what's going on in my life. . . . I'm so confused."

"Ah," the man said. "That's when you go to what you know."

"What do I know?"

The man's laughter this time sounded a bit scolding. "A great deal, I should hope. You took your vows as a believer in front of everyone just a few months ago! Would you so soon forget it all?"

"Well. Seems like I've still got a lot to learn."

"That, I can help with." The man turned a page. "Here's another one. 'Whoever conceals his transgressions will not prosper, but he who confesses and forsakes them will obtain mercy.'"

"Yeah, I've had plenty of experience with that."

"Why did you come today? Anything in particular you want to read?"

Simon shrugged. "Well, I was thinking I could go back to Philippians. Dad—" Simon choked on the word. "He said we have it all."

"We do indeed!" The attendant flipped near the back of the album and pulled one of the chairs to a far corner, allowing Simon space to take his time reading.

As Simon read, it served as a flashback through the past few months. He remembered Zeke's comment about being afflicted but not destroyed. He remembered his last visit here and hearing that "to live is Christ, and to die is gain." Simon thought about his dad's most recent question. *What is there to lose?* Simon turned to chapter three and smiled at Paul's version of the answer: "But whatever gain I had, I counted as loss for the sake of Christ. Indeed, I count everything as loss because of the surpassing worth of knowing Christ Jesus my Lord. For His sake I have suffered the loss of all things and count them as rubbish, in order that I may gain Christ."

Simon continued to read, pulled into this letter from a believer who knew his time was likely near the end. Finally, Simon reached the last chapter and remembered what his dad had said about forgiveness just a month before he was killed. Simon read on: "I know how to be brought low, and I know how to abound. In any and every circumstance, I have learned the secret of facing plenty and hunger, abundance and need. I can do all things through Him who strengthens me."

"Good morning, Sol."

Simon turned to see Dr. Roth walking up to the tent. "Hello, Simon. What are you reading?"

"Philippians."

Dr. Roth nodded. "'I press on toward the prize of the upward call of God in Christ Jesus.'"

Simon laughed. "Lots of good stuff in there. Paul knew a few things."

"I'll say. Did you know he was at one time a persecutor of the Church?" Dr. Roth asked.

Simon shook his head. "Can't be the same guy."

"Oh, he most definitely was. You'll have to read his story in Acts. He was the one who oversaw Stephen's stoning, for example. He wreaked havoc on the believers of his day. Sought them out for the purpose of stopping their ministry. But Jesus called him, forgave him, and used him in remarkable ways. In the end, it's pretty safe to say that Paul suffered more than most for the Gospel."

Simon needed to wrestle with this new information. Mark, he had learned, was a coward who was restored. Judas had spent every day with Jesus for years and then betrayed Him. And Paul's mission had been to destroy the Church, not strengthen it? The lives of disciples were messy. Messy like a believer who kept clouding up when life got hard. *Messy like my life.* Simon closed the album and faced the other two.

"Death stinks. I know that my parents are with the Lord and we'll all be restored on the Last Day. But the here and now—that's the rough part. I'm all alone."

He sat on the chair near the Bible passages.

"There's so much left undone. So many plans left unfinished. Dad wasn't even able to help you with that translation, Dr. Roth."

"I'm sorry?"

"The translation. That night? Dad said you needed some help with a translation."

Dr. Roth furrowed her brow and slowly shook her head.

"No, we haven't had much come in lately. I didn't send for his help."

Simon's head filled with confusion, then realization, then anger. The cloud came back, but Simon forced it aside. There was work to be done, and he was going to need to focus as much as possible. He began to walk out of the tent with determined steps.

"Oh, Simon! Wait. I wanted to find you to let you know: it's Charity's birthday today."

Simon stopped short. Today was getting complicated. He needed to go somewhere to sort things out.

"Thanks, Dr. Roth. Thanks, Sol." Simon would have to catch the rest of his name later. There was a lot of work to do.

That night, Simon was ready—at least as ready as he ever would be. As he made his way to the Room of the Twelve, he prayed that all would go well. He was thrilled to see his usual crowd nearby. Charity was painting the finishing touches on Judas, adding details to his sandals and feet. Jack and Micah were carrying her ladder to another archway: Charity's next project, no doubt.

"Pretty good-looking guy, that Judas," Simon commented as he walked up. "Clean-cut and all. Kept everyone in line, I bet."

Jack and Micah looked at Simon strangely as they lifted the ladder and set it in place.

"Yeah, for an evil guy," Jack added.

Simon shrugged. "Never can quite tell, after all."

"Amazing how a reckless disciple can put everyone else in danger, isn't it?" Micah mused.

"I don't think I'd call Judas reckless. He was a planner," Simon responded.

Jack shrugged. "Whatever. Here's what I wanna know. Anything fun happening tonight?"

Simon smiled. This was going smoothly so far. "Well, it's Charity's birthday today. Any party plans, Charity?"

"Thanks for noticing," Charity said as she cleaned off her brush. "I could use a little adventure myself."

"I think we can do that," Simon agreed. "Let's meet here around ten o'clock. I'm thinking that City Hall is the way to go tonight. You all in?"

"Of course," Charity answered.

"I'm game," Jack replied.

"Sorry, guys." Micah shook his head. "I have a mission tonight. Have fun, though."

"Be safe, Micah," Simon cautioned.

The rest of Simon's day was filled with plans and prayer. He struggled with knowing how many people to get involved, but there were still so many unknowns. He decided that the fewer involved, the fewer in danger.

An hour before nightfall, he knocked on Charity's door. "Meet me in the Courtyard?"

Ten minutes later, the two sat at a table in an otherwise empty eating area. Simon had a small bag at his feet, and he nervously handed it to Charity. One by one, she pulled out paintbrushes.

"I finally started looking through my dad's stuff today." His voice was unstable, but he pushed through. "I know these are mainly for staining and doing basic stuff for furniture, but I thought you could use them."

"They're great," Charity affirmed earnestly. "Thank you."

"There's another thing." Simon looked around and noticed that some City residents were beginning to filter into the marketplace nearby. He was glad their table wasn't in direct line of sight for many. He took off his watch.

"My dad gave me this for my birthday . . ."

"Simon, don't—"

"I'm asking you to take care of it for me tonight. Just keep it safe. And if anything goes wrong . . ."

"Simon?"

People were beginning to make their way into the Courtyard now as well.

"Charity, please listen." Simon leaned closer and lowered his voice. "There's been a change of plans. When you meet with Jack tonight, go to the bus stop near the

East Sector Preparatory School. Take this." He handed her a sheet of paper.

She opened the paper and read slowly, her smile growing as she read it successfully. "'At the name of Jesus every knee should bow, in heaven and on earth and under the earth, and every tongue confess that Jesus Christ is Lord, to the glory of God the Father.' P—Philippians chapter two, verses ten and eleven."

Simon felt a rush of emotions surge toward him, but he kept them at bay. In less than a year, he and Charity had both grown so much, and they had grown together too. The next few hours were going to be pivotal. "If you don't see me back in Grand Station tonight, you'll need the watch. The Word is the key."

Charity looked alarmed and mirrored Simon as he stood up.

"Happy birthday, Charity."

She grabbed him in a tight hug, catching him completely off guard. He wrapped his arms around her, hoping he'd see her again tomorrow. *Was it worth the trouble? What is there to lose?* But Simon didn't want to think of all that was at stake tonight. Without thinking, he kissed the top of her head, near the place she had been bleeding about six weeks ago. It didn't happen the way he had pictured it, but another line of his summer checklist was now complete.

Chapter Twenty-Eight

The figure at the end of the boardroom table stood.
"Can you be sure?"

Roderick Druck and two Security guards nodded.

"That's what he said."

"This would be the perfect time to catch him in the act and stop this once and for all. But can we still trust the informant?"

"What do we have to lose?"

Out of the shadows, she walked toward her minions. Her severe face turned sinister with foreboding.

"You have no idea. Just see to it you don't disappoint me like usual, Roderick. My life is full of disappointment, and I'll not endure it any longer."

"Yes, Mother." Mr. Druck bowed and turned, set on his new mission.

Simon did not want to enter the empty building, but he had given himself no choice. He opened the door and stepped into the hallway. He closed his eyes and searched for something to give him strength. Psalm 139 came to mind, and he slowly went through it.

O Lord, You have searched me and known me! You know when I sit down and when I rise up; You discern my thoughts from afar.

He walked closer to the first room on the right. He felt the familiar haze creep over him, but he fought against it.

You hem me in, behind and before, and lay Your hand upon me.

Simon walked to the door and opened it. It was just as it had been. He felt a pang of guilt when he saw the broken crate. He realized he hadn't seen Malachi since that night, which had been Simon's demand.

He took a step inside the room and stared at the dark circle where his dad had lain. Simon felt grief and rage well inside, but he knew that he couldn't let emotions control his actions tonight. His motivation should be only to protect those in danger and to expose the truth.

If I say, "Surely the darkness shall cover me, and the light about me be night," even the darkness is not dark to You; the night is bright as the day, for darkness is as light with You.

Simon left the room and closed the door behind him. He walked steadily on.

Search me, O God, and know my heart! Try me and know my thoughts! And see if there be any grievous way in me, and lead me in the way everlasting!

Simon walked down the stairs and into the tunnel, toward Ella's basement.

On the second knock, Ella opened the door to her home. Her wide eyes and silence communicated her confusion about what to do next.

"Ella, I'm so sorry. I don't deserve to be your friend, and I don't deserve your trust either."

"I forgive you."

"I know this must be hard, but—"

"I forgive you."

"What?"

Ella rolled her eyes. "Simon. Enough. I forgive you. Pretty sure I would yell at someone if I thought they killed my dad."

"Yeah, but—"

"Enough. What do you need?"

"I . . . Well, I wrote that email. On paper, that is. Would you mind sending it?"

Ella took the piece of paper Simon offered and examined it.

Dear Caleb and Jane,

I don't believe we have met, but you may know of me. We both know Jonathan. I knew him all my life, as he knew you all of his. I hope this message finds you well.

Worthy is the Lamb,
Simon

"Looks good to me. I think you're vague enough. 'The Lamb' is probably just right," Ella commented. "I'm on it."

"Thanks, Ella."

Ella nodded. "Oh, hey! Have you seen our Bot lately? It's really shaping up."

"I'll have to check it out sometime," Simon obliged. "See ya."

"Bye. Be safe."

"Thanks. I needed that."

And Simon was down the stairs and walking back toward the tunnel.

The night air was warm enough that Simon wanted to pull off his hood, but he kept it on for cover. He decided a knit cap would have worked better; the hood was discreet, but it inhibited his view. He wound his way through the alleys, staying in the shadows of the buildings, and approached City Hall. When the front of the building was in sight, he crouched low and scoped everything out.

Sure enough, there was a pair of Security guards hidden in the shadows on either side of the front gates. He drew a little closer and saw the silhouette of a Bot on the far corner of the building. He felt sure of his theory now, but how would he prove it? He stood up and took a step, preparing to get a better look, when a hand clamped firmly over his mouth and an arm pulled him backward into the darkness of an alley corner. Simon smelled the sickening combination of anise and ammonia, and his heart sank.

This was not the plan. Simon stood at the end of a long boardroom inside the City Hall building. Mr. Druck stood behind him, and two Security guards stood on either side of him. On the other side of a table, he saw the silhouette of a woman he recognized.

"Nice to see you, Grandmother."

"Silence!" The reaction took Simon aback. Mrs. Louise Baden-Druck stood up in protest. It seemed to Simon that his particular greeting was an accusation she would not allow. "Insolent boy. How dare you address me?"

Simon stood silent, but allowed a subtle smirk to play across his otherwise blank face. He'd had much practice.

"You, Simon Clay, are a blight on society. You allowed yourself to be duped by the tired platitudes of your father despite our best efforts to show you the error of his ways."

Simon felt his skin crawl as he recognized that their "best efforts" included the torture he endured as a thirteen-year-old at the hands of the man who stood behind him.

"And my mother."

"Excuse me?"

"And the platitudes of my mother."

"You don't know anything about your mother. Don't talk to me about Abigail. She was the jewel of New Morgan and the promise of the future. Everything her brother is not."

Simon felt an involuntary twinge of pity for his uncle. Was this common conversation for the two of them?

"You're just like your father—nothing but trouble for us all."

"You know nothing about my father," Simon countered coolly.

"I know he deserved his fate," Mrs. Baden-Druck said slowly with a sly smile. She began walking toward them. "Isn't that right, Roderick?"

Simon couldn't believe his ears; there was silence.

"Roderick!"

"Yes."

It appeared the simple answer did not satisfy Roderick's mother, but she moved on.

"What a despicable genealogy I must endure. I married my husband and offered my own renowned Baden name to the estate and family we would lead together. But after years of waiting for children, we settled on adoption." She looked over Simon's shoulder to Roderick. "A poor, scrawny, Revemondian child. He began obediently enough, slow as he was. It wasn't until we bore our own little Abigail that we saw his flaws so clearly."

She stood now directly in front of Simon, looking down on him.

"Then that Revemondian father of yours had to steal away our Abigail—a cruel fate for us to endure."

"And then your stooges killed her."

Mrs. Baden-Druck swung her hand against his face in a mighty backslap.

"The Darkness is to blame for her death. And for your father's. And now," she grinned, "for yours."

"You said we would teach him, Mother." Roderick's voice sounded weak compared to the confidence he exuded two years ago in the dungeon room at Druck-Baden Manor. "You said I would have another chance. We would carry on the family legacy."

"What legacy?" she spat. "Our proud family has been decimated to cowards and criminals. Clearly, this brat before us has no intention to rise above either role. There is no more to do."

A light knock on the door behind Simon interrupted them.

"Mrs. Baden-Druck? We can't find him."

Simon watched his grandmother sneer.

"That's because we already have him, you fool. But come! Come in. Let Simon personally thank you for all your efforts."

The new visitor came around the Security guard on the left. Simon turned and looked directly at him.

"Hello, Micah."

"Good evening, Simon. Surprised to see me?"

"I'm afraid not, actually."

Micah squinted his eyes doubtfully.

"You are the reason Charity was kidnapped."

"No, Simon. You are. You're the one who invited her to join us. I warned you, remember?"

"You are the reason I could never get a mission completed lately without finding a Bot or pair of guards in the way."

"You, Simon, are the one who craved all the attention. You were getting what you asked for."

"You are the reason," Simon continued, keeping his voice as level as possible, "my father was murdered. You told him he was needed for a translation, but that Message didn't exist."

Micah sneered. "They were after *you*. You're the one who brought this on us all. If it wasn't for your craving for attention and your brazen messages on the streets, we could have continued to do work—good work, Simon. But you put us all in danger."

Simon had little he could say to this one. "So you decided to get rid of me."

Micah nodded. "We can get back to our business when you're out of the way. You wanted action, Simon? Well, now you've got it."

"Micah, how on earth do you think you're going to be able to continue being a Messenger now? You've put them in more danger than I ever did."

Micah's only answer was a solid punch to Simon's gut.

"Take the boy away," Mrs. Baden-Druck ordered the guards. "We'll deal with him tomorrow."

Simon lay on a cold slab of concrete. After the guards had tossed him in the cell, he had stood on the slab to look through the small open portal. He was up several stories, overlooking the area near the North Gate entrance. *If they only knew.* Simon prayed for a pair of Messengers on a very different mission tonight. He prayed that they were safe.

Now, lying down, he waited to hear the large City Hall clock to see what time it was. He had no way of knowing how much time had passed.

Click, click, creeeeeak. Simon turned his head to see a pale white face poke into the open doorway. Simon's heart thudded as he braced himself for whatever would come next: water, weights, weaponry. Maybe Mr. Druck would have syringes ready for him again.

"You have forty-five seconds before I lock this again."

"What?"

"You're on your own after that."

"Umm, thank you?" Simon had no idea what to say to this man who had only hurt him, who had progressively taken away everything important to him.

"Don't mention it. Please."

Roderick Druck disappeared back into the hallway. By the time Simon closed the door behind him, he was alone.

Chapter Twenty-Nine

Simon had no idea where he was going. Down halls, up stairs, around corners. He dodged Security guards by ducking out of sight as soon as he heard footsteps. Always present was the *tick, tick, tick* of clocks, but he could never find one to discover the time. Tomorrow was going to be the last day of his life, but if he was caught out of his cell, he knew they wouldn't wait.

Peering around one corner, Simon saw two guards descend a set of stairs and exit on their right. As he crept down the same stairs, an excruciating alarm screeched throughout the building, causing the walls to tremble. *They know.* Simon rushed down the stairs and through the door to the outside, diving behind a row of large crates stacked on pallets. He peeked around the crate on the end, saw four guards run into the building, and breathed a sigh of relief. He was in a loading dock area, a concrete courtyard surrounded on three sides by the imposing building. As soon as Simon had enough courage to get up again, he heard another sound: the strikes of the City Hall clock. *Eleven*. If all went well, Jack and Charity would be safely back by now. He crept out from behind the crates and aimed for the closest alley.

"Stop!"

Simon spun to his right, expecting a Security guard. Instead, he saw a Messenger. If he could be called that.

"Micah."

"Don't move! You're under arrest!"

"Micah, who are you helping?"

"You don't know how to play by the rules, Simon. You don't know how to play it safe. The Messengers are better without you and your tactics that put lives at risk."

Simon thought suddenly of Ella. "Micah, Messengers share the Word. And sharing the Word saves lives."

Micah's eyes flashed darkly in the night, and he held up a device, pressing the button with his thumb. At first, Simon didn't think anything had happened, but he quickly learned that the small object was a remote alert device. *Thud, thud, thud*. Metal glinted in the streetlight as Maximalus rounded a corner and came up from behind Micah, looming large and closing up the partial square of the three walls surrounding them. A low grating sound pulled Simon's attention above to a window that opened from within City Hall, and Simon saw his uncle and grandmother peer down on the scene as Maximalus backed Simon and Micah up against a wall. Micah started to move out of the way, but the Bot lurched toward him. Micah, Simon, and even the Bot paused to focus on Mrs. Baden-Druck.

"Dispose of them. Both of them."

Micah's look of horror and despair was painful for Simon to see. He tried to focus on the Micah he had learned from, the Micah he had trusted. All he saw now was a hopeless traitor abandoned by his conspirators.

"Grab a pipe." Simon filtered through the horrible memory of his father's death and snatched on to the help it provided. He remembered Malachi's resourcefulness.

"What?" Micah asked.

"Grab a pipe. Or a beam. Anything that can be used as a weapon."

The two scrambled into the concrete cove, picking up whatever they could find. Micah grabbed the lid of a metal storage container for a shield. Simon found a crowbar and pointed it toward Maximalus. The machine spewed smoke out of its three spouts as if laughing at the pitiful prey it would soon destroy. Simon reminded himself of the torch and blade Maximalus possessed.

"Try to outrun it."

"What?! How?"

"Its weapons are dangerous, but it's pretty slow." Simon gestured toward the six thick legs that pounded into the ground.

"Why are you helping me?"

Simon didn't know what to say. He shrugged and looked at the one who had been so protective of him in the past.

"You're my brother."

Micah shouted in anger, but it wasn't directed at Simon.

Maximalus stomped toward them, and they scurried around to a corner, on a platform. It blew fire in their direction, but the flame could not reach. The spinning saw came next, demolishing the poles that supported the platform. They both fell, and Simon landed hard on his left shin. Screaming in pain, Simon knew he wouldn't be able to run away.

"Go. Get out of here," he called to Micah.

"No. I've done enough harm. This is all my fault."

Micah grabbed Simon and attempted to drag him to safety, but Maximalus was gaining on them. Simon closed his eyes, certain that pain would come in moments. He heard the crunching of Maximalus's footsteps, but he heard something else too: another engine.

"Look!" Micah shook Simon and pointed.

Another Bot came from behind Maximalus, and Simon wondered why they would expend so much energy on two people.

"Wait a minute!" Simon said. "I know that Bot."

The sleek Bot with titanium scales zipped into the scene, its rectangular hammer spinning like a blade. Full speed ahead, the new Bot attacked one of Maximalus's legs and then quickly retreated. The mighty Bot fell back a few feet, but steadied itself. Meanwhile, the new Bot came slamming back into the mechanical beast, maiming it again.

"Now's our chance," Micah said.

The two hurried together, Simon limping through the pain. The top compartment of the new Bot opened, and Ella popped her head out.

CHAPTER TWENTY-NINE

"Quick! At the back! Strap yourself in!"

That was all the opportunity Maximalus needed. One leg pounded into Micah with unbelievable force. He flew back and hit against a pile of crates, which fell, burying half of his body.

"Micah!"

Micah coughed, gasped, and spluttered, but no words came. His lips moved, and Simon was sure he saw the word "sorry."

"We've gotta get you out of here." Simon started to limp toward his friend.

"Simon! You have to hurry!" Simon looked back to see Ella climbing out of the Bot and waving frantically at him.

"Micah, listen," Simon pleaded. "Listen to me, Micah." Micah's wild eyes focused on Simon just long enough.

"I forgive you. I forgive you, Micah."

It was hard to see in the dark, but Simon was sure he saw Micah give one more nod before staring off into the night.

Simon felt himself yanked backward. Ella pulled his jacket.

"Come on, Simon! No one wins against Maximalus."

The monstrous Bot was doing its best; three legs were down now, but its dodging maneuvers were just fast enough to avoid further damage.

Simon was finally close enough to see Spence at the controls of the new Bot. Ella pulled Simon up to the back of the machine, where two seats with straps allowed for rescue missions. Simon collapsed into one chair while

Ella buckled herself into the other, forgoing the seat inside, and pounded on the back of the Bot. Taking the cue, Spence set the Bot on full retreat, disappearing deep into the city. Just before they left, Simon looked up to the window where his grandmother had been, but there was no one there. Evidently, she had been too sure of her victory to stay and watch her grandson's demise.

"Hey," Simon called over the noise of being strapped on the outside of a rapidly escaping vehicle. "Nice Bot."

Chapter Thirty

"I think we should name it David," Ella declared. She and Spence were gathering tools in order to fix their Bot after its first time seeing action the night before. At the moment, it was in an empty building not far from the South Gate, but they would need to reconsider their storage strategy before long.

Jack and Simon were helping to tidy up Spence's cellar, but Simon's leg kept him mainly in one place. He sorted nuts, bolts, and screws into containers. It had been almost twenty-four hours since the most recent time Simon nearly lost his life, and his body protested accordingly. He looked around the cellar, one room of his new neighborhood, and watched his friends work together.

"Almost feels like home," he admitted. He caught the sympathetic look Ella offered, and he appreciated it. The pain of losing his dad wasn't incapacitating anymore, but he had a feeling he would be grieving for a very long time.

"So, what genius plan are you two cooking up next?" Jack inquired. "Some drone army to overthrow New Morgan? 'Cause, you know, I'd help with that."

Spence rolled his eyes. "And then what?"

"Then you could name me king." Jack hopped onto the work counter and struck a regal pose. "I promise to lead a benevolent monarchy and to offer plenty of favors to friends who helped me along. Of course, I'll need to find a queen." Jack flashed a winning smile at Ella, who rolled her eyes while simultaneously bowing. She extended her arm with emphasized grandeur to offer the monarch a wrench for a scepter.

"So, Simon, interested in a position as a bodyguard?"

"With this leg?"

"Hmmm." Jack frowned. "Good point. Maybe we'll make you a scribe. Or the cupbearer—to see if anyone's going to poison me."

"I have experience."

"Actually," Spence cut in through the nonsense, "my next plan has more to do with stealth than strength."

"Wait, wait, like Messengermobiles?" Jack guessed.

"How do you manage to make anything sound ridiculous?" Ella teased.

Jack did his best impression of being stabbed from behind, complete with a dramatic fall from the counter. "The crown has fallen!"

"You're no help at all," Ella continued. "Don't you have something better to do?"

Jack looked up at the clock hanging on the wall.

"We all do. Time to go, loyal subjects!"

On their way to the chapel, Simon's mind wandered through the events of the past day.

"Ella, how'd you know where to find me last night?"

"Oh, right. Well, after your visit, my parents and I went to the City as planned. I was on my way to help Spence when I saw Jack and Charity in the Room of the Twelve."

"We had just completed our mission, and we never saw you," Jack added with a touch of gravity.

"Charity pulled out your watch and told us the thing you said about the key."

"I figured that part out," Jack said proudly, waving his ring.

"And there was your message in the watch: 'Micah is our Judas.' That freaked us out a bit. Okay—a lot," Ella admitted. "We didn't really know what you meant, but it didn't sound good."

"So then what? Where would you go? You didn't tell us where to find you," Jack pointed out.

Simon suddenly felt foolish. Apparently, he wasn't the best at planning undercover reconnaissance missions.

"But Charity remembered your Plan A for last night and figured you'd be at City Hall," Ella added. "I knew Spence was almost done with our Bot, so I ran over there to help. His cellar has a fairly wide ramp to bring his big tools in, but we still had to move the Bot out in a few pieces and assemble it in an alley. It's a wonder we got there in time."

"Unbelievable," Simon agreed.

"Don't mention it," Jack said, stretching his arms.

"Thank you, Spence," Simon directed to their silent companion.

"All in a day's work," Spence said calmly.

Simon thought of Micah, and he felt a jabbing sensation. Should he have said anything about Micah? So far, he had only told his small group of friends, but he knew word would spread. Would people believe him? Would they hate Micah? Would they be heartbroken? Simon didn't know the answer for himself yet. He realized that the shock waves of this event would take time to course through the Messengers as they coped with their loss.

The group was nearing the chapel, and Ella slowed down a bit, motioning for Simon to do the same.

"This morning, when I got home, I found this in my email inbox." Ella handed Simon a folded piece of paper.

Simon took a deep breath and opened the paper. Ella had copied the brief message neatly:

Dear Simon,

Yes, we know of you. We know Jonathan very well. We are eager to hear news of how you all are doing.

The Lion of Judah is King,
Caleb and Jane

Simon celebrated the end of the email and the fact that Ella's work had connected him to his grandparents. But he grieved at the middle. *Where do I start?* He would have a lot of explaining to do.

He limped forward and sat next to a Messenger sitting near the back.

"Long time no see," Simon greeted.

"I've been working on a few things. Did they take you to the medical hall?" Charity asked.

Simon nodded. "They kept me overnight for observation. Jack broke me out an hour or so ago."

"Are you going to be okay?"

Simon shrugged. "I'm supposed to go back after the service; a doctor will be in then. And how about you? How was your birthday?"

Charity gave her classic look of incredulity. "I've had better. I've had worse." After a pause, she clarified. "It was pretty great, actually, except for the time I was wondering whether or not you were alive. That put a damper on things."

"Yeah, but that was only, like, ninety minutes of your actual birthday, so . . ." Simon dismissed.

"Right. Silly me. Why should I complain?"

"Thanks, by the way."

"For what?"

"For saving my life."

Charity shrugged, smiling, and faced forward as the Elders came to the front. "It's what I do."

Simon turned too, steeling himself for what was to come. It was the third funeral service he had attended in less than two months. If it weren't for Micah, his dad's funeral would not have happened. If it weren't for Micah, this funeral could have been avoided too. Simon pictured Micah in those last few minutes, suffering both pain and regret.

The gathering confessed the Apostles' Creed, and Simon thought about the power of those words—words that set a life-changing trajectory for so many in such a short time. Ella was here now. His dad was not. He hadn't seen Malachi for days. So many concealed truths were brought to light—and not all of them pleasant. He looked around at those who confessed their faith alongside him, and he was surprised to see two new figures: Ben and Dr. Pharen.

As they began the Lord's Prayer, Simon felt a knot in his gut and a haze hover nearby. Pushing the fog away, Simon bared the wounds that only his Savior could heal.

"And forgive us our trespasses as we forgive those who trespass against us; and lead us not into temptation, but deliver us from evil."

The words stung, but they granted healing as well. Simon was ready to move forward.

" 'My own eyes have seen the salvation which You have prepared in the sight of every people: a light to reveal You to the nations and the glory of Your people Israel.' "

Again, the words of the Message did their work as Simon and all those around him spoke them together. He wondered what more God would reveal to him and his nation in the months to come.

After the service, Ben and his dad hurried over to talk to Simon, who was still sitting by Charity in the pew.

"I hear you're hurt, Simon. Mind if I take a look?"

"Not at all. Thanks, Dr. Pharen."

Dr. Pharen opened his medical case. He performed a few standard checks—shining a light in Simon's eyes, moving his neck and arms, tapping his knees with a tiny hammer. He finished by gently pressing on Simon's legs with his fingers, but Simon saw stars when the probing reached his left shin.

"You've had several injuries here, haven't you?" Dr. Pharen asked.

"Sad but true."

"We're going to have to take a closer look; you'll likely need to rest that leg for a while."

Simon groaned.

"Been there, done that," Charity inserted. Simon took the hint to limit his degree of complaining.

"Simon!" Ben cut in, clearly impatient for the examination to be over. "Your words—the Message. Everyone's talking about it. I don't know why the government didn't notice last night. It's like Security was distracted or something, and the Word was waiting for everyone this morning."

"Can't take credit for it this time," Simon admitted.

"Well, maybe half the credit," Charity corrected.

"By the way," Simon added with a smile, "glad to see you here, Ben."

"Glad to be here." Ben beamed. "I'll have to stop by and visit every once in a while."

"You know, maybe you can help with some library runs," Simon suggested.

"We could trade research," Ben replied.

"Well, Doc, is he gonna make it?" Jack walked up and placed an elbow on Dr. Pharen's shoulder.

"He'll need to slow down for a while, but I think he'll survive."

"Slow down? Ha! Good luck with that, Doc. Come on, Simon. I'll be your crutch for the evening."

The group slowly parted ways, and Simon and Jack finally arrived at Simon's room. Simon instantly noticed the difference: a simple but bright message was painted on his ceiling. "I can do all things through Him who strengthens me."

Simon made it to his bed, and Jack saluted before closing the door behind him. The back of the door was painted too: "To live is Christ, and to die is gain."

Simon felt at home.

Epilogue

Mrs. Louise Baden-Druck stared at the piece of Maximalus set before her on the table.

"This. Is. Unforgiveable!" she shouted.

The three figures on the other side of the table cringed.

She stood and wielded the scrap of metal.

"Our family reputation is at stake. Our government is at stake. How is it that we cannot silence one insignificant *boy*?!"

She walked toward them.

"Let me tell you one thing, Roderick. And listen to me closely. One of you will survive another year. You or Simon. It's up to you to decide who that's going to be."

Acknowledgments

The Lord uses all of us to serve one another according to His will. I thank Him that He has used me in this small way, and I pray that this book is a blessing to you. I thank Him that He has used you to encourage me and so many others as we, together, share the Message worth dying for.

Thank you, Matt, for your countless prayers for me and our family. Thank you for your prayers for all those who read this book. You are most certainly a shepherd, and I thank you for demonstrating the love of the Good Shepherd every day. I treasure our "evening compositionals," including the one as I write now. Thank you, Noah and Anna, for cheering me on and for praying for me. Thank you for being proud of your mom and begging to hear the book—especially when it meant a later bedtime.

Peggy Kuethe, I'm thankful for your encouragement and expertise. Thank you for encouraging me to write, even years ago when I was just beginning! Laura, your willingness to set aside time for Simon will always be appreciated. Your honesty and support are priceless. Katie, Colleen, Heather, Melissa, and Erin, your early encouragement gave me the motivation to keep going. My team: Mark, Lisa, Lorraine, Cindy, and Pete. Thanks for being patient with me and for cheering me on. Pam and Joe: your enthusiasm is contagious. Thanks for the pep talks. Holli, Cheryl, Elizabeth, Lindsey, and Hannah, you spoil me. Your passion for what you do inspires me. Tim, Vicky, Mike, Sara, and Alex: you know how to make the Messengers look good. Jamie and Emily, it's such a comfort to know you've got my back. (And you edit a book really well too!) Jamie, you're a superhero. Emily, you're a rock. Mark, Jeremy, Matt, and Bob: thank you so very much for hanging out in Spence's cellar, helping him blow things up and save some lives.

Bill, Karen, Jon, Gail, Tim, Heather: thank you for your love and support. *Discovered* and *Concealed* Launch Teams: thank you for spreading the Message and making me laugh! Teachers, students, pastors, youth, parents, and leaders: I can't tell you what a joy it has been to be a part of your lives this past year. Dear Ascension family: I love you all.

This book does not belong to me. Many hands labored to create, improve, share, and read it. We made this book together, with the help of God. To Him be the glory.

The λόγος abides.

Discussion Questions

CHAPTER ONE

Simon and his dad talk about Mark 8 (where
Jesus warns others not to talk about Him)
and Romans 10 (where Paul questions how
people will believe if they do not hear the
Word). Discuss this tension, and weigh in
on Simon's recent actions.

Ben is acting unusual. What might be going
through his mind? Ella is acting unusual
too. What has changed?

CHAPTER TWO

A tiny hole in a stone wall: discuss how this
could both relieve and build tension

for Simon and his father. What are the risks for them? What are the risks for the Messengers?

Write a list of things that Simon has endured since his Arena incident two weeks ago. In what ways are these examples realistic? Discuss the likelihood of this happening in your environment. Discuss the likelihood of this happening somewhere else in the world.

Chapter Three

This chapter begins with an outsider's perspective—the same one who ended the narrative of *Discovered*. Who might this person be?

Consider both Ella and Charity. What challenges does Simon have in associating with Ella? with Charity?

Chapter Four

This past year, Jonathan often focused on two questions, and now he introduces a new one. What are they? Consider these questions in Simon's life. Consider them in yours.

Nearly a year ago, Jonathan was reluctant for Simon to become a Messenger. Or was he? Jonathan begins to explain the main concerns that he had when Simon met Jack and Micah. What was there to lose?

CHAPTER FIVE

Any guesses as to the speaker of the opening narrative yet? Do you think this perspective is realistic? Can you think of any examples of these attitudes today?

Discuss Ben a little bit. What is he afraid of? Is he a reliable friend? Do you agree with his points?

CHAPTER SIX

Discuss the interaction between Jack and Simon. Have they changed much since the first book? Whom are you most like?

The Bots are being used in a new way now. Discuss what this could mean for the Messengers.

CHAPTER SEVEN

Zeke quotes 2 Corinthians 4. How does it apply to this point in the plot? How does it apply to your world today?

Talk about the scene in the Meyers' apartment. How is Jonathan serving them right now? Have you experienced a similar time?

CHAPTER EIGHT

The shadowy person is back. Who do you think it is? What do you think the person wants?

Simon's role is changing among the Messengers. How so? How will this affect his community? his life?

CHAPTER NINE

Discuss the conversation Ella and Simon have on the way home from school. Is your story more like Ella's or Simon's?

Talk about the night scene. What happened? Do you think Simon made the right decisions?

Chapter Ten

Christian persecution was prevalent in the Early Church. It's even more common today. What would motivate someone to persecute others?

Ms. Stetter gives a history lesson. What issues are raised in her lecture? Do any of these problems exist in our world today?

Chapter Eleven

Ben is starting to share his faith more. Why? What concerns does he still have?

Discuss the Arena scene. Can you think of real-world examples where this has happened? Could it happen today?

Chapter Twelve

Think about Malachi. What role does he have among the Messengers?

Why is the situation especially bleak for Charity? How does her role as an outsider make life more difficult? How might this apply to your community today?

CHAPTER THIRTEEN

The shadowy figure is now indoors, talking
with Security guards. What have we learned
about this person's intentions?

Discuss the risks of Charity being in the Clay
apartment. Why was it so important for her
to leave?

CHAPTER FOURTEEN

Simon is making more friends: Ella and Spence,
for example. How do they help Simon? How
does Simon help them?

The chapter ends with Simon praying for his
friends. Discuss the problems these Messengers face. Think about problems you and
your own friends have.

CHAPTER FIFTEEN

Both Charity and Ella thanked Simon for
"saving my life." In what ways is this true?
In what ways is this not? How are the
situations different?

Simon finally meets Aunt Sarah, a woman he had only heard about up to this point. What is your impression of her?

CHAPTER SIXTEEN

Simon asked Jonathan more details about the Bible. In what ways was its censorship systematic and intentional? In what ways did it simply fade away from New Morgan?

What does Charity remember about her imprisonment? How does Simon respond? How can this inform Simon's own experiences with Mr. Druck?

CHAPTER SEVENTEEN

The Message in the vial talks about truth that is covered and hidden. According to Matthew 10, what should the Messengers do with the truth? What does the passage say about fear? Discuss this in light of the question "What is there to lose?"

The librarian acts differently now. Why do you think that is? Discuss how Simon's witness has affected various people, even people Simon doesn't know well.

Chapter Eighteen

Mr. Druck's pin already connected him to Charity's brand. Now, it seems that Mr. Druck is involved with a slave ring. In what ways is slavery ignored in New Morgan? In what ways is it ignored today?

The Messengers must question whom to trust. Can Ben trust Simon? Can Simon trust Ella? There's always a balance between honesty and safety. This chapter begins with a clear reality: there is an informant among the Messengers. Who might it be?

Chapter Nineteen

Simon realized he was falling out of the practice of turning to Scripture. How might this affect his thoughts and actions? How would this practice affect your own life?

Consider Ella. Is she trustworthy? How does she act around Simon? around Ben?

Chapter Twenty

The chapter opens again with an ancient voice. In the darkness, he contemplates the Light of the world. Consider how it sometimes takes a moment like this for someone to face reality. Any guesses as to who this person could be?

If you were one of the Elders, what would you say to the Maxons?

CHAPTER TWENTY-ONE

Under the tent, Simon hears the passage, "To live is Christ, and to die is gain." How does this apply to some of Jonathan's questions? (What did you learn? Was it worth the trouble? What is there to lose?)

Jonathan ends the chapter saying, "People aren't the enemy, Simon. They're the prize." How can this help Simon with his struggle to forgive? How might it inform the way Simon interacts with Ella? with Mr. Druck?

CHAPTER TWENTY-TWO

Think about Ben's gift. How is it similar to Simon's birthday gift? How does Ben respond? Take time to discuss how Ben has developed over the past two books.

Watch Malachi throughout this chapter. How does Simon respond to him at the end?

Chapter Twenty-Three

Simon ended the school year and reveled in the hopes that the summer would bring. Now what?

If you're willing, consider yourself in Simon's place. Do you think you would react in a similar way?

Chapter Twenty-Four

Zeke visits Simon and talks about tragedy. What do you think about what he said?

Charity tells Simon that they are stronger together. How does God use His people to build one another up? Give examples from the book as well as from real life.

Chapter Twenty-Five

Paul's life doesn't mirror Simon's life, but there are similarities. What are they? What other characters have similarities to Paul?

Consider Zeke's sermon. Who is the enemy? Who is the victor?

CHAPTER TWENTY-SIX

Simon allows a haze to fall on him during the service. Why? Do you know of instances when this occurs today?

In what ways is Ben a Judas? In what ways might Simon be his own Judas?

CHAPTER TWENTY-SEVEN

Simon has a terrible realization about the fog-like cloud or haze that had become so familiar. What was happening to Simon? Has this ever happened to someone you know?

After talking with Dr. Roth, Simon is suddenly angry again, but he pushes back the nearby cloud. Why?

CHAPTER TWENTY-EIGHT

This chapter reveals the shadowy figure whose identity had been concealed throughout the book. Who is it? How did you respond to the realization?

Simon learns of another Judas. He isn't surprised. Were you?

Chapter Twenty-Nine

Throughout the book, Simon has been fighting many internal battles, including the one about forgiving others. Why do you think Simon is able to offer forgiveness in this chapter?

There are at least three characters in this chapter who have sinned against Simon. If you were in his place, how would you respond to each of them?

Chapter Thirty

Simon received word from Revemond! What do you think will happen next?

This last chapter shows the Messengers supporting one another. Give a few examples. Also share a few examples from your own life.

The Messengers
Revealed

by Lisa M. Clark

Chapter One

—*Two thousand years ago*—

Why, oh why, must I always do everything with my brother? We work together. We eat together. And now, we travel the land together. Some men may be fine spending day in and day out with family, but they clearly do not know this thunder-head of a brother I have! Always putting himself first—I cannot bear the way he pushes his way nonstop. You would think that our Teacher would notice what a pain he can be. You would think I could find some time to get away from him. But no, even when Jesus pulls me aside for a special lesson or time away, He invites my brother along too. I tell you the truth; as soon as I can find the occasion, I'm going to get away from him and do things my way for a change.

■ ■ ■

—*Right about now, not far away*—

"Simon . . . Simoooooooooooon . . ."

Under his quilt, Simon heard the low groan from outside his bedroom door.

"It's time, Simoooooon."

The creak of his door and the floorboards declared that the intruder was closing in.

"The Darkness, Siiiiimon. It's coming for yoooooooooooooooou!"

The warning voice rose to a shrill shriek, and Simon's shout rose to meet it as icy cold water splashed through the quilt and onto his head and torso.

Simon leaped up, tossing the soaked blanket aside and standing on his bed to face his attacker.

The culprit, however, was already subdued, curled into a circle, failing miserably at warding off the hysterical laughter that shook his frame.

"Jack Lane!" Simon spluttered. "I—you—why do I even put up with you?!"

Simon hurled his pillow and blanket onto the unapologetic teenager, who made no attempt to get up or compose himself.

Simon dropped down clumsily to sit on his mattress, assessing the situation as best as anyone could after such a rude awakening. The brick walls of his bedroom were still new to him, as was the thin mattress and close quarters. It was nothing like the room he had known all his life. A pang of sadness grabbed his chest, and Simon didn't push it away. Still, there were familiar things: wooden furniture his dad had crafted, a picture of his family from years ago, and a watch that had become a part of him even in the short time he had owned it. There were new things too—new things that provided comfort rather than a sense of loss: a mural on his ceiling, a painted message on his door, and the handmade quilt Mrs. Meyer had given him. The one that half-covered Jack with condemnation and water.

"What are you doing here? You have a home, don't you?"

Simon didn't mean for the comment to come out as an accusation, but his fatigue and irritation laced the words in a way that Simon regretted. He was learning that seemingly innocent phrases could take on new meaning. Jokes that had once been good-natured could sour. Jack had a home, and Simon was constantly reminded that he did not.

"Hey, bright eyes," Jack tossed back, graciously ignoring the jab, "look at the time."

Simon reached for his watch on the top of a bookshelf and tried to make sense of what he saw. It was noon already. Simon rubbed his forehead and remembered the day: Saturday, August 1. Census Day.

"How did you get here during the day anyway?" Simon knew that crowds in Grand Station grew during the weekends, but most Messengers only dared to visit after dark. Still, there were others who found ways to come during daylight hours.

"I have my ways." Jack shrugged and sat up. "Paid a visit to good ol' Mrs. Meyer. Besides," he added, tossing the quilt aside with dramatic flair, "Ella needs me."

Simon grabbed the quilt and draped it on a wooden chair. So Jack had used Mrs. Meyer's tunnel to the City to impress one of the newest members of the Messengers.

"If you say so. But why are you up here?"

Jack jumped to his feet and dusted himself off. "Someone had to check to see if you were alive." With a wave, Jack was gone.

After a suitable shower, Simon found his assailant faithfully offering his services to a damsel in distress.

"So this is the tool you need then?"

"No."

"How 'bout this one?"

"Nope."

"This one?" At this point, Jack hopped onto a counter, shoving bolts, gears, and a variety of small gadgets aside. With hands stretched wide in invitation, he clearly suggested himself as the cure-all solution.

"No! Honestly, Jack! Can't you find something better to do?" Ella pulled back her safety goggles in exasperation and faced her self-proclaimed hero. Her light hair was tied into a tight knot, but thin wisps escaped any form of entrapment and waved wildly around her face.

"Honestly, Ella? I can't." Jack's grin grew to preposterous levels, and all Ella could do was toss a greasy towel at him and turn back to her work.

Simon had witnessed the exchange through the entryway, and now he descended the few stairs into the room they called Spence's cellar to get a better look at their current effort.

Ella finally noticed his presence and offered a hearty wave.

"Hey, Simon!" She pulled her goggles back on and crawled under a skeletal structure that looked just big enough to seat two people.

"What's new?" Simon stood near the counter that separated him from the workspace and rested his elbows a few feet from Jack's . . . feet.

"Ella's more of a New Morganian than ever," Jack proclaimed. Simon wasn't sure if this was a passive attack or a strange compliment.

Ella finished tightening the machine in a few places and stood up. Reaching into her back pocket, she provided explanation.

"Census Day, of course! With my birthday last month, my new card for the year shows my Provisional Adult Status. Did you get yours?"

Once again, an innocent question inflicted silent barbs into Simon, as the sting of his altered reality did its damage.

"I didn't go."

Ella stared for a moment, uncomprehending.

"You didn't go? Simon, all citizens have to go. Today is Census Day! You can't just—wait. It's only noon, right? You still have two hours left to go before City Hall closes, and it's just out the North Gate—"

"Ella! I'm not going. I can't go."

Ella shook her head, her pale eyes showing alarm through the large goggles.

"Ella. If I go, they'll arrest me. I can't have any resident status anymore—much less Provisional Adult Status. Who cares how old I am? If my grandmother has her way, I won't be getting any older."

The full weight of reality hit Ella at once. She dropped to the concrete floor and sat with her legs crossed; a socket wrench escaped her fingers and clanged dully in an anticlimactic protest.

"It isn't fair," she said absently.

"Nope." Simon didn't know what more to say. Jack, who had righted himself to a seated position on the counter during the back-and-forth, leaned forward and rested his forearms on his knees.

"This world is a mess," Ella uttered with quiet solemnity.

"Yep."

In dissonant affirmation, a crash came from behind the back wall of the cellar. All three rushed to an open doorway that led to a wide ramp and, eventually, a hidden passageway. Spence had one arm full of random Bot parts, mechanical odds and ends, and tools. His other arm worked to gather the pieces he had just dropped.

"Gotta create a dramatic entrance, eh, Spence?" Jack's greeting was no surprise to his friends, but Spence responded only with an unimpressed sneer.

Jack bent down to pick up a few stray pieces, but he was interrupted by a reprimand.

"Just leave it, Jack. I don't need your help."

Simon caught Ella's eye before she stooped down to help her mechanically minded companion. Something wasn't right. After all the newfound treasures were stored in appropriate—albeit cluttered—compartments, Jack cleared his throat. The brief hesitation betrayed that he was slightly less confident than usual.

"Well, Ella, your big day isn't over yet, is it?"

"The best is yet to come!" Ella's face lit up as she bounced around the workroom in celebration.

"Just remember, Ella," Spence muttered into a box of wire coils, "you're about to renounce the devil and all his ways. I'd be careful if I were you."

Simon didn't know what was going on with Spence, but Jack didn't seem too surprised. His grin was nowhere to be seen, however, and his shoulders fell with an invisible weight. The next few moments were strange as Jack exited the cellar without much excuse or farewell. Simon shrugged to Ella and followed after.

Jack maneuvered through the hallway with speed, weaving around other Messengers passing in and out of the main marketplace. Simon instantly noticed the absence of his friend's loud salutations or hearty waves that typically added to the hum of the City. Jack ducked left into the large space filled with booths of all shapes and sizes, and Simon almost ran into a middle-aged man carrying a large crate in an attempt to keep up.

The two gathered under a tent in the middle of the marketplace, and the man standing post nodded quietly as Jack approached.

"Hi, Sol," Simon greeted the man who was seated on a folding chair near a tent pole. The kindly gentleman waved and faced forward. Evidently, Sol picked up on Jack's need for little interference.

"Where is it?" Jack called.

"What's that?" Simon turned to his friend, who was flipping through the pages of an album, hunting for something within the collection of writings in front of him.

"Where's that part about Judas?"

"Which part do you mean? He was in several places, you know."

Jack shot a look of annoyance at Simon as his only comeback and flipped more pages.

"Hey, easy with that," Simon warned. He knew these were merely copies of the Word, duplicates of texts that were kept safely in the Archive Room as well as five other Archives throughout the city of Westbend, but any collection of the Scriptures was precious. This was the Message worth dying for, as Simon was keenly aware.

Jack closed the book and turned toward Simon. Jack's eyes burned with anger and hurt, and Simon couldn't make sense of the expression—he'd never seen Jack make it before.

"When Judas dies. What do people say about him? What do they do? Are the disciples all pointing fingers at each other or are they, you know, talking more about Jesus and the end of the world as they knew it? Did they just shrug their shoulders and move on, or did they tear each other apart?"

Simon could only stare back. He had no idea where all of this was coming from, and he definitely had no idea what to say.

Jack shook his head and started to walk back into the aisle. Two steps out from the tent, Jack stopped as a young woman holding a baby called out to him.

"You, there. Jack, is it? You were friends with that Micah character, weren't you? You could probably tell me, couldn't you? I've heard that he—"

But that was all she could get out before Jack vanished in the crowd.